THE OSMIUM MARBLES

Ian Bradley

ISBN: 099435553X
ISBN-13: 978-0-9943555-3-9

DEDICATION

To Lottie who is the Future.

ACKNOWLEDGMENTS

I would like to thank my editor and wife, Anne Lucas; my cover designer and son, Lucas Bradley; and my friend, Patrick Besso, for his knowledge of morgues, cadavers, and the smell of death.

Prologue

Before the end of the Fifth Millennium as measured by the World's oldest religion, or early in the Third Millennium as measured by one of the World's newer, more invasive religions, everyone knew that life on the planet would end billions of years before the yellow sun expanded, turning the inner planets of their System into burnt crisps and the outer planets into wisps of gas floating across the Universe.

The reason was simple: the only true religion was Greed; too many compliant politicians were owned by too many mining magnates and industrialists. Together they stood like Canute against the relentless tide, protecting their vested interests and destroying the planet.

By the time the rises in temperature and sea level were so obvious that they could no longer be ignored, and the storms had become so violent that humanity was retreating en masse to cyclone-proof structures, it was too late to reverse the process.

The only hope now was to move to another planet; but how? The cost of transporting the entire population across the universe in some huge flying ark was too great for even the richest industrialised nations to consider. Besides, the technology didn't exist that could lift such vast quantities of living matter off the planet, let alone into deep space. And even if it did, a single ark might travel through space for millennia without ever finding another habitable planet.

As the world's greatest minds pondered the problem, they turned to the question of what exactly it was to be human. What was so unique? What was so worth saving?

A leading physicist and dreamer, himself a victim of amyotrophic lateral sclerosis, argued that the body was irrelevant. What made humans human was the brain, regardless of the body that housed it. It followed, therefore, that if you could cryogenically freeze just the brain you could then send it across the universe to find new habitable environments and new host bodies.

With nanotechnology and bio-molecular science well advanced, the ability to duplicate the brain wasn't an insurmountable problem; and because the payload was so small it would be possible to dispatch millions of brains across the universe to millions of potential host-planets. But the idea had other problems. Even in purpose-built, evolutionarily modified bodies, humankind had managed to destroy itself. Would the pioneer brains be any different?

It was an ancient but still immensely popular naturalist who came up with the answer.

"Look to nature," he said.

Many species, *most* species, he argued, had existed far longer than humankind without destroying themselves. The new humans should be instilled with a natural and ethical survival system derived from nature. Each colony of brains would have to act as one to survive, just as many colonies of insects and fish had done for millennia.

Each colony would have one dominant female member, defended by an army of males and obeyed by the masses. If the dominant female died, the dominant male would change sex and take over the mantle of dominant female. The colony would survive intact and unaffected. Grafting this behaviour pattern onto the pioneer brains took scientists decades, and even then they weren't sure how successful they had been.

When the scientists and naturalists and engineers thought they had finally achieved their goal, a young girl stood up before the Assembly of their United Nations. She pointed out that the one trait that had led to the imminent destruction of the planet, and therefore of human life, was their species' disregard for its environment. The new humans, she said, should be imbued with an instinct to protect their living environment at all costs; even the cost of their own lives. Only then would their continued survival as a species be ensured.

The physicist in his wheelchair agreed, and the young girl's brain was one of the first to be duplicated, and prepared for a journey that would end light years away, on the other side of the Universe.

1 - *Forward to the Past.*

Steve Moss had spent the first half of his thirty four years dreaming of becoming a soldier, and the second half watching the dream turn into a nightmare. Perhaps he was too idealistic for the life; perhaps it was just bad timing.

The week Steve was accepted into the SAS, two planes flew into the twin towers of the World Trade Centre in New York. So for the next twelve years he was deployed alternately in Iraq or Afghanistan with just a few weeks leave between each deployment. The problem was that no matter how many patrols he went on, how many insurgents, terrorists or self-styled freedom fighters he killed, when he returned to either theatre of war after a break of a year or so, the situation was no better. There were still as many enemy to kill, as many patrols to make.

Slowly it dawned on him that all this killing was pointless. If you could knock out a leader, a Bin Laden or a Saddam Hussein, it might make a difference, albeit temporarily. But killing foot soldiers was counter-productive; it just produced martyrs, and more martyrs produced more volunteers.

Despite his misgivings, Steve remained an effective killing machine to the last. On his final patrol, his squad was attacked by a superior force and pinned down by machine gun fire. Steve single-handedly took out the machine-gun post and fought a rear-guard action while his companions returned to safety, some of them so badly wounded that they would never fight again.

He was recommended for the Victoria Cross for his actions; but that would have meant presenting him to the Queen, and even more awkwardly, to the world's media. He had become so frank and open about his views on the futility of the "War on Terror" that this was considered an unacceptable risk. Instead he was given open-ended sick leave in the hope that time would eventually re-ignite his thirst for battle. The Army was loath to lose him; they had spent a lot of money training him to kill.

Although still technically in the SAS, Steve packed his kitbag and retired to the isolation and peace of the bush. With no great faith in the future, he took solace in the past. Not the European history of the country, which went back just two hundred years, nor even the Indigenous presence there, which was reputed to go back fifty thousand years, but the history of the land itself. A sunburnt land that had been under the sea three hundred million years ago, and was still a swamp when the first pioneer brains on the other side of the Galaxy were despatched on their mission to find new worlds.

He ended up renting a small house in Winton, in Far West Queensland, and settled into life in an outback town.

His choice of Winton was not a random one. As he wandered aimlessly north, shortly after being given sick leave, he had hitched a ride with a pair of Grey Nomads. They were headed for a tourist attraction known as Lark

Quarry and Steve, with nothing better to do, went along for the ride. He had no idea that he'd just made a life-changing decision.

Lark Quarry is the site of what many believe to be the world's only known record of a dinosaur stampede. Despite this, like most Australians, Steve had never heard of the place. In the cool shelter of the purpose-built Conservation Building, he listened to the guide tell how, one day, ninety-five million years earlier, a carnivorous theropod had happened on a herd of smaller dinosaurs grazing at the water's edge. As the hunter attacked and his prey scattered, their tracks were etched into the wet earth to be preserved for millennia by the eruption of a nearby volcano. Volcanic ash settled into their footprints on the drying and hardening clay, protecting them from the sandstone that gradually built up over the area as the swamp dried up. Ninety-five million years later, archaeologists were able to simply peel back the sandstone to reveal the story that lay beneath.

Steve wondered at tracks millions of years old where ancient creatures, predator and prey, had run for their lives; the prey to survive, the predator to eat, to survive. The story was timeless. It put the twelve years of the Iraqi and Afghani conflicts into perspective. Who would remember them in ninety-five million years? Intrigued, Steve followed up with a visit to the Australian Age of Dinosaurs Museum, in Winton, 110 kilometres further north of Lark Quarry or just up the road, in Outback language.

The museum was situated on a high mesa overlooking the town and the plains below. The mesa itself was relatively new in archaeological terms, maybe only fifty million years old, so no fossil finds were ever made there. But it housed a replica of the stampede site as well as an almost complete skeleton of Australovenator Wintonensis the theropod whose tracks were preserved at Lark Quarry. And it offered programs that were designed to encourage the general public to become involved in the work of the museum. Steve joined up immediately.

During his "Dig-a-Dino" week, Steve helped search for fossilised bones scattered on or just below the surface of the black-soil plains around Winton. These dinosaur remains should, by rights, have lain undisturbed, buried metres deep in the earth. But during drought the fine soil cracks and dries, causing extensive fissures that reach down to the fossil layer. When it rains, the flood washes topsoil into the cracks, forcing the fossils upwards. Eventually, this movement thrusts the rock-encased, fossilized bone to the surface. For decades, graziers had been finding these odd-looking rocks on their properties. Now palaeontologists, with the help of volunteers like Steve, were digging the loose earth away and encasing the fossils they found in Plaster of Paris, to protect them on their journey back to the lab.

During his "Prep-a-Dino" course in the lab, Steve learned how to retrieve the fossils from their plaster tombs; firstly cutting away the Plaster of Paris, then using a device like a dentist's drill to chip at the pale rock encasing the fossils until it revealed the darker bone matter beneath. Steve learned that distinguishing bone from rock was not a particularly scientific process. When the rock changed colour he would lick the fossil. If his tongue didn't stick, he knew he was still working on rock. If his tongue stuck, he knew it was bone because the minute cavities in the bone caused a vacuum when covered in spittle, turning his tongue into a small suction pad. Steve then learned to paint silicone over the revealed bone and leave it to harden before work could commence on removing the entire fossil from the rock that enclosed and protected it.

It was slow, painstaking work and it suited Steve's mood ideally. On completion of both courses he qualified as an honorary technician, able to work in the laboratory whenever there was a space available. During the non-tourist season, that was practically all the time. Each day he would spend eight hours or more preparing fossils. Nights he spent deepening his knowledge of the southern night sky.

The skies over Winton were so clear and there was so little ambient light that he almost didn't need a telescope. This didn't stop him from buying one, of course, and the one he bought came with a laser pointer. During the tourist season, when he often couldn't get into the laboratory, he would give star-gazing lectures for tourist buses and caravanners camped overnight in Winton. So it was that on one clear, starry night Steve found himself with a bunch of tourists at Long Waterhole Camping Ground, some miles out of Winton on the Winton-Jundah Road.

Long Waterhole was Steve's favourite location for giving his star-gazing lectures. In the Outback tradition of making use of everything, the reserve also served as a Cross Country Moto-Racing Track. The land surrounding the waterhole had been cleared right back as far as the Jundah Road. The waterhole itself was surrounded by willows and gum trees and was a haven for birds and wild life, but all around it dirt ramps had been built and roads cut through the scrub.

Apart from the few days each year when the Moto-Cross was in progress it was an idyllic place to camp… and it was free. Even better from Steve's point of view, the built-up road ramps formed an ideal viewing platform from which to observe the stars, with unrestricted vision in every direction.

The tour was run by a husband and wife team, Greg and Aimee Ahearn, from Cairns. Greg drove the huge bus and Aimee did the cooking. They shared the daily task of erecting and dismantling the luxury tents the tourists slept in. Occasionally the tourists would help them. More often they would just sit and watch, which is what the current group were doing now. They sat around in silence, drinking coffee and waiting as Steve took a platform from the back of his 4WD and laid it on one of the road ramps. Aided by Greg, Steve checked it with a spirit level and bolted his reflector telescope onto the platform. The telescope wasn't of the size and power used in an Observatory but it could self-align to any object in the heavens without any input from Steve, and it was certainly powerful enough to view the usual suspects that the tourists wanted to see: the Rings of Saturn, and the myriad stars of the Kappa Crucis Cluster, more commonly known as the Jewel Box.

While Steve finished setting up his telescope Aimee Ahearn picked up a bottle of scotch from a trestle table and carried it to the waiting group.

"Anybody like something to warm up their coffee?"

Alan Ready was the first to his feet.

Alan was always ready when something was being given away. Unlike the others, men and women alike, who all wore the safari uniform of khaki shirts and shorts with stout socks and desert boots, Alan was dressed in jeans, a sweater and a very expensive pair of runners that were finding the Outback conditions hard going.

Alan liked to look different. He liked to stand out. He saw himself as a pretty shrewd operator, always on the look-out for an advantage or something for nothing.

The truth was he was a bit of a loser who still lived with his mum in Logan, a suburb south of Brisbane. He didn't really have a friend in the world except her and she didn't like him much.

He'd come on the tour because he had nobody else to holiday with, and he hadn't made any friends on the trip, either. Still, he affected an air of bonhomie as he held out his coffee mug to be topped up.

"Thanks Aimee. Bloody freezing out here."

Luc Reinhart, a German in his seventies, who showed a European disdain for the cold by wearing micro shorts and a shirt with torn off sleeves, called across to him.

"You should get yourself a good woman to cuddle, Alan."

"Maybe he could cuddle up with Danny."

Luc's wife, Leda, joined her husband in their favourite pastime of baiting Alan, who was always complaining about something. Danny Ridge looked up at the sound of his name.

"Not if he doesn't want his balls blown off," he scowled. "I'd rather sleep with me dog."

"Language... Ladies present, Danny."

The comment came, surprisingly, from a young, student type, David Symonds. He pulled the blanket he was sharing with his girlfriend Gina a little tighter around their shoulders, as if to protect her from the bad language. He needn't have bothered. Gina Bennett wasn't as delicate as David liked to think. She grinned at Danny.

"Don't think the dog would enjoy it much," she said.

"What would you know?" Danny snapped back, irritated that the conversation, which had at first been aimed at poking fun at Alan, was now poking fun at him.

Danny was a man of indeterminate age, with skin tanned deep brown and wrinkled by too many years in the sun. Travelling the Bush was a real Busman's Holiday for Danny. He was a wildcat prospector with his own private reasons for travelling with the group. He wouldn't have been seen dead with this lot, otherwise.

Keen to head off what looked like developing into a row, Aimee filled Danny's coffee mug with scotch and tried to lighten the conversation.

"That's how the blackfellas survive out here," she said, to no one in particular. "Sleeping with their dogs. A cold night's a two-dog-night. A three-dog-night, and it's like tonight, bloody freezing."

Conversation lulled as Danny slurped his spiked coffee and Aimee filled Leda's cup.

Not wanting to upset anybody, Leda, a tall, pencil-thin woman, dressed like her husband in micro-shorts, tried to distract Danny by asking:

"You have a dog, Danny?"

"Yeah, only company I need," he growled, pointedly.

"Just as well," Gina laughed, more than happy to continue teasing him.

Leda ignored her.

"You don't keep him with you?"

"He comes with me when I'm prospecting"

"You should have brought him along on the tour."

"Nah. He'd have driven you all mad; stupid mutt."

"What breed is he?"

"I dunno, Blue Heeler, I s'pose. A bit of dingo, probably."

"I love dingoes," said Leda.

Danny snorted; a laugh that wasn't a laugh.

"Tell that to Lindy," he said.

Leda looked puzzled.

"Lindy Chamberlain," Gina offered. "Her baby was taken by a dingo, like, decades ago."

"Ah yes," said Leda. "I remember now. They made a film, yes? With Meryl Streep?"

"That's the one," Gina nodded.

The conversation moved on to other stories of the Australian Outback but Danny didn't join in. He didn't like talking much. And he'd bet London to a brick someone would bring up Lassiter's Reef; then they'd start asking him questions about prospecting and maybe about why he had joined an organized tour in country that he normally travelled alone. Danny certainly didn't want that.

The truth was that gold was getting harder and harder to find, but Danny knew a dealer back in Cairns who was offering good money for fossils and Aboriginal artefacts. Rumours abounded that a major new fossil site had been found somewhere south of Winton and that the Ahearn Tour included this site; although it always kept the location a secret.

Danny had joined the group so that he could mark out the fossil site on a GPS he had hidden in his rucksack. He had managed to record the coordinates without anyone suspecting what he was doing. Now he was marking time. Once the tour was over he'd be back out there with his dog, Dog, and a few sticks of dynamite. Much easier than the painstaking way the volunteers at the Museum eased the fossils out of the ground.

Satisfied with the set-up of his telescope, Steve joined the others around the fire to warm himself. It was amazing how quickly the temperature dropped after sunset in the semi-desert, even this close to the equator. Leda watched as he squatted on his haunches and held his brown hands out to the flames.

"Did I see you working at the Museum, Steve?" she asked.

During their tour of the laboratory attached to the museum, several people had been working there, freeing fossils from the rock that encased them.

"Yes, I'm working on what we think is part of the skeleton of a theropod. Like the one whose tracks you'd have seen at Lark Quarry."

Leda nodded.

"So are you an anthropologist or an astronomer?".

Steve grinned.

"Well, neither really. I'm a soldier. At least I was."

"You retired?"

Steve stared into the flames, the grin still fixed in place.

"I just came to think it was pointless," he said.

After a pause, Leda nodded again.

"It was the same in my day," she said. "We had a saying: fighting for peace is like fucking for virginity."

Alan, who wasn't anywhere near as worldly as he liked to make out, gasped audibly at this frail little old lady speaking like that. Gina giggled and glanced at David, who fidgeted a little uncomfortably. Leda looked across at them, wrapped cosily together in the blanket.

"Not as much fun, though," she added, with a smile.

Having all their meals provided, as well as evening entertainments like Steve's star gazing lecture, made the tourists in the Ahearn party fairly privileged. The daily routine of most Grey Nomads who travel through Winton is dictated by the rising and setting of the sun. All the cafes and restaurants in the town close at six o'clock. If you want to eat later than that you have to join the locals at one of the three pubs in the main street, or cook for yourself.

So it was that, long before nine p.m., all the caravans parked around Long Waterhole were in darkness and their occupants fast asleep. The Ahearn's campfire had been allowed to die down to a faint glow and the group moved their canvas chairs up onto the ridge near Steve's telescope to listen to his lecture.

There were no clouds or moon, and the stars covered the heavens like sparkling jewels in a giant, upturned bowl. The urban travellers, used to a night sky dimmed by the ambient light of cities, had never seen anything like it. Only Danny, the prospector, could identify the Southern Cross. The rest were fooled by the False Cross, a formation of stars between Carina and Vela, brighter than the real thing and in more or less the same area of the sky. If used for navigation, however, it could put you anything up to 45 degrees off course, east or west, depending on the time of the year.

Steve used the laser pointer to pick out the False Cross and then moved on to the Southern Cross, which was dimmer and further away. Some of the stars, he told them, were so far away that they may no longer exist. They may have exploded or imploded years before, in a galactic cataclysm, the light from which could take a thousand or more years to reach the earth; always assuming that Earth was still in existence by then.

As the group stared up into the night, trying to get their heads around this, Steve moved the laser to pick out other stars and constellations. Centaurus, Lupus toward the east, and higher up, Libra.

"Anybody here born under Libra?" he asked." What star signs are you?"

"Cancer," Leda called back.
Luc found her hand in the darkness and gave it a reassuring squeeze. He alone knew that not only was she born under Cancer, but she would die under it; probably in the next year. They had decided to spend their last time

together visiting the most ancient land on earth. Leda was grateful for his silent support, but she was already strangely comforted by the thought that she was gazing on stars that perhaps had not existed for millennia. It made her feel that when she was gone somebody would still see her; still remember her.

Steve swung his laser beam off to the west in search of the constellation Cancer.

"Cancer's way off to the west, high in the sky. See it? Way up there. Look for the False Cross and go higher; Vela, Pyxis, Cancer."

His laser picked out each star and constellation as he spoke its name.

"What's that bright star there?" asked Gina. "The one just above the False Cross?"

Steve brought his laser beam back down and picked out the star. At first he had no idea what it was. There shouldn't have been a bright star in that area at all.

"Not sure. It could be a plane. Or a shooting star."
The whole group was now concentrating on the one object. In the laser's beam it seemed to be getting bigger.

"Aren't shooting stars supposed to shoot across the sky?" asked Gina.

"Not if they're coming straight towards you."
As they watched, the object was definitely getting bigger and brighter, and it wasn't coming straight towards them but moving from west to east in the southern sky. As it got closer its speed increased, until it suddenly flashed across almost directly overhead. For a brief instant the whole camping ground was illuminated as the object passed over then disappeared beyond the horizon.

A second brief impact flash and it was gone.

Darkness settled again over Long Waterhole

"What was that?"

The exclamations buzzed around Steve. But Steve was already taking out his phone, switching on his space tracking app and pointing it in the direction of the flash over the horizon. The app recorded Steve's GPS position and the exact compass reference for the dying flash.

He tried to answer their questions as he operated the app:

"There are a lot of things it could be; a comet, an asteroid, most likely space junk. There are over six hundred thousand pieces of space junk circling the earth. About twelve thousand of them fall back to earth each year."

Steve keyed in the time lag between the object disappearing over the horizon and the impact flash; less than a second. The app would automatically transmit this information, he told them, to a computer in a Space Tracking Station in far-off Perth, on the other side of the continent. If other amateur astronomers with the Space Tracking App had also seen the object crash to earth and had entered their own co-ordinates into the app, the computer would be able to pinpoint exactly where the co-ordinates dissected and give a fairly precise location for the crash.

The group of strangers, who had sat around practically in silence before the crash, were suddenly animated and united with a common purpose.

"Let's go see if we can find the crash site," said Gina.

"In the dark?" asked David, a touch nervously.

"*Not* in the dark," said Greg.

Steve agreed.

"It could be anywhere up to fifty kilometres away. And anywhere in a band as wide as ten kilometres. We'd never find it in the dark."

"We could go in the morning," Leda said.

"We've got to get back to Cairns tomorrow," Greg pointed out. "You heard what Steve said. It could be fifty kilometres away in a band ten kilometres wide. That's five hundred square kilometres."

"We could at least try," insisted Gina.

"There's probably not even anything to find," said Steve, backing up Greg. "Most of the stuff that falls back to earth just gets burnt up in the atmosphere. A whole American space lab crashed about twenty years ago, and they found almost nothing. A TV station in the States actually offered a hundred-thousand-dollar reward for anyone who could find a piece of the wreckage. A man in Perth collected a small piece of metal from off his roof and flew to the States to claim the reward. And that was it. As far as I know the rest of the lab was never found."

It was a mistake. Mention of a reward just made the group even more eager.

"So what's the harm in trying?" Alan joined in, echoing Gina. Now that he knew there might be a dollar or two to be made, he was all for it.

"It could be a piece of a Star or a Comet," pleaded Leda, "Something a million times older than the dinosaur fossils we've seen. Something that would last forever."

Luc put his arm around Leda. He knew why she wanted to find something that would last forever.

Steve didn't, but Leda's need was clearly so urgent, so desperate, that he found himself saying:

"Look, if anybody else has called in the crash, the tracking site will tell me. They'll have co-ordinates. They'll be able to pinpoint the crash."

He looked at Greg.

"Maybe you can swing by there in the morning, then? On your way back to Cairns."

Greg shrugged.

"Sure," he said. "But we'd need exact co-ordinates. Or we'll be at it all day."

Luc smiled down at Leda.

"Das object war hell. Andere leute mussen gesehen haben," he reassured her, quietly.

The object was bright. Other people must have seen it.

2 - *Duty Calls.*

Having left the travellers to go to bed dreaming of finding star fragments or some priceless treasure at the crash site, Steve returned to his small house in Winton. He still hadn't heard back from the Perth Tracking Station. Perhaps nobody else had reported the incident.

Despite the lateness of the hour, Steve was sufficiently intrigued to log into the station's website. There was nothing there. Not even his own report. He was wondering if he should call Perth - it was still only just after eight pm there - and ask if they'd received his report, when he was startled by the sound of his phone ringing.

He could tell from the phone screen that it was a Perth number but it wasn't the tracking station. Steve recognized the mocking, elite-private-school drawl immediately, without any need for the caller to identify himself; which was just as well because he didn't identify himself.

"Corporal Moss, just wondering how you were getting along?"

It was Colonel Robinson, the Commanding Officer of his SAS Regiment. Steve was immediately on the defensive.

"I'm not ready to come back if that's what you're asking."

"No, didn't think you were," the drawl became even more pronounced. "Bit of a reverse Catch 22, isn't it? If you're still mad, we don't want you. If you're not mad, you won't want to come back."

Steve let him enjoy his little joke in silence, then...

"The thing is, Corporal, you do realize that, technically, you are still in the Regiment."

"I'm not coming back."

"No, no. Don't want you to. Not in the state you're in. But you can do something for us. Nothing involving military deployment. Something right up your alley. Something you're already involved in."

Steve listened, intrigued despite himself.

"Seems the Froggies have lost an Ariane Rocket. Probably the object you reported seeing earlier this evening. They've asked for our help in recovering it. We've got some co-ordinates besides yours, so we know pretty much where it is. We're sending an astronomer up from Canberra to locate it. Thought you might meet her off the flight tomorrow morning. Drive her out to the crash site."

"So it did actually crash then? Not disintegrate in mid-air?"

"Almost certainly."

Steve could think of no reason not to help, but his Commanding Officer's next question did sow the smallest seed of doubt in his mind.

"Do you still have your service pistol?"

"No."

Steve didn't have any guns; didn't want any guns, not even a rifle for shooting feral pigs and cats.

"Well, probably no need anyway," the mocking voice

continued. "Just meet the astronomer at the Winton airstrip. Her name's McDonald. Oh, and Corporal, you're to tell nobody about this. Nobody. Understood?"

The line went dead without waiting for Steve's replay.

Robinson's call kept Steve awake for some time. It wasn't the prospect of helping the astronomer that bothered him. In fact he was keen to see the crash site, himself. But why had Robinson asked if he had his service pistol? How had he known about Steve's report when it hadn't made it onto the tracking site yet? And why had he insisted that Steve tell nobody?

Eventually Steve convinced himself that the answer to all three questions was probably just Robinson's obsession with security. He hadn't seemed concerned when Steve said he didn't have a gun. He was probably just paranoid about others getting to the crash site before them.

Nevertheless, Steve couldn't resist googling details of the Ariane Rocket and its mission. According to the Internet, the mission was supposed to last for another week. There was no mention of the rocket falling out of orbit prematurely.

It was midnight when Steve finally switched off his computer, went to bed and fell asleep. For once he didn't dream about wars and killing. But his sleep may not have been so peaceful had he made the connection between the early demise of the Ariane Rocket and the fatal crash of an American Manned Space Vehicle just a few months earlier.

3 - *Fallout.*

American interest in space exploration seemed to evaporate after the collapse of the Soviet Union and the end of the Cold War. With the threat from the Russians gone, the Military-Industrial Complex that ran the Space Race turned instead to spending its billions on more practical things. Like nuclear submarines and aircraft carriers as large as a small city, which ultimately proved totally useless and unsuited to the guerrilla-style wars that the Twenty-First Century brought.

Two decades later, when America announced a program designed to one day take man to Mars, it wasn't "reaching out." In the half-century since Kennedy's ambitious Lunar Program, innumerable countries had gained the expertise to put satellites into space. Russia, Europe, China, Japan, India, even Google. The Mars program was designed to re-establish America's superiority. Even so, there were those who thought America would be better off spending the money developing spy satellites and space-based weaponry, rather than missions to Mars.

Who knew what the Russians or Chinese were up to?

In a Space War, being able to reach Mars would be of little use.

These doomsayers claimed a victory (although, publicly, they called it a tragedy) when an American manned space capsule suddenly dropped out of the sky and crashed in the Australian Outback. It had virtually burnt up on re-entry, despite having a heat shield and a parachute. Of course, there was a myriad of possible explanations. The most likely was that it had collided with one or more of the six hundred thousand pieces of space junk that had accumulated in a vast band circling the earth over the previous fifty years; a vast rubbish dump that continues to build as humankind sends satellite after satellite into space and discards them when their useful life is over.

The American spy agencies weren't convinced, though. They descended on the crash site with more technology than they had used to excavate the mass graves from the entire Serbian/Croatian conflict. And they used experts from that excavation to examine minutely any remaining part of the American astronaut or his craft that might yield a clue to the cause of the crash. Among the experts they used was a forensic pathologist from the Australian Federal Police.

Kelly McDonald was used to dealing with an excess of physical evidence in mass graves in Croatia or in stinking, makeshift mortuaries after the tsunami in Aceh. But when she arrived at the crash site, there was virtually nothing for her to work on. As it turned out, however, the task of putting together what went wrong with the American space capsule wasn't as difficult as Kelly had first envisaged, although the results posed more questions than they answered.

The heat shield of the capsule was still virtually intact,

yet the capsule had all but disintegrated during re-entry. Metal and human tissue had vaporized, suggesting that the capsule had been spinning when it encountered the atmosphere. The astronaut must have been already incapable of righting the vehicle by then, and almost certainly the skin of the capsule had been punctured; but by what?

All that remained of the spacecraft was a molten mess, and all that remained of the astronaut was a couple of lower vertebrae. They had been protected from carbonizing in the heat by a strange blue-grey substance that stuck to the small bones. It didn't take Kelly long to identify the substance as osmium. But what was it doing in the space capsule?

The American Space Program hadn't touched osmium since it abandoned its use for coating mirrors in the space shuttle because they deteriorated so quickly. But if the Americans weren't putting osmium into space, somebody or something else was.

The American spy agencies were awash with conspiracy theorists, convinced that the osmium might have been utilised in some mode of space weaponry, either by the Russians or the Chinese. So Kelly was politely sent back to her Canberra laboratory and sworn to secrecy about what she had found, while scientists in top secret laboratories back in the States continued studying the osmium residue in an attempt to find any new, previously unknown properties.

What they found was the densest element in nature. It was immune to all attacks by acids or alkalis. It was also very difficult to machine or work, because of its hardness, brittleness, and very high melting point. Apart from that, the only notable effect was that osmium oxides left a dark smudge wherever they reacted with fatty tissue.

It made osmium ideal for making pen nibs and lifting fingerprints from crime scenes but pretty useless for anything else. Or had they missed something?

With paranoia on high alert, the dishes at the American top secret spy facility at Pine Gap were ordered to keep searching the skies over Australia for any more objects threatening to return to earth unexpectedly.

Meanwhile, unknown to them, the Americans were not the only ones still investigating the space capsule crash.

Forensic pathologists, used to having their results questioned in court, always take a B Sample of all the evidence. In this case, the B Samples were sent directly to America for back-up. But Kelly McDonald had worked at the International Court in The Hague. She understood that, in places like Croatia for example, the local authorities had a vested interest in destroying evidence of War Crimes against Serbians; while in Serbia, the Serbians had a vested interest in destroying evidence of War Crimes against Croatians. So Kelly had developed the habit of taking a secret, third sample of the evidence: a C sample. She had sent her C Samples back to her lab in Canberra.

Intrigued by the mystery of the osmium residue, Kelly had checked the C samples in her spare time and made an amazing discovery. The C sample of DNA in her Canberra Laboratory didn't match the sample she had tested on site. It seemed that she had somehow gathered the DNA of whoever was responsible for putting the osmium into the space capsule. Excitedly, she had reported her findings to the Americans and asked them to check the B samples they were storing. The response was less than friendly.

Kelly had no right to have taken evidence from the

crash site without their permission, they said. The C Samples were to be sent to Washington immediately. And the Americans didn't need Kelly's advice to carry out tests on the B Samples. They had already done so, and they were identical to the A samples. The explanation for the discrepancy she had found was obvious. The C samples had been contaminated. And the cause of the contamination was equally obvious. Since the A and B Samples were identical, the contamination must have taken place in Kelly's laboratory.

Kelly was naturally upset by the tone of the US response, but she was absolutely livid that the Americans should question her professional competence. She complained to her superiors at the Australian Federal Police. Eventually, her complaint reached the desk of the Assistant Director General for Counter Espionage and Interference at ASIO, the Australian Security Intelligence Organisation. The Deputy Director, like Kelly, had reasons not to be fond of the CIA. In her opinion, they were arrogant, secretive, and leaked like a sieve.

Her opinion was coloured by the fact that she was the ASIO agent who had authorized the bugging of the phones of the Indonesian President and his wife in 2009. The result was a considerable political embarrassment to Canberra when the feral CIA agent, Edward Snowden, fled to Russia with volumes of CIA and ASIO secrets and started broadcasting them to the world.

Nonetheless the Deputy Director couldn't be seen to be acting against the interests of the Americans. She advised Kelly that she must comply with the request and send the C Sample to Washington.

But she promised that if and when any other spacecraft crash-landed in Australia, Kelly would be given the first and exclusive opportunity to investigate the crash; without American involvement.

Kelly was hardly pacified. The chances of another spacecraft falling out of the skies with DNA on board seemed to her too remote to contemplate. She went back to her normal forensic duties vowing never to co-operate with the Americans again. But just a few months later, the Ariane rocket crashed somewhere south-east of Winton. Kelly packed her bag and prepared to catch the early morning flight out of Canberra, unaware that half a continent away, the Americans were already making their own, rather more urgent travel plans.

4 - The Middle of Nowhere.

Alice Springs lies in the dead centre of the Dead Heart of the World's driest Continent. The casual observer might wonder why anybody would want to live in such an isolated place but there are a myriad of reasons for the Alice's existence; most of them to do with Communications

Permanent waterholes in the area were meeting places for the local indigenous peoples tens of thousands of years before the arrival of the Europeans, who came to build and operate the Adelaide to Darwin Telegraph Line in the nineteenth century.

The Telegraph Line was a gargantuan endeavour, especially in the Red Centre where the MacDonnell Ranges formed a barrier running several hundred miles from East to West. The only easy way through was a pass formed by the Todd River, which only flowed intermittently but had nevertheless carved a gap in the Mountains, over millions of years.

A few miles north of this pass, known colloquially as The Gap, they discovered a permanent spring, or more accurately, a permanent waterhole because the place they call Alice Springs has no spring at all.

The Todd riverbed is usually dry with only the occasional waterhole holding permanent water. On the site of the future Alice Springs, when the water does flow, even in a trickle, it cascades over rocks and into a pool where the sides of the overhanging rock have been slowly worn away, causing the flow to drop suddenly, deep into the pool. It then bubbles up against the rock face, giving the impression of water rising from an underground spring. And while there was no actual spring, the fact that there was a permanent water hole was still reason enough to justify building the Alice Springs Telegraph Station there.

It would be hard to exaggerate the importance of the telegraph when it was first built but its day has now long gone. The Reserve, containing the telegraph offices, living quarters and even a school, is maintained as an interesting attraction for the thousands of tourists who visit the Alice every year. However, as Alice Springs has lost its importance as an Australian Communications Centre, so it has gained importance as an American Communications Centre.

Across the river, behind the Casino and Golf Course, are street after street of modern well-kept single-storey bungalows with well-watered gardens that would look far more at home in Middle America than in the Central Australian Desert. This surprising wealth is due to the even more surprising fact that Alice Springs has more University Graduates per capita than any other town or city in Australia. It also has more lesbians, and more CIA spies.

The CIA "operatives" work at the American Tracking Station at Pine Gap, situated eighteen kilometres south-west of the town. Just as the Europeans took over Alice Springs from the Indigenous Peoples so the Americans have now taken over from the Australians, because the work at Pine Gap is so secret that not even the Australian Government knows what goes on there. The facility is heavily guarded and surrounded by high fences. But if anybody wants to take a look, they can simply book a place in a hot-air balloon operated by Outback Ballooning.

Immediately above Pine Gap is, of course, restricted airspace, but as the hot air balloons take off from their base south of the tracking station, prevailing winds invariably take them high enough and close enough to view the structures, looking like giant dimpled golf balls, which house the tracking and listening devices.

In Alice Springs itself it is equally easy to find the CIA. If the buttoned down American accents in the air-conditioned shopping malls aren't a giveaway, one simply needs to drive across the river to the well-kept single storey bungalows. Being in the middle of the desert, Alice gets very hot in summer and very cold in winter, so each of these bungalows has both air-conditioning and wood stove heating.

Australians, being a pretty laid back lot, tend to use up their entire wood supply during winter and not replenish it until the following autumn. The CIA, however, takes rather better care of its operatives and ensures that their dwellings always have a full supply of firewood, even in summer. Drive along the suburban streets during summer and wherever you find a house with a neatly stacked pile of firewood standing against it, you know the occupants work for the CIA. And on the night of Steve's star gazing party the phones in these neat suburban bungalows were running hot.

Steve had used the Space Tracking App on his phone at nine p.m. Because of the half hour time difference between Queensland and Central Australia, it was still only a quarter to nine local time when a large sedan pulled up outside one of the bungalows with the neat woodpiles.

The driver wore jeans, a checked shirt and cowboy boots, but the fact that all the clothes were brand new and that he was wearing sun-glasses even though it was pitch black outside, indicated that he was not a cowboy.

No sooner had the car come to a halt than a second man came out of the bungalow wearing exactly the same uniform as the driver and carrying a leather travelling case. He put the case in the trunk and got into the front seat on the left-hand side of the car, because although this was an American car, it was a right-hand-drive vehicle. The CIA didn't want to appear conspicuous.

Despite their apparent similarities, the two men in the car had had very different careers in the CIA. The occupant of the single storey bungalow, Bamberger, had spent his time in the war zones of Asia. His transfer to Australia as the Allies withdrew from Afghanistan had been in the nature of a reward for a life spent under constant threat of death. Ramirez, on the other hand, had spent almost his entire career with the CIA in the Nevada Desert, at a highly classified base known as Area 51.

Area 51 has attracted an almost mythical reputation over the years. Its main purpose is to test military aircraft; spy planes and stealth bombers. But Ramirez's job at the base was to investigate reports of UFO sightings and other unexplained phenomena; a sort of real life Agent Mulder, but without the excitement of ever actually encountering any aliens.

There are rumours that Area 51 contains the remains of crashed alien spacecraft and even aliens themselves, but in his twenty years there Ramirez hadn't encountered a single confirmed instance of alien contact. It was natural therefore, when it was suggested that the DNA on the dead Astronaut might not be human, that Ramirez would volunteer to travel to Australia to wait for another piece of space junk to fall from the sky. He expected that there would be a mundane explanation; the DNA belonged to one of the higher apes or was simply modified human DNA. But Ramirez lived in hope. Just once, before he retired, he wanted to encounter an alien. If for no other reason than to convince himself that he hadn't wasted his entire life.

So, as usual when he set off to investigate another UFO sighting, Ramirez couldn't help feeling a rising excitement as he drove the sedan quickly and quietly across the Todd River Bridge, through The Gap and down to Alice Springs Airport. From there, an unscheduled flight would get them to Townsville on the Eastern Seaboard in about three hours. Taking it in turns to drive and sleep, the two men could then travel from Townsville to Winton by 4WD and be at the local airstrip long before dawn, when planes would resume flying in. There were no night flights into Winton from anywhere because Winton Airport had no landing lights.

5 Urban Terrorists.

There are no lights at the Long Waterhole camping site either. Greg had to turn on the light inside the tour bus to find his way to the bathroom shortly before dawn.

The bus was a converted ten-wheel-drive military vehicle, designed to take troops and equipment into war in trackless wastes. The original front seats had been removed and replaced with twelve deeply cushioned tourist seats, complete with seat belts, which would deliver a safe and comfortable ride over the roughest terrain. Behind the seats was a small toilet and washroom. Next was a storage area where each camp chair, table, bed and even the barbecue had its allotted place. All were secured and tied away to prevent them crashing around as the bus headed out to remote waterholes and sacred sites deep in the bush. When the bus was traveling, the tents that the tourists slept in were also stacked in the middle of the storage area. In camp, when they were removed and set up, Greg and Aimee lowered their foldaway bed from the wall of the bus, and this is where they slept.

As Greg stumbled out of the bus into the darkness to light the campfire, he noticed that the light in Leda and

Luc's tent was already on. He'd got the fire going and had just turned his attention to lighting up the barbecue when he was startled by a voice immediately behind him. It was Leda, talking in that strange way she had, which was part order, part statement, and part question.

"You have phoned Steven?"

"It's a bit early, Leda. He won't be up yet."

"Text him. He can choose his own time to reply. Luc, light the barbecue while Greg sends the message."

Without waiting for a response from either of the men, Leda strode off to the other tents.

"Bit of a Nazi, your wife," said Greg, good-naturedly, as he pulled out his mobile phone. Luc took the statement literally.

"Nazi? No, quite the opposite, in fact. Leda hates the Nazis."

"No, I meant she likes giving orders."

Greg shrugged off his faux pas with a grin. But although Luc enjoyed teasing members of the party, he showed no other signs of a sense of humour at all.

"Of course. She has been a University Professor back in Germany for the last forty years."

What Luc didn't tell Greg was what Leda had done before she was a University Professor and why, really, she was so accustomed to giving orders. She did indeed hate the Nazis. So much so that she had been a cell leader in the left wing European student rebellions of the seventies; the Red Army Faction and the Baader-Meinhof. This frail little old lady had been a highly proficient urban terrorist, bank robber and kidnapper of leading Industrialists.

It was only when she realized, like Steve, that her efforts were counter-productive; that the more capitalists she kidnapped, the more repressive and Nazi-like the

State became to counter the threat, that she negotiated an amnesty with the authorities.

They waived all charges and in return she repaid all ransom monies and undertook never to join any military or security organizations again, nor to seek election to any political office. Instead, she returned to the University where she had studied and there, for forty years as a lecturer in Political History, her leadership skills forced a lot of otherwise quite average students to obtain quite exceptional results.

Her leadership qualities were still to the fore as she went about gathering the group around the breakfast table while Greg messaged Steve, who was already awake.

Aware of his Commanding Officer's warning to speak to no-one; Steve didn't want to leave a text reply on Greg's phone. Instead, he called Greg straight back. What he told Greg was the truth; but not the whole truth, nor nothing but the truth.

He said he hadn't heard from the Perth Tracking Station, which was true.

He also said that he'd checked the tracking station website and there was no mention of any object falling from the sky the night before, which was also true.

He said he assumed they must have been the only people to have seen whatever it was, which wasn't true and that there were no other co-ordinates, which also wasn't true.

Finally he said that it was probably a waste of time anyway, because whatever it was had probably disintegrated in space, which might have been true.

Leda took no notice of any of this when Greg reported the conversation to her. She spread the map on the breakfast table and spoke to the assembled group.

She had drawn a line in red from the Long Waterhole

Campsite running in the south-easterly direction in which they had seen the object crash the previous night. She had also drawn a second blue line running down the Jundah Road almost until the bitumen ran out. The blue line then turned left along a dirt track leading towards Warrnambool Downs, an isolated cattle station south-east of Winton. Before the blue line on the map reached the cattle station it merged with the red line heading across Bladensburg National Park, parallel with the Winton-Longreach Road, which itself ran off to the southeast.

Leda thought that if they all pitched in they could break camp in about forty-five minutes. Aimee could prepare egg and bacon rolls; food they could eat on the run. If they followed the blue line, they would enter the search zone about twenty kilometres east of the campsite. She reasoned that if the object had crashed nearer than that they would have seen the crash. They could travel along the track of the object for an hour, enough time to spot anything if they were lucky. If not they could simply turn left onto the Longreach/Winton Road, backtrack and head north to the Undara Volcanic Tubes and Cairns, as they'd previously planned.

Greg put up a series of half-hearted objections, all of which Leda answered without even thinking about it.

It was a long drive. No problem. If Greg had to stop and rest; they'd stop and rest.

Some of the party weren't staying in Cairns that night; they were travelling on. Again no problem. They could change their plans.

Vision wasn't that good from the bus. Leda had thought of that, too. They would put one of the younger ones up on the roof rack with a clear view for miles.

Gina immediately volunteered. Dave objected. Gina's parents would kill him if anything happened to her.

He volunteered Alan instead.

Leda agreed. Alan was the perfect choice. He had very sharp eyes.

Alan didn't know whether to be flattered or scared. Instead, he decided to be greedy. If he were the first one to spot the wreck, he said, he should get first choice of any souvenirs.

"Anything we find, rocks or metal, we take it back to Cairns and get it cut into eight parts; one each," Leda insisted.

"But if there're nine pieces, I get the extra piece." Alan wasn't going to give up, and Leda didn't have time to argue.

"Okay, if there are nine pieces, you get the extra piece. Now, let's get this camp dismantled. Aimee, cook bacon and eggs rolls, brew some coffee."

And as they'd done for over forty years, everybody did exactly what Leda said.

The tour bus headed out of Long Waterhole campsite before seven a.m. and turned left; south on the Jundah Road. There was no need for a lookout up top at this stage and Greg gunned the motor with everybody safely strapped into their deeply cushioned seats. But a few kilometres south of the camp where the bitumen ran out, and the truck turned off onto the dirt track, the truck started bouncing around. Aimee insisted they slow down but although the speed gauge dropped slightly the bus still hurtled along throwing up a huge cloud of dust.

After about twenty minutes, Leda called out for Greg to stop. She had been consulting her GPS. They were at the point on the map where the blue and red lines converged.

They piled out of the truck, and while Greg attached

luggage straps to the roof rack for Alan to hold on to, Aimee went looking for a pillow for Alan to sit on. Leda swapped hats with Alan; his baseball cap for her wide-brimmed Akubra, with a cord to go under his chin to keep it on in the wind. Gina covered Alan's exposed face neck and hands with her 50+ sun cream. Alan hadn't had this much attention from a group of women since he was a breech birth at Brisbane Hospital, thirty years earlier. An incident his mother had never forgiven him for.

With Alan on the roof rack, hanging on to the straps for grim death, Greg slowly eased the bus off the track and into the bush.

Leda had now taken the seat beside him and was guiding him with her compass and GPS. But it was impossible to keep driving in a straight line because of the gullies and occasional trees that dotted the landscape in the Bladensburg National Park. Aimee wasn't sure Alan would survive too long on the roof.

"After an hour, David can replace him," Leda said, looking up briefly from her GPS, but only to check the vista ahead.

Gina grinned excitedly at this news, but David looked decidedly uncomfortable and hoped they'd find what they were looking for, long before then.

After crossing a couple of dry riverbeds and narrowly avoiding the trees that lined their banks and threatened to sweep Alan off the roof with their upper branches, the going began to get a lot easier. The soil in the area was poor at the best of times and the drought had made it even worse. In the Bladensburg National Park, which they had now crossed, the occasional tree and shrub survived, but now they were on private land. Grazing cattle had eaten any vegetation and killed off any small trees struggling for survival. The only prominent landmark was a small hill up ahead, directly in their path. It looked quite close when they first sighted it, but twenty minutes later it still seemed as far away as ever. It was nearly an hour before Greg eventually pulled the bus to a halt at the foot of the hill.

"Why are you stopping?" Leda asked, too intent on the task at hand to notice the passage of time.

"The hour's up," said Greg. "Time to relieve Alan."

David wasn't at all happy about swapping places with Alan. He was even less keen when they found Alan clinging to the bus so hard that he couldn't let go and they had to prise his hands off the luggage straps. Greg's insistence that they'd have to abandon the search in about half an hour anyway and turn off for the Longreach-Winton Road didn't reassure David either. He looked around for a way out; then he looked up.

What if he climbed the hill? You should be able to see for miles from up there. If there were nothing to see, it could save them a lot of time.

So, while Greg, Luc and Danny man-handled Alan down from the roof, David started to climb the hill, followed by the ever eager Gina.

It wasn't so much a hill as a single rock that at some stage had been deposited on the surrounding plain, and had defied all of nature's attempts over the ages to wear it down. Nothing but a few tufts of grass grew on the rock, and the ascent got steeper and steeper even though there was a clear path where previous visitors had made their way to the top.

It wasn't long before Gina overtook David and clambered on up, while he proceeded more slowly, almost on hands and knees.

The truth was, he suffered from vertigo. Not badly, just badly enough to tremble every time Gina took him to the edge of a waterfall in Kakadu, or a rock face in Northern Queensland, to enjoy the view.

He needn't have worried. Gina got to the top of the rock long before him, took a deep breath of the warm, clean air and started to do a slow three hundred and sixty-degree inspection of the surrounding plain. She took her starting point from the parked bus, looking out to the south-east, in the direction the bus had been travelling.

Since she was turning in a clockwise direction, it wasn't until she had completed almost a full rotation that she stopped and yelled to the people below.

"I've found it. Over there. Quite close. A huge crater."

David never did get to see the view from the top of the rock, but he didn't get to sit on top of the bus either, and that was more than enough compensation. He also didn't mind Luc teasing him, saying that if there were a ninth souvenir, Gina should be the one to have it since she saw the wreckage first.

Alan, however, took this statement rather badly. After all, he'd had to endure an hour clinging to the top of the bus, getting splattered with flies and insects as they rushed past, and having the life shaken out of him. It wasn't fair.

He spent the short time it took to drive the bus around the rock and across to the crater's edge, stamping his feet and rubbing circulation back into his arms and legs. So that when the bus stopped, he was the first one out. And while the others stood around taking photos of the ten-meter wide crater and the rocket nose cone half-buried at the bottom of it, Alan clambered down to the wreckage. It was a steep and dangerous slope. He could easily have slipped and broken his neck but that wasn't going to stop Alan. He'd earned the right to lay first hands on whatever treasure the rocket held.

The Ariane Rocket nose cone was in surprisingly good condition. Alan knew it was an Ariane rocket because the word 'Ariane' was printed on the side. It was built to carry a payload, usually of scientific instruments or a satellite, and to return safely to earth, so it wasn't a surprise that it had survived re-entry. What was surprising was that it had done so with a neat round hole cut in its side.

Alan scrambled down the side of the crater, skidding on the loose earth and shale that had been thrown up by the impact. He bent down to inspect the nose cone and the hole in its side. He tentatively touched the edge of the hole then pulled his hand back in shock. It was cold.

"It's cold," he called up to the others.

Leda, the University Lecturer, pointed out that the temperature in space is close to absolute zero. The heat shield at the tip of the cone would have heated up during re-entry, but the bulk of the rocket would remain cold.

Aware of what to expect now, Alan touched the smooth round hole in the side of the rocket for a second time. It was so neat and perfectly round that it seemed like it had been cut by a machine. As Alan ventured his hand further into the dark interior of the nose cone something brushed up against his fingers. He yelled and quickly withdrew his hand as a large blue-grey marble rolled out of the hole and fell to the ground at his feet; followed by another and another until there were eight marbles lying there.

Alan bent down, scrabbling to pick them up.

"What have you got there?" Greg called from the edge of the crater.

"Ball bearings, I think."

Greg threw his wide-brimmed hat down to Alan.

"Put 'em in there. We'll divvy them up."

"I found them."

"Put 'em in the hat... unless you want to walk back to Cairns."

Alan snatched up the hat and started dropping the marbles into the upturned crown. But not even the threat of being marooned was enough to stop him from wanting more than his fair share. As he scrabbled in the dust with one hand, he picked up a couple of marbles with the other and surreptitiously tucked them into his sock. So that when he climbed back out of the crater and handed the hat back to Greg, there were six marbles inside, not eight.

Leda had been hoping for something alien, a little piece of a star, not the wreckage of a rocket, so she was more than happy to give up her marble and share one with Luc. Under the impression that they were the only ones who knew where the wreck was and therefore he could come back at any time to retrieve the whole rocket, Greg also generously agreed to share with Aimee.

The others took a marble each. Alan stuck his into his pocket immediately, trying to hide his triumph. Gina rolled her marble around in her hand.

"It's dirty. It rubs off on your hand," she said.

"Probably a powdered lubricant, like lithium," said Danny the Prospector. He wrapped his marble in a dirty handkerchief, stuffed it in his pocket and attempted to wipe his hands clean on his equally dirty shorts.

David had put his marble onto a clean tissue, which he now held out to receive Gina's marble. As she dropped hers onto the tissue, it kissed the second marble, and the two of them seemed to dance around each other, coming together occasionally to touch. Gina smiled with delight.

"They're dancing."

"They're lovers," said David, putting the marbles away and wrapping his arms around Gina. "Like us."

He didn't know how right he was.

And Steve didn't know how wrong he was when he drove north out of Winton towards the airstrip, a little over an hour later, at a few minutes to ten. Ahead of him he saw the Ahearn's bus, travelling north, past the airstrip turnoff and on to Hughenden, heading for the Undara Lava Tubes and Cairns.

They must have had a lie-in, Steve thought. *Well, at least they're not somewhere out there, searching for space junk.*

6 - *Lost in Space.*

Winton Airport is situated three kilometres north-east of Winton on a right turn, off the Hughenden Road. There is only one sealed landing strip, crossed by a shorter dirt runway for the local bush pilots. The airport is run by the local council and the gate to the car park, the only access to the Airport, is locked unless a scheduled flight is due in the next hour. Then a council worker comes out and unlocks the gate. The council worker also unlocks the small building that serves as a terminal, re-stocks the chips and drinks in the vending machine that serves as a cafeteria, and waits for the plane to land. When it takes off again, he relocks the gate and returns to the air-conditioned comfort of his Council Office.

As Steve drove into the car park, he recognized every vehicle there. There was the Council vehicle; the Australia Post van waiting to pick up the mail; a couple of taxis and a tour bus that had brought passengers for the outgoing flight and would pick up another group from the incoming flight; and the local paddy wagon. The presence of the police vehicle was unusual. Winton Airport wasn't exactly security conscious. They weren't expecting any terrorists to pass through any day soon. The two cops were waiting inside the small terminal building, breakfasting on chips and soft drinks from the vending machine. Steve knew them both and had always thought they made an odd couple. Both were overweight but there the similarity ended. Sergeant Bill Maher had a shock of ginger hair and the type of light freckled skin that led to the coining of the phrase "redneck" when the Celts first ventured to warmer climates from Scotland and Ireland. Not that Bill was a racist; he just didn't care about anybody but himself. His partner, Carl Miller, was aboriginal. He was half as old as Bill and twice as smart; a fact he didn't bother to hide because Bill wouldn't have recognized it anyway.

Steve, having walked in out of the glare of the early morning sun, stood at the door letting his eyes get accustomed to the gloom. Carl called a greeting, and he crossed over and sat down beside the two policemen.

"What are you two doing here?"
Bill didn't bother to lower his voice.

"Same as you, meeting the suit from Canberra. We're supposed to follow you to the crash site. If there's anything to find, we're supposed to bung it in the back of the wagon and bring it back. If it's too big, we've gotta organize a truck."

Steve said he thought it was more likely there would be little or nothing to find. That the rocket had disintegrated during re-entry. It was certainly burning brightly enough as it passed overhead, the night before.

"Yeah, bloody waste of time, I reckon," Bill agreed.

"Rockets'd be expensive, but, eh?" Carl chipped in, in the strange way Queenslanders have of making a statement and asking a question, both at the same time.

Bill just stared at him, which was okay because Carl

wasn't expecting a response.

A man in a check shirt, jeans, cowboy boots and sunglasses, who had been standing nearby at the vending machine, pondering his purchase, suddenly seemed to make up his mind. He bought a can of coke and walked out of the terminal into the car park. It was Ramirez.

If Steve had thought about it, he might have wondered how Ramirez had got to the airport because he didn't belong with any of the vehicles parked outside.

If Carl had thought about it, he might have wondered why Ramirez was at the airport waiting when they arrived but left before the plane arrived.

If Bill had thought about it, it wouldn't have made any difference. He was back at the vending machine getting another packet of chips.

Ramirez walked out into the car park and around behind the paddy wagon so that he was out of view to anybody in the terminal. He stepped up on the wheel hub and lifted himself high enough to reach the top of the metal box that was fitted on the back of the paddy wagon as a mobile holding cell. He placed a magnetized tracking device in the middle of the metal roof, where even people as tall as Bill wouldn't be able to see it unless they, too, climbed onto the wheel hub. Then he waited until Bamberger arrived in a brand new 4WD to pick him up.

They drove out of the airfield and into town, where they parked outside a convenience store. After checking that the transmission from the tracking device was working properly on the screen in the 4WD, the two men went into the convenience store to stock up on food and water. They knew the police vehicle was heading for the bush and they had no idea how long they might be out there.

Best be prepared, because they were pretty much making it up as they went along.

When the Americans learned that Kelly had discovered DNA in the crashed Space Module that they'd somehow missed, they resolved next time not to involve the Australians. Instead, they'd sent extra agents, including Ramirez, to Alice Springs to wait for another opportunity and conduct any search or investigation required. They were confident that their superior equipment at Pine Gap could track any object falling to earth long before the Australians got wind of it. But thanks to the app created by an enterprising astronomer in a small Perth tracking station, amateurs all over Australia could record the time, position and direction of their sightings simply by switching on their mobile phones. So while the Americans had Pine Gap, the Australians had a thousand pairs of eyes scattered across the continent.

Of course, Pine Gap listened to every message ever sent across Australia. In fact, they had a weekly flight back to the States from Alice Springs just to carry this data home. They particularly listened to messages sent by the star-gazing app. They recorded Steve's message from Winton indicating that the crash site was to the south-east. They recorded the message of an amateur astronomer in Longreach who reported the crash site as being south-west. And they recorded a message from Windorah that reported it being in the north- east. They had the triangulation; they knew where the crash site was, but they were surprised by the speed of Canberra's response. They were even more surprised to find that Canberra was just sending a single, female pathologist and giving her just one soldier with a history of mental disorder to help her. They figured the Australians had done this to try to keep a low profile, which was fine because it made their task much easier. They'd simply let Kelly and Steve find the crash site. Then they'd close in and remove the wreckage, using as little force as necessary. They already had a team of two more Agents in Mount Isa hiring a helicopter for the purpose. Now all they had to do was wait.

Regional Express Airline, or REX as it's better known, runs the regular flight service between Townsville and Winton. With just one flight a day they don't have permanent ground staff at Winton, so as the small Fokker came in to land it was the council employee who guided it to its final resting place. He then pushed the stairs out to allow the passengers to disembark; then he drove the trolley out to collect the luggage.

Kelly was the first passenger off the plane, carrying only hand luggage. She strode across the tarmac and shook hands with Steve, having recognized him because he was standing with Bill and Carl.

Steve thought she walked more like an athlete than an astronomer, although in truth he'd never met a female astronomer before so he had no one to compare her with.

He was surprised by her urgency. She was keen to get straight on the road. Steve pointed out that he needed the coordinates first. She had them ready and while she visited the Ladies Restroom, Steve laid a map on the table in the terminal, and looked for the quickest and easiest way to reach the crash site.

There were two alternatives. Straight down the Winton-Longreach Road and then across open country was the quickest.

The other option was to travel to the Long Waterhole campsite, get under the flight path of the rocket and follow it across the Bladensburg National Park into open farmland.

The advantage of the second route, as Steve explained to Kelly when she returned from the restroom, was that for the last twenty or so kilometres they'd be travelling along the flight path. If anything had fallen off during the rocket's descent they might find it.

"Not much chance of that," muttered Bill, who thought the whole exercise wasn't really police business.

"How much longer would it take on the Flight Path route?" asked Kelly.

"About an hour."

"It could be worth it," said Kelly. "We're in no hurry." As if to contradict herself, she picked up her hand luggage and headed for the exit.

"Shall we go?"

Kelly was out the door before Steve even had time to fold up his map, and Bill almost forgot to recover the last of his chips from the table.

They drove out of the car park in convoy; Steve and Kelly in his 4WD, followed closely by the paddy wagon, driven by Carl. Turning left on the main road they drove south through the town and past the 4WD still parked outside the Convenience Store. Bamberger and Ramirez waited until the convoy was out of sight before starting the engine and following slowly.

Steve drove in silence through the town and south onto the Jundah Road.

Eventually, he couldn't resist asking the question that had been bugging him ever since his Commanding Officer's call the previous night.

"Why send an astronomer?"

"Sorry?"

"Why send an astronomer to a crash site? Why not an Aerospace Engineer? Somebody from Australian Aerospace? They're fully owned by the European Aeronautical Defence and Space Group, aren't they?"

"How do you know that?"

"I googled it."

ASIO had anticipated this question. The truth was they didn't want the Europeans crawling over the wreckage before Kelly had completed her examination any more than they wanted the Americans. But they also didn't want to reveal that she was a forensic pathologist. Who knows what strange tales of little green men might circulate if the locals heard a "Forensic Scientist" was examining a "Rocket from Outer Space"?

They'd come up with a plausible cover story that Kelly had learned off pat.

"This is just a P.R. exercise, really. You probably know Australian Aerospace has nothing to do with the Space Program. They just build Defence aircraft. We track the European Satellites through our Observatories at Stromlo and Spring Sidings, so I know the Europeans well. My job is just to find the nose cone, wrap it up and send it back to them; provided it's intact, of course."

Steve nodded as if this made perfect sense and the pair drove on in silence until they left the sealed road and approached the Long Waterhole camping grounds. Steve drove up onto the ramp where he had delivered his lecture the previous night and stopped.

As they got out of their 4WD, the Police paddy wagon pulled up behind them. Carl clambered out, but Bill stayed put with the engine and the air-conditioning running.

Kelly was intrigued by the strange artificial ridges, tracks, and ramps.

"What is this place?"

"It's a Moto-Cross track. At least it is for a couple of days a year. The rest of the time it's a great camping spot and an ideal location to deliver my Star Gazing lectures. I was standing right here when the rocket passed overhead."

Steve positioned himself exactly where he had been standing the night before.

"I was using a laser pointer to pick out Cancer in the east."

He pointed with his finger.

"One of the tourists was a Cancer. I was pointing out her constellation. Find the False Cross, look up, past Lupus, Pyxis, to Cancer."

He paused. Kelly nodded knowingly. Behind her, Carl looked confused. Steve caught his eye, smiled slightly and carried on with his report.

"Then, just above Lupus, there was this bright object that shouldn't have been there. It came flashing across just south of us and almost passed overhead. Lit the place up, I can tell you. Then it disappeared over the horizon in that direction. There was a flash, and shockwaves not a second later, so I guessed it must have crashed, and crashed pretty close."

"OK, let's follow it," said Kelly and led the way back to the 4WD.

Carl hung back a bit, waiting for Steve to walk past him.

"Where's this woman from, Steve?"

"Mount Stromlo Observatory in Canberra apparently." Steve got into his 4WD while Carl hitched his trousers and gun belt and clambered back into the paddy wagon.

Bill hadn't missed the exchange.

"We got a problem?"

"Dunno. But she's not an astronomer."

"How would you know?"

"Lupus is nowhere near Pyxis, this time of the year."

"Yeah, right," said Bill, not having a clue what Carl was talking about.

The paddy wagon followed Steve's 4WD around the Moto-Cross track north of the water hole. They needed to go straight across the National Park to pick up the flight path of the doomed rocket cone, but they couldn't drive due east from here. Even though the country was in its usual drought-ridden state the river bed at Long Waterhole was still filled with water, which stretched for quite a distance south, hence the name: Long Waterhole. To the north however, the riverbed was dry, and Steve crossed there then headed south to pick up the flight path.

A short while later, Ramirez and Bamberger drove up to the Waterhole. They didn't know the local terrain, which is why they'd decided to let the Aussies find the nose cone for them in the first place. But it also meant they didn't know where the river crossing was. Steve and Kelly had obviously got across because the tracking device on the roof of the paddy wagon was slowly moving further away. Since it was moving southeast, it was counter-intuitive for Ramirez and Bamberger to travel north around the waterhole to find a crossing, so they moved south. When, eventually, they did find a crossing, they found the terrain to the south heavily covered in tough scrub and crisscrossed with dried up river beds and ravines.

More than once Ramirez and Bamberger had to retrace their steps and find another way around an obstacle, just to keep moving in what was now a due easterly direction according to the tracking signal. They weren't concerned about losing the paddy wagon. The tracking device was satellite-guided and had an infinite range. However, it did mean they wouldn't reach the crash site before Kelly had time to examine the nose cone, and that was the last thing they wanted. They considered contacting the Agents who were hiring the helicopter in Mount Isa and asking them to help. But after some thought, they decided they didn't want to admit they'd stuffed up, and just pushed on.

After an hour or so of hard, frustrating driving, they emerged from the National Park into open, sun-parched grazing land. Bamberger gunned the engine and they surged forward at a reckless pace, knowing they were still likely to be too late. The tracking device up ahead had stopped moving. The Aussies had reached the crash site.

7 - *Who's Lost Their Marbles?*

Steve's 4WD and the paddy wagon were parked near the edge of the crater. Kelly had insisted that the vehicles didn't get too close, and the men themselves stand back so that they wouldn't contaminate the crash site. So the three men stood back, watching, as she circled the crater taking photos of the nose cone and its surroundings. Bill watched Kelly as if she had lost her mind. Carl hitched his trousers and gun belt and grinned at Steve.

"Astronomer, eh?"

Kelly completed her circumference of the crater, talking into her recorder as she went.

"The crater is quite shallow, suggesting that the nose cone came in at an oblique angle. If the ground had been harder, the wreck would probably have just skidded along the ground but it's dry and crumbly from the drought. The earth surrounding the wreck is just dry dust."

Kelly bent down and picked up some of the dust which she let run out through her fingers. There was virtually no wind. The dust hung in the air before it drifted away.

She clambered down to the nose cone. As she did so,

the earth shifted, and more dust cascaded down to fill her footsteps, leaving just tell-tale ridges to show where she had been.

At the base, she started to examine the nose cone itself, still talking all the time into her recorder.

"The nose cone is remarkably undamaged; at least it is on the top side away from the impact. The only anomaly seems to be a neat cylindrical hole in the side of the cone."

Kelly took a pair of spotless white gloves from her pocket, took out a flashlight and started to examine the hole in the nose cone.

"CSI," said Carl, who watched a lot of television.

Steve nodded. He called out to Kelly.

"Was it carrying an astronaut?"

Kelly called back, irritated at being interrupted.

"Of course not, it's a French Ariane rocket. The French don't send astronauts into space. If they want somebody up there, they hitch a ride with the Russians to the International Space Station. This nose cone was designed to deliver satellites into orbit."

Kelly turned back to her inspection but now held the recorder closer to her mouth and spoke more quietly.

The men moved closer to the edge of the crater and strained to hear as she described her actions.

Kelly shone the torchlight through the cylindrical hole into the dark interior of the nose cone and virtually whispered into the recorder.

"There's quite a lot of damage to the equipment inside the nose cone. It seems to have been caused by impact from a shell-like object. Ammunition shell, not sea shell. It seems to have pierced the side of the nose cone and lodged itself inside. I'm going to try to recover it."

Before putting her hand into the dark interior, Kelly

held her camera over the hole and took enough flash photos to cover the whole interior of the cone in minute detail. She then removed the camera and tentatively placed her gloved hand into the cone. Kelly could easily get her hand around the diameter of the shell-like object and prize it loose, but holding the cylinder meant her hand was now too large to retract through the hole. She let go of the shell, which fell back to the bottom of the cone.

She shone her torch into the cone again, looking for a way to grip the shell and pull it out through a hole barely larger than itself. Having moved the cylinder she could now see that it was hollow. She photographed the interior then continued recording, quietly, as she tried once more to recover it.

"The cylinder is hollow, pointed at one end and the bottom or blunt end is open. Inside is a round structure or band, which may be there to add strength to the cylinder, or it may have held something in place. I'm going to try to retrieve the cylinder by holding on to the band and pulling it out lengthways."

Kelly took a pair of pliers from her shoulder bag, reached in and clasped the band with the pliers. Then she started to withdraw the cylinder through the hole, still recording as she went.

"The band is firmly fixed inside the cylinder so both are coming out of the hole."

She held the cylinder in the sunlight and examined it closely. She put her pliers back into her bag then put her gloved hand into the cylinder to touch the band. When she removed her hand, the fingertips of the pristine white glove were covered in blue-black smudges.

"Yes, the band was apparently used to hold something in place. There are eight round depressions in the band, each large enough to hold a sphere or ball bearing. The inside of these depressions are coated in what looks like an osmium oxide. It forms when powdered osmium comes into contact with the air so the ball-bearings, or whatever they are, must have still been in the cylinder when the cone re-entered the earth's atmosphere. I'm going to have a look now to see if they were dislodged inside the nose cone."

Kelly shone her torch into the nose cone. The interior wasn't very large, and there weren't many places the marbles could hide. They would have simply rolled to the bottom of the nose cone. They weren't there.

"There's nothing inside the nose cone, I'm going to look at the surrounding area. They may have been dislodged during impact and fallen out through the hole."

As Kelly reached down to search in the dust, Carl called down to her.

"If you're looking for what fell out, you're too late."

Kelly looked up at him, startled. She had been so engrossed in what she was doing she'd practically forgotten the men were there. She certainly didn't think they could hear what she was saying into her recorder.

"What d'you mean?"

Carl's people had been following tracks in this country for fifty thousand years.

"Someone"'s been here before us," he said. "See where you scrambled down to the wreck? The ridges you left in the dirt? There's another set of ridges right next to it."

Kelly looked where he was pointing. Even after he had pointed out the tracks they seemed vague and indistinct.

"And something was on the ground," Carl went on. "You can see where they been scrambling around to pick it up. Finger marks. Fresh; a couple of hours ago at most. They'd blow away pretty quick."

Carl was still standing on the edge of the crater, several metres from the cone. It irritated Kelly that he could see things she had missed, although admittedly she'd been concentrating on the nose cone, not the ground. She was even more irritated by the fact that somebody had beaten them to the wreck site.

"I suppose you can tell me who it was, too," she said, sarcastically.

Carl wasn't offended.

"Greg Ahearn and his Tourist Bus, I reckon. The mob Steve was talking to when the rocket crashed. We've bin following their tyre tracks for the last few miles. Bloody big buggers they are. They drove off towards the Winton-Longreach Highway. If we'd come that way, we probably would have bumped into 'em as they were leaving."

"We wouldn't," Steve said. "I saw the bus heading north out of Winton when I was driving to the airport. Thought they were running a bit late. They must have come out here at first light."

Kelly put her recorder back into her shoulder bag and clambered up the side of the crater using her hands and feet. By the time she reached the top, her pristine gloves were the colour of the black dirt of the plains. She confronted Steve.

"Why didn't you say something?"

"Say what? I saw a tourist bus driving through town. If you'd told me what you were up to, maybe I could have been more help."

"I'm not up to anything. Have you got this man's mobile number? Ahearn, whatever his name is?"

"Sure."

"Phone him. Tell him the things they took from the crash site are the property of the European Space and Defence Agency. I want them back; all eight of them.

Otherwise, they're in deep trouble."

Kelly angrily and impotently tried to brush the black earth off of her gloves as Steve moved off to dial Greg's number.

Bill stood there impassively, no idea what was going on, while Carl felt a little guilty that he'd shown Kelly up. Perhaps he should have said something earlier.

"Them old fellas, they taught us young'uns to follow tracks from the time we were three or four," he said in a conciliatory tone. "We notice things other people miss. When you're hunting for food, your life depends on it."

Kelly wasn't mollified.

"Yes, well, my career depends on me noticing things, too."

Steve wasn't getting any answer on the phone.

"There's a surprise," said Kelly. "Leave him a message. Tell him what I said. Where is he now?"

"Half way to Cairns."

"Right, well, we're going after him."

And Kelly climbed into the 4WD without waiting for a reply.

Bill walked up and tapped on the 4WD window. With the engine turned off, Kelly had to open the door to speak to him.

"Do you want us to come with you?" he asked.

"What use would you be?" Kelly snapped, then realized she was going too far. It wasn't their fault.

"Stay here and guard the nose cone. I'll arrange for someone to come out and collect it."

"How long's that gonna take?"

Bill's whining set Kelly off again.

"As long as it takes."

She slammed the door shut again, and Steve switched the engine on and drove off in a cloud of dust.

Bill stood there impassively as the dust swirled around him.

"Bloody woman. If she was married to me, I'd bloody drown her."

Carl grinned.

"If she was married to you, she'd probably drown herself."

He hitched up his trousers and gun-belt and started down the crater.

"Come on; let's have a look at this rocket. We might find somethin' else she missed."

But as Carl scrambled down to the nose cone, Bill remained motionless, determined to be bored.

A few hundred yards away Ramirez and Bamberger were watching from the cover of the rock. They had recorded everything since they'd arrived with the latest and best surveillance equipment money could buy. Even so they hadn't been able to hear or see what Kelly had been doing when she was in the crater, so they had only the vaguest notion of what was going on. They did, however, know that somebody else had beaten Kelly to the crash site, and that was a relief. If Kelly had found something before they'd arrived, they would have had to admit they'd gotten themselves lost. This way they could call in with vital information without revealing that they'd messed up.

Using a satellite phone, they called the American Embassy in Canberra and just a few minutes later the American Ambassador called the Australian Foreign Affairs Office to advise them that an Ariane Rocket had crashed to earth over Australia.

They, the Americans that is, had pinpointed the crash site, and they had a helicopter in the region. The Ambassador was offering to collect the wreckage and deliver it to wherever the Australians wished.

The Head of the American Desk at DFAT received this news as if it were the first he had heard about any Ariane Rocket, which in fact it was. However after a brief discussion with the Defence Department and ASIO, the Head of the American Desk was back on the phone to the Ambassador. He accepted his gracious offer and requested that the nose cone be taken to the Australian Aerospace Facility at Brisbane Airport. As the Ambassador would know, the AAF was a wholly owned subsidiary of the European Aerospace and Defence Corporation who owned the Ariane Rocket. They could provide a Crash Investigation Officer and Aerospace engineers to determine the cause of the crash. The Americans would, of course, be most welcome to co-operate in the investigation.

The Head of the American Desk didn't mention Kelly or the missing marbles because he knew nothing about them. But his offer did tell the Americans that if the Aussies were happy to let them inspect the wreck then whatever had caused the crash was no longer at the crash site. Accordingly they started deploying the various teams of agents they now had headed towards Far North Queensland; one team to trace the Ahearn Bus, a second to pick up Kelly and Steve on the road to Cairns. In both cases, the orders were to observe and report back.

Meanwhile, as Carl was still examining the interior of the nose cone and searching the crater for more debris, two Americans in check shirts, jeans and sunglasses suddenly appeared at the rim of the crater and introduced themselves as being from NASA. They told Bill the nose cone was theirs, and that they'd organised a helicopter to collect it. Bill and Carl would soon be getting a call from their superiors confirming this. In the interim, they'd appreciate it if Carl would get out of the crater and stop contaminating the scene.

Apart from this, they were friendly enough and shared their sandwiches and soft drinks with Bill and Carl while they waited.

Sure enough, Bill received a call from Brisbane shortly afterwards. He was more than happy to hand everything over to the Yanks and get back to Winton and a cold beer in the beer garden at the North Gregory Hotel.

Carl, however, who recognized one of the men from the Airport in Winton; who knew that the rocket cone was French, not American; and whose mother had read him Lewis Carroll when he was a child, thought things were just getting curiouser and curiouser.

As he and Bill drove from the crash site, he used his hands-free to call Steve and tell him what had happened. He also asked Steve to tell Kelly he'd conducted a thorough examination of the nose cone interior and the surrounding area. There was definitely no sign of any ball bearings. Ahearn and his tourists must have taken the lot.

8 - *Two Lonely People.*

The atmosphere had been pretty frosty when Kelly and Steve started their journey back to Winton.

Firstly Kelly queried whether they weren't going the wrong way as Steve drove north-east from the crash site. Winton was north-west, wasn't it? Steve pointed out that they would get to the highway much quicker heading north-east. Then they could gun the motor up the highway.

Next Kelly queried whether Steve had told Ahearn where the wreck site was. Steve pointed out that he didn't know where it was until Kelly gave him the coordinates. The tourists were curious. Who wouldn't be? Kelly shouldn't blame herself. She couldn't have got to Winton any sooner.

Kelly resented the suggestion that she was blaming herself, and the vehicle filled with an uneasy silence. It was Steve who finally broke the silence.

"Are you an only child?"

"What's that got to do with anything?"

"You're not very good at sharing things, are you? Not even the blame."

Kelly sat there in silence. She was an only child. Kelly had never understood why her mother had her. Her mother had hired a Nanny and was back at work before Kelly was six weeks old. She had never known her father to be anything other than 'at work' too. When she turned six she was bundled off to a boarding school. She spent most of her school holidays with her maternal grandparents who were as confused as Kelly as to why their daughter had presented them with a grand-daughter when she clearly wasn't interested in children.

With nothing else to occupy her emotionally or intellectually, Kelly had excelled at school and University. She studied Medicine, but she found the patient contact confronting. In her sixth year at Uni, she decided to specialize in Pathology; in particular Forensic Pathology. She felt more at home with dead bodies.

Steve felt sorry for her without knowing exactly why, but she was a hard person to comfort.

He tried pointing out that if the crash site were so important, Robinson should have sent him out to the site at first light to secure the area. Bill and Carl could have brought Kelly out later.

Kelly didn't even know who Robinson was. Besides, she told Steve, she hadn't wanted anybody tampering with the crash site before she got there.

Steve gave up trying to be nice.

"I was in the SAS for twelve years. I'm used to securing positions."

"This is different."

"How? What's the difference between securing a gun position and securing a space wreck? I'm not stupid. Why do you think I asked you if it was a manned spacecraft? I've worked out you're a pathologist."

"Well, that wasn't difficult."

"Then why keep it a secret?"

"Because we didn't want to cause a panic."

As soon as Kelly said it, she regretted it. She clammed up, but Steve wasn't going to let her get away with that.

"Panic about what?"

Kelly was damned if she told him. Damned if she didn't. She decided that taking him into her confidence was the lesser of two evils.

"This isn't the first spacecraft to crash back to earth. There was a manned American Capsule a few months back."

"I read about it."

"The Americans asked me to examine the remains; the remains of the astronaut. There wasn't much left, a few vertebrae with osmium attached to them."

Steve had heard Kelly mention osmium when she was recording her findings at the crash site.

"Like the marbles or whatever they were?"

"Like the marbles. It looks like somebody is deliberately knocking space vehicles out of the sky. Have you any idea what a panic there'd be if that got out? Without satellites, there'd be no communications, no television, no GPS and no International flights. There'd be chaos."

"You think the shell in your bag is what they're using?"

"It looks like it."

"So what's the significance of these osmium marbles?"

"We don't know, but I found something else in the original crash. DNA attached to the osmium. Not the astronaut's DNA. You can tell a lot from DNA. There are key indicators that tell where a person comes from. It may have told us who made whatever it is that is knocking these spacecraft out of the sky.

The Americans took all the DNA samples. By now they've probably analysed them. They may even know who's attacking the spacecraft, and how."

"Probably not how. You've got the shell."

Kelly took the shell out of her bag and examined it again. It was completely hollow except for the band in the middle.

"But how is this propelled through space?"

"Maybe it's a nose cone too," said Steve. "Maybe the rocket has burnt up and dropped off."

Kelly examined the base of the cylinder. There were indentations where something had been latched onto the exterior. The bottom edges of the cylinder were scorched. Steve was right. It had been propelled by a rocket that had burnt out.

"But why shoot down satellites and space capsules? It makes no sense."

"Maybe they didn't mean to knock them out. If they did, the shell would be filled with explosives, surely?"

"So what's the significance of the osmium marbles?"

Steve grinned.

"Don't ask me. I'm a genius, but you can't expect me to do all your work."

Kelly smiled back at him. She was beginning to feel better about things. Obviously she was holding the most important part of the puzzle in her hand. And it shouldn't be too difficult getting the marbles back from the tourists. All she had to do was get the police to wait at Ahearn's base in Cairns for the bus to get there. Then make sure nobody left before they handed over the marbles. Not even Carl's call spoilt her mood. So what if the Americans took the nose cone? She had the important bit. The wreck could tell them nothing she didn't already know.

As they drove into Winton, Kelly suggested they fill up

with diesel, food and water. They probably wouldn't catch up with Ahearn before he reached Cairns, but if they took it in turns to drive and drove straight through, they wouldn't be far behind. Kelly had handled 4WDs in Aceh and Croatia; she was sure she could manage a few outback roads in Australia.

Of course much of the Outback isn't covered by road; it's covered by dirt tracks that are so overgrown they are barely discernible from the scrub. Several hundred kilometres north of Winton, Ahearn's bus was parked on such a track, seemingly in the middle of nowhere.

There was no sign of Ahearn or his group but there was a faded sign, almost illegible, which read: Undara Lava Tubes. And, if one looked closely, there was a large, faded arrow pointing to a flat nothingness, and a small walking track disappearing into the scrub. No sign of Lava Tubes, whatever they were. No sign of anything.

This part of the Tablelands was formed nearly two hundred thousand years ago when the Undara Volcano erupted, spreading billions of cubic litres of lava over the vast plateau. As the lava cooled, it formed a crust on the surface; but below, the molten lava continued to flow. And the lava at the edges of this flow also began to cool, forming a hard wall and creating a tunnel. As the volcano erupted again and again, the red hot lava burned through the cooling crust to the tunnel, just like rain collects in a riverbed. It continued to flow until it erupted out into a valley at the escarpment's edge. Even then it didn't stop. It backed up until the lava filled the valley. The surface crust hardened again but the flow of lava below continued, leaving behind the longest lava tunnel created by a single volcano anywhere in the world. Eventually, the tunnel ran for over one hundred and sixty kilometres.

Fifty thousand years ago, when this area was first settled by humans, they must have known about the tubes because they named the volcano Undara: *The Long One*.

By that time, the roof of the tunnel had collapsed in places. Sometimes this blocked off the tunnel. At other times, where the tunnel was high and the crust thin, the rock would just fall to the bottom of the tunnel to create a long winding depression in the otherwise flat landscape.

Almost invisible until you were immediately on top of them, these depressions began to create their own microclimates. Sunlight only penetrated when the sun was directly overhead. Water caught in the rock pools and didn't evaporate as it would have done on the surface. Lush vegetation grew in the shade. Colonies of Rock Wallabies made their home in these subterranean oases, unaware that as the climate became drier and hotter they would be cut off from the rest of the world. Unaffected by changes in climate on the surface of the plains, they continued to thrive in their small world. Tiger Snakes also thrived there, feeding on the microbats that lived in the huge Lava Caverns. It was a habitat completely in balance, regardless of the hostile conditions that surrounded it; an Ark in a barren sea.

The Ahearns always included the Lava Tubes in their Outback Safaris. These were reached by descending steps into one of the exposed depressions and walking directly into the open tunnel entrance. They never spent more than an hour or so in the tunnels. They are designated Bad Air Tunnels with measured Carbon Dioxide levels as high as 5.9%. Staying too long can cause headaches and nausea. The air in the open depression, however, is cool and pure. Normally Aimee would set up the lunch there, always ensuring that she took any remains of the meal away with her, to avoid affecting the ecology.

While she prepared the meal, the tourists would wait in silence until the Rock Wallabies became used to their presence and emerged from their hiding places to stare at them. They were as curious about their visitors as their visitors were about them.

Today, however, having got away from Winton a couple of hours late, the group missed the pleasures of having lunch with the Rock Wallabies and went straight back to the bus. There they found another message from Steve, asking them to return the eight marbles. This time Steve explained that this was the second spacecraft that had crashed of late and that the powers-that-be suspected engine failure of some sort; perhaps caused by faulty ball bearings. That was why they needed them back. They suspected they might have developed a flaw or become misshapen.

Steve and Kelly had settled on this story after some thought. They had considered suggesting that the marbles were radioactive, which would most certainly have got the group to hand in the marbles straight away. But this could well have started rumours of nuclear-powered spacecraft, a rumour no more desirable than stories of impending star wars.

The chosen story, however, had little effect on the group. Gina did inspect one of the marbles and decide that perhaps it wasn't perfectly round, but Luc pointed out that they only had six marbles, not eight. If any were broken, he said, it was likely to be one or both of the two that evidently didn't roll out of the hole.

Alan, trying to cover his guilt by contributing to the discussion, said if the marbles were so valuable they ought to be paid for them. Greg, who didn't want any trouble from the authorities, was inclined to hand his marble in.

As had become normal of late it was Leda who had

the last word. The anarchic views that informed her youth had begun to resurface as she approached her final days on earth,. Not that she would advocate urban terrorism again; but she had become more and more angry about the gradual loss of individual freedom and the fact that it was so often stolen by Governments passing laws supposedly designed to protect the very freedoms they threatened.

"Surely it is a matter of personal choice," she said. "If you wish to return your marble, Greg, that is your choice. If Alan wants to sell his, or we wish to keep ours, that is our choice. We should return to Cairns where everybody can make their own decisions."

Although nobody, except Luc, understood the ideals that motivated Leda's little speech, everybody could see the sense in what she said. They agreed to press on to Cairns.

"But what do I tell Steve?" asked Greg who, without realising it, had now virtually handed over the running of the tour to Leda.

"Text him. Tell him we are heading for Cairns where the authorities may negotiate individually with the owners of the marbles."

This rather stiff message had the effect of lulling Steve and Kelly into a false sense of security. Greg was admitting they had the marbles and that they were willing to negotiate handing them over. No point in pushing it and appearing overanxious.

Steve replied:

'Thanks, C U in Cairns.'

Kelly contacted the ASIO Deputy Director asking what sort of reward they could offer to recover the marbles. Again, they didn't want to appear overanxious. The Deputy Director suggested five hundred dollars a marble.

9 - *Gateway to the World.*

Considering its position as the Gateway to the Barrier Reef and Tropical North Queensland, first impressions of Cairns are quite disappointing. There are no palm tree fringed beaches; in fact, there are no beaches at all. The town is set on a bay ringed with mangrove swamp. And the airport is built on reclaimed mangrove swamp, because flat land is so scarce. To the north of the town, the mountains come so close to the coast that there is no room for settlement, other than a few outrageously expensive homes clinging precariously to the mountainside, overlooking the sea.

The seafront of the town itself has been nicely thought out, with a wide Esplanade and Parks running from north to south, but look over the sea wall and there's the mangrove swamp again.

Cairns does have a decent, although not very large, harbour at the river mouth. Big enough for tourist boats and pleasure craft, but not big enough for industrial tankers; which suits the mood of the town perfectly.

All the money has been spent around the harbour.

The Casino and the other luxury hotels are there.

A large complex known as The Pier houses a dozen bars and restaurants with views over the water, together with specialty shops, entertainment areas, nightclubs and tourist booking offices advertising daily trips to the Reef.

A block back from the harbour is the backpacker accommodation and the food halls, where you can get almost any cuisine on earth and eat it at communal tables.

One more block back and you hit the dual-lane highway, which runs from Brisbane to Port Douglas. Cross the highway and you are in suburbs that are so flat you get no sight or sense of the sea. You could be anywhere in the north-eastern half of Australia.

It was on one of these wide nondescript streets that Greg and Aimee housed their Outback Safari Travel Business. They had no permanent staff other than themselves. Bookings were made in the travel agency offices at The Pier, or more usually over the Net, and the bus took the computer, and therefore Aimee's "office", with them.

Even so, as Kelly and Steve drove into Cairns shortly after sunset, they were surprised to find the place in total darkness, with a police car parked outside on the street. Steve and Kelly had given the bus about three hour's start out of Winton. They had expected to pick up an hour or so, on the road; another hour or so, while Greg and Aimee showed the group the Undara Lava Tubes. By their calculations, the bus should have arrived by now.

Steve parked and went to talk to the waiting policeman. As he did so, the bus appeared, coming from the direction of the City Centre.

Greg pulled up, and Aimee got out to open the gates to the yard. Steve crossed over and climbed into the bus. Apart from Greg the bus was empty.

Greg explained that, because they were running so late, he had driven around dropping people off at the airport and their various hotels before returning to base. They had even stopped at a long-term carpark, where Danny had garaged his truck.

Kelly climbed onto the bus behind Steve. After a nine-hour drive she was in no mood to be polite. She didn't even introduce herself.

"You knew we wanted to talk to everybody. You messaged Steve saying you'd meet us here."

Greg shrugged.

"If people don't want to wait, you can't make 'em. You can't make 'em miss their flights or hang around."

Then, by way of apology, he handed Kelly the marble that he had kept in his drink holder next to the driver's seat. If he was expecting gratitude from Kelly, he was disappointed.

"Where are the rest of them?"

"We shared them out. And there was six of 'em, not eight."

"There were places in the nose cone for eight."

"I can't help that, lady. There were six. Aimee and I shared one, so did the Reinhardts. Everybody else had one each."

Kelly was sure Greg was lying.

"We searched the crash site thoroughly. There were eight there, we found the device that held them in place. They're all gone. There was nobody else there. You must have taken them."

At last even laid-back Greg was getting angry.

"Are you calling me a liar?"

Steve had conducted a lot of interrogations in the SAS. He always found he got better results staying calm.

"Who found the marbles, Greg?"

"Alan Ready."

"Is it possible he might have squirreled a couple of them away without anybody noticing?"

Greg had considered this possibility as soon as Steve had texted that there were eight marbles, and they only had six.

"Possible? It's almost bloody certain. Greedy little bastard, Alan. Always first in the queue. Always wanting seconds. Always after something for nothing."

"So where is he now?"

"Halfway to Brisbane, I reckon. He was flying out tonight."

In the calm of the little onsite office, Aimee ran off the contact details of all the passengers from their booking sheets, while Greg recounted where he had dropped each of them off.

Alan had been first at the airport. He'd said he had a flight to catch, but maybe he was just trying to get away fast before anybody realized he had three marbles, not one.

Then Greg dropped Danny at the long-term car park. Greg didn't know if Danny was driving straight home to Charters Towers or staying in Cairns.

Gina and David didn't have any accommodation lined up in Cairns, so Greg dropped them in the Backpacker District.

He dropped the Reinhardts at the Shangri-La Hotel at The Pier. They were staying there overnight, flying back to Germany the following day.

"So the only people we know how to find are the Reinhardts," concluded Kelly.

"Well," said Steve, taking the contact sheet from Aimee, "Let's start with them. Then we'd better find ourselves a room somewhere; if your budget runs to that?"

"My budget runs to two rooms," said Kelly, just so there would be no misunderstanding.

When they arrived at the Shangri-La, Steve parked his truck in the set-down area outside the hotel. A Porter stepped forward to collect their bags. Steve explained that they were just visiting somebody and rushed after Kelly who was already in the foyer, leaving the Porter protesting that he should not be parked there, in that case.

Kelly was at the desk, asking for the Reinhardts, who had just booked in. The Receptionist pointed her to an in-house phone at the end of the reception desk. Kelly picked up the phone and asked to be put through to their room. While they waited, Steve suggested he speak to the Reinhardts. After all he knew them. The real reason he offered to talk to them was because he was afraid Kelly would rub them up the wrong way, as she seemed to do with just about everybody else. But when somebody answered the phone, Kelly's tone was sweetness itself.

"Mrs. Reinhardt, sorry to bother you after your long journey.. my name's Kelly McDonald from the Australian Aerospace Corporation. It's about some space junk that crashed to earth last night. In Winton."

Leda's manner on the phone was equally warm and open. Steve watched as Kelly listened to Leda telling her how exciting it had all been.

"The highlight of the tour, really," Leda concluded.

Kelly smiled in the way people do on the phone; as if the person on the other end can see them.

"Yes, it must have been very exciting. I wonder if I could talk to you about it in person...?

... Yes, we're here at your hotel.... Yes, in the lobby, so we'd really appreciate... Room 1414? Thank you. We'll be right up."

And Kelly headed for the lifts, followed by Steve, and watched by the Porter, who wasn't at all happy about a dusty old truck being parked outside the hotel but was far too well trained to yell across the foyer.

Leda and Luc had a corner room with views out to both the city and the sea. The sea was now just ink-black. Up the coast, the lines of street lights along the Esplanade seemed to point to the even brighter glow of the airport terminal in the distance. They had all their clothes laid out on the bed and were obviously packing for the long trip home to Europe. Nonetheless, they were very courteous, inviting Kelly and Steve to sit down, taking clothes and a roll of cling wrap off the chairs to make room.

Leda noticed Steve frowning at the cling wrap and smiled.

"I use it to wrap my dirty hiking boots. It keeps my other clothes clean," she explained, as she casually threw the cling wrap onto the bed.

"Can we get you anything? A drink? Did you drive from Winton, Steven? You must be exhausted."

"Yes, we are tired, "Kelly agreed, "So we'll get straight to the point. We'd like the ball bearing that you took from the crash site."

Leda's smile didn't waver for even a fraction of a second. If anything, it might have got broader.

"Oh, we don't have one."

"Greg says you do."

Still the smile didn't waver.

"Well, yes, we had one, but we're flying home tomorrow. We thought we might have trouble with Customs so we gave our marble to Alan. When he heard the marbles might be valuable, he was keen to have it."

Steve seemed to believe every word Leda said.

"It seems Alan might have collected quite a few of the marbles," he said

"Really?" said Leda.

Kelly was making no pretence.

"Mrs. Reinhardt, would you mind if we had a quick look through your luggage?"

The sweet smile disappeared in an instant.

"Yes, I would mind."

Luc put a pair of calming hands on Leda's shoulders.

"It seems that you are calling my wife a liar," he said to Kelly. "If you don't mind, we'd like you to leave now. My wife is not well, and she should not be distressed."

"Yes, we're sorry, Luc, Leda," said Steve. "Sorry to have bothered you. Have a safe trip home."

And he practically wheeled Kelly around and out the door.

Kelly stood in the corridor, very indignant.

"They're lying."

"Of course they are. But what do you want to do? Strip search a little old German Lady Tourist? You don't even have a warrant. You'd start a whacking great diplomatic row. They're flying out tomorrow. I'm sure you can use your influence to get Customs to do the searching for us."

Kelly smiled.

"You're not as stupid as you look, are you?"

"No, but I am bloody tired and hungry. Why don't we find that room?"

Kelly considered.

"Why don't we stay here?"

Steve wasn't used to five-star luxury.

"It's a bit swish isn't it?"

"Well, we need to keep an eye on the Reinhardts. We'll just have to put up with it."

Luc watched Steve and Kelly through the spy hole in the door as they walked away to the lift. He turned back to Leda, who had already gone back to her packing.

"They don't believe us, you know?"

Leda was unperturbed.

"Of course they don't. But what can they do about it?"

10 Under Surveillance.

Kelly and Steve took the lift down to the foyer where Kelly asked to see the Duty Manager. She flashed her Australian Federal Police I.D., making sure the insignia and her photo were clear but keeping her thumb over the words "Forensic Pathologist". She explained that she was keeping two of the Hotel's guests under surveillance, Mr. and Mrs. Reinhardt in Room 1414. She believed they were smugglers working for a major crime syndicate.

The manager was shocked. They seemed like such a nice couple.

Kelly agreed. That's what made the AFP's work so difficult; the syndicates were using the most unlikely looking people as mules, these days. The manager nodded, sympathetically.

Kelly gestured toward Steve, standing in the middle of the foyer. In his outback khaki shorts and boots, he looked as little like a Federal Police Officer as one could imagine.

"My partner, Sergeant Moss, has been tailing them for days," she said.

The Manager knew the Reinhardts had just returned from

a tour of the Outback and were flying out the following day, so all this made perfect sense to him. He had no hesitation in agreeing to give Kelly two rooms right next to the Reinhardts.

"One either side?" he suggested.

"Perfect."

Kelly called Steve over to the desk.

"We're checking in. Don't put your rank or occupation on the Register, Sergeant. You never know who might be checking the hotel computers."

While the manager went off to check the Reinhardt's movements for the evening, Steve and Kelly signed the Register.

"Actually, I'm a Corporal," he murmured, as he stood alongside Kelly, signing in.

"I told him you were Federal Police," Kelly murmured back. "And the Reinhardts are smugglers."

Steve looked at her in disbelief.

"Well if they take the marble out of the country, they are, aren't they?"

Steve thought Kelly was taking the subterfuge a bit far but could see the sense of it when the manager returned. He told them that the Reinhardts were clearly exhausted from their journey and were staying in their room for the evening.

"They've ordered room service."

"Good, that'll give us a chance to eat. Could you put some toiletries in the Sergeant's Room, please? This was such a rushed job he didn't have time to pack."

The Manager smiled at Steve conspiratorially; at least Steve thought it was conspiratorially. He wasn't at all sure about the warmth with which the Manager gave him his room key.

Kelly turned to Steve.

"I'll just drop my bags in my room and freshen up. We'll meet back here in half an hour and get dinner, ok?"

She walked off to the lift, feeling quite pleased with herself, while Steve headed out through the foyer to find somewhere to buy a change of clothes, and to pacify the Porter, who was hovering once more.

A short while later, two men who looked and dressed exactly like Queensland Detectives approached the Duty Manager. They were with Inspector McDonald and Sergeant Moss, they said. Part of the surveillance team. Could they have another room near the Reinhardt's, preferably something between theirs and the lift? Just the one room; they were happy to share. They weren't on the Inspector's expense account, they joked.

Swept up in the excitement, the Manager forgot to ask them for their IDs.

In her room, Kelly didn't immediately head for the shower. Instead, she took the shell and Greg's marble out of her shoulder bag and placed them on the desk. The marble wobbled unevenly on the desktop. She opened her suitcase and took out some rudimentary examination devices: a pair of callipers, a dental probe, and a small set of scales.

Then she noticed her hand was already dirty from handling the marble. She wiped the smudge off with a tissue. She had taken enough fingerprints in her time to know the smudge was an osmium oxide. The marble was definitely made of osmium. She put on another pristine pair of white gloves and examined the marble through a magnifying glass.

The surface was smooth, apparently unmarked; or did she discern a couple of small circles on the marbles?

They were so faint; it was difficult to tell. She measured the marble's dimensions with the callipers and fed the results into her computer. The dimensions weren't exactly symmetrical; the marble wasn't exactly round.

It was oval in shape, like a fat egg. Obviously, then, it wasn't a ball bearing; the irregularity of its shape made that impossible.

She weighed the marble on the scales and fed that data into the computer.

She pressed a couple of keys on the computer and got the result she wanted. Osmium is the densest element found in nature. The marble was far too light to be solid osmium all the way through. It was hollow, or at least filled with a substance far less dense than osmium. The cavity inside the marble was between 60% and 85% of its volume, depending on the density of the material inside. What that might be, Kelly couldn't even guess, although it struck her that if the marble were hollow, the small circles on its surface might be portals to the interior.

She picked up the dental probe with the intention of seeing if she could prize the marble open. As the probe neared the marble, there was a flash and a sharp crack. A blue light arced across to the probe, sending a shock wave through Kelly's hand.

She dropped the probe in pain; then noticed that the hand that had been holding the marble remained totally unaffected. The marble had just reacted to the probe; protected itself.

Tentatively Kelly picked up the probe again, brought it slowly towards the marble. At a distance of about three inches, the blue arc again flashed from the marble. This time the shock was barely discernible. Apparently its intensity increased the closer the probe came. The marble was computerised, she concluded, programmed to protect itself. But what was a computer, or more precisely what were eight computers doing inside a projectile? She thought that perhaps they were a navigation system.

Deciding she could take the examination no further with the limited equipment she had, Kelly put the marble on the desk and placed the shell over it to prevent it from rolling off onto the floor. She then headed for the shower, which was unfortunate. Had she stayed she would have heard the marble start rolling about inside the shell, bumping into the edges, rolling back and forth; probing, pushing, trying to find a way out.

Meanwhile, the two men who had identified themselves as policemen had checked into their room, closed the door and attached a small camera to the peephole in the door.

The camera gave them a fisheye-lens view of the corridor, which one of them watched on a small screen while the other took off his shoes, lay on the bed and closed his eyes.

The man watching the screen saw room service being delivered to the Reinhardt's room. He saw Steve return from his shopping expedition. A short time later he watched Kelly come out of her room carrying her large shoulder bag, and tap on Steve's door. The device they had set up on the peephole was a microphone as well as a camera. As Steve and Kelly waited for the lift and discussed where they were going to eat, the man on the bed got up and watched, listened, and waited.

As soon as the lift door shut, the man, still in his stockinged feet, opened the door and crossed to Kelly's room. Using a master key-card, it took him just seconds to open the door and disappear inside while his accomplice watched the corridor.

Inside Kelly's room, the man quickly searched Kelly's suitcase, which was now empty.

He opened the wardrobe and expertly patted down the clothes to check that nothing bulky was hidden in them. He checked the floor of the wardrobe and the shelves. He checked under the bed and did a quick search of the bathroom.

He checked drawers in the desk and found Kelly's callipers and scales, but he wasn't interested in them. Obviously what he was looking for was still in Kelly's shoulder bag; which was what, in the end, he'd expected.

He didn't entirely waste his visit to Kelly's room, however. He attached a small listening device to her suitcase then exited the room and closed the door, leaving everything totally undisturbed.

Steve had walked out through the foyer earlier, when he'd gone shopping, and had walked directly into The Pier, which isn't actually a pier but a huge shopping, eating, and entertainment complex overlooking the harbour. Even in late afternoon the place was brightly lit in a range of garish colours that the architects must have thought reflected the Far North Queensland ambiance of sun, sea and beach but which made Steve squint. It was packed with locals and tourists alike; more people than Steve had seen in one place for over a year.

At first the lights and noise assaulted his senses and he felt slightly disorientated. He soon realized that if, instead of trying to take it all in at once, he concentrated on his immediate vicinity, he could check out the various shops and restaurants, buy what he needed and find a place to eat that wasn't too noisy or too bright.

The shops mostly catered for the beach and the tourists, with souvenirs and straw beach hats.

Nevertheless, he managed to buy a pair of chinos, some underwear that he normally wouldn't be seen dead in, and a couple of short-sleeved white shirts. The latter, he knew, were the business uniform of choice in North Queensland and would help him blend into the surroundings.

When Kelly knocked on his hotel room door to go to dinner, she thought the white shirt set off his tan beautifully and that he looked quite handsome in a rugged sort of way. Steve, seeing her for the first time in a dress, thought she had terrific legs.

Both quickly put the thoughts out of their minds. Neither of them was good at one night stands. Tomorrow they would recover the marble from the Reinhardts. Kelly would continue the pursuit of the other marbles in Brisbane or Sydney or wherever, and Steve would return to his fossils in Winton. There was no point in starting something that was never going anywhere.

Things don't always work out as planned, however.

Steve had selected an upmarket Chinese Restaurant in The Pier. They had a Chinese restaurant in Winton, but it was nothing like this; more a takeaway, with decidedly non-Chinese dishes on the menu like Fish and Chips and Burgers, alongside the deep-fried Dim Sims.

And Kelly often ate in the Chinese restaurants in Dickson, in Canberra, but they were just noodle houses.

The Restaurant in The Pier was the Chinese version of fine dining.

They were pleased to see that both of them ate with chopsticks, and they spent some time discussing what wine to order.

Being from Perth, Steve favoured West Australian whites. As a matter of pride, Kelly had to stand up for the cold climate whites being produced around Canberra. In the end, since there weren't any wines on the menu that came from vineyards either of them recognized, they settled on a bottle of trusty New Zealand Sauvignon Blanc.

Deep in conversation, and thirsty from the long drive, they were surprised to find the first bottle empty before they were half way through the meal. So they ordered a second bottle.

They found they had a lot in common. For a start, neither was married.

Steve said he had never thought it fair if you spent half your life in war zones. Not only would the woman have to bring up any kids virtually alone but she would also live with the constant fear that he wouldn't return.

Kelly also blamed her profession for the fact that she wasn't married. The truth was, having been passed around all her young life she had never really learned to trust anybody enough to rely on them. She liked the fact that she had only herself to rely on and to answer to.

Still, halfway through the second bottle, she again started to think that Steve was very handsome, and surprisingly thoughtful, too. A soldier who was now questioning his whole life; thinking there must be a better solution to the world's problems than the constant killing. It was a problem she too grappled with. After all, she had dug up mass graves in Croatia and Serbia. She felt strongly that somebody had to stand between the killers and their victims. But how did one tell who was right and who was wrong? Who were the good guys and who were the bad?

The conversation was beginning to get maudlin, and they had virtually finished the second bottle of wine.

Steve called for the bill and Kelly was thinking perhaps, just this once, a one-night stand wouldn't be such a bad thing.

She was insisting on paying the bill when, suddenly, everything changed.

Her shoulder bag was gone. She couldn't believe it. How could she be so stupid? What was she doing drinking bottles of wine when she was supposed to be recovering the marbles? She knew they were after the marbles as well.

Steve didn't quite follow: Who were "they"?

"The Americans, the CIA."

Steve found this a bit far-fetched.

"You think the CIA stole your handbag?"

"Yes!" said Kelly rather too vehemently, then she leaned forward to whisper, "They don't want us to know what's going on."

Steve was pretty convinced it was just a bag snatcher. He said he'd pay the bill. They'd ask the waiter if anybody had picked up her bag and handed it in. If not, they'd go back to the hotel, call the police, put a stop on her credit cards. It would be fine.

Kelly shook her head.

"It won't be fine. I shouldn't have let my guard down. They're going to think I'm totally stupid. Shit!"

"The CIA are going to think you're stupid?"

"No. ASIO."

Now Steve was convinced Kelly was drunk. He checked with the waiter, but the bag hadn't been handed in.

He paid the bill and tried to give Kelly a helping hand. She shrugged off his hand, strode through to the hotel foyer and on towards the lift.

Seeing her approach, the Duty Manager called out:

"Inspector! Inspector!"

Steve whispered in Kelly's ear,

"That's you."

Kelly stopped and with a great effort straightened herself up and crossed to the desk.

The Night Manager placed her shoulder bag on the counter. The shock of seeing the bag temporarily sobered Kelly up. She opened the bag and started checking the contents. Steve asked who had handed the bag in? The Night Manager wasn't sure. Just somebody walking through, found it at the entrance to The Pier.

Kelly had finished checking the bag's contents. She smiled at the Night Manager.

"Everything's here. Wallet, money, credit cards, phone, everything. Can I give a reward to the person who handed it in?"

"I'm sorry. Whoever it was has gone."

Kelly nodded, thanked the Night Manager and headed for the lift, seemingly calm and relaxed.

As the lift door closed, she started to swear,

" Shit! Shit! Shit! Shit! Shit! Shit! Shit!"

Steve guessed that everything wasn't still in the bag.

"What's missing? The shell and the marble?"

"No," said Kelly. "I put those in the room safe. But they've got everything else they wanted. They've had my phone, checked all the numbers I've called, all the texts I've sent; which means they have the names of everybody who has one of the marbles. They know the Reinhardts have a marble and won't give it back."

Kelly and Steve didn't talk as they got out of the lift. She was wondering what to do next. He was wondering how much of what she had said was real.

So while Kelly sent a brief note to the Deputy Director of ASIO saying - *'The CIA got hold of my phone. They know everything'*- Steve went to the Reinhardt's room and knocked gently on the door.

It was still relatively early, but it took a while before he heard the sound of a chair being dragged aside and Luc opened the door as far as the safety chain would allow.

"What do you want?"

"Just checking on your wife, Mr. Reinhardt, is she alright? We didn't upset her too much, earlier, I hope?"

"She is sleeping. She needs to sleep."

"Of course," said Steve. "Goodnight… and keep your safety chain on. There are some strange people about."

Luc closed the door without responding. But as Steve listened he was sure he heard the chair being dragged up against the door again. Everybody was certainly acting suspiciously. Perhaps there was something in what Kelly was saying, after all.

Steve returned to Kelly's room. Luckily, she hadn't locked the door as he'd left because she was already fast asleep on the bed. He checked her phone. She really had texted ASIO.

He looked at her lying there, fast asleep. If anybody wanted to break into the room, it wouldn't be difficult; even easier to open the room safe. If he left her, he couldn't put the safety chain on. The room wouldn't even be that secure. So he pushed a chair up under the door handle, as he imagined Luc had done, and put the chain on.

He lifted Kelly to one side of the oversized bed and covered her with a blanket. He then took off his shoes and lay on the bed and starting scrolling through the rest of Kelly's texts.

11 - The Bodyguard.

Kelly's room faced east over the Coral Sea so by six o'clock, as it did all year round this close to the equator, the sun started to rise over the water, turning the sea into a shimmering mirror.

Steve squinted as he opened the curtains; then shook Kelly's foot. She awoke, bleary eyed. She too squinted to avoid the brilliant sunlight; then she sat bolt upright.

"Have you been here all night?".

Kelly checked under the blanket to ensure she was still fully dressed. Steve shrugged.

"I had to. You passed out. Anybody could have gotten into the room and the safe. If the CIA really are following you, they'd have had the shell and the marble by now."

In the room opposite, the man at the screen turned to his companion.

"Why didn't you look in the safe?

"I didn't think it'd be small enough to fit in there. They said it was a nose cone. It must be more like an artillery shell."

The first man returned to the screen, disgusted.

Obviously the CIA kept their operatives as well informed as ASIO did.

Steve told Kelly she'd received a text. ASIO was sending somebody to take over. All they had to do was make sure they didn't lose the Reinhardts before they got on their plane.

Kelly barely heard anything more than his first sentence. She was too angry that he had read her text. She looked at her phone.

"And you've sent a reply!"

"Somebody had to. You were out of it."

"And whose fault was that, plying me with wine?"

Steve didn't even bother to answer that. He'd ordered breakfast for 6.30, he said. Kelly had better shower and dress.

"I'm going to do the same. I'll be back for breakfast."

Even worse.

"You ordered breakfast in *my* room?"

"We're Federal Police Officers. Why wouldn't we have breakfast together? Provided you're dressed and decent. Look, don't get your knickers in a knot. Your ASIO man will be here at seven. Then he can take over. You can go back to your dead people, and I can go back to my fossils."

Steve stepped out into the corridor, quietly closing the door behind him.

Before he'd reached his room, the lift doors opened, and a waitress emerged with a breakfast trolley. It was for the Reinhardts. Steve waited until Luc opened the door and let the waitress in. He heard the waitress ask how everybody was. It was another perfect day outside, she told them. He heard Leda agree that it was perfect.

Reassured that the confrontation the previous night hadn't killed Leda off, Steve went into his room.

There is a two hour time difference between Perth and Cairns. The flight between the two cities takes around four and a half hours. So if the plane leaves at a bit before midnight in Perth, it arrives in Cairns at dawn where the passengers disembark looking tired and groggy; hence the nickname for the flight, The Redeye.

But as Colonel Robinson, formerly of the SAS, now of Military Intelligence, alighted from the plane, he was neither red-eyed nor tired. He was alert and ready for anything. As was his bodyguard; a rather nuggetty individual who had a bearing not unlike Steve's.

They were both dressed in immaculate but loose fitting suits with plenty of underarm room for the guns they carried. Robinson carried an overnight bag; the Bodyguard carried two suit-carriers.

They went straight to a federal police car and drove to the Shangri-La.

Steve and Kelly were sharing a rather silent breakfast when Robinson arrived, unannounced. He left his bodyguard in the corridor but had brought one of the suit-carriers into the room.

Steve stiffened visibly when he saw him. He had not expected the "ASIO man" would turn out to be Robinson.

Robinson carried on as if he hadn't noticed. He was used to people not being pleased to see him. He nodded to Steve.

"Corporal."

"Colonel."

After a slight pause, Steve made the introductions:

" Kelly this is Colonel Robinson of the SAS."

"Actually, It's Military Intelligence these days," Robinson smiled and shook Kelly's hand before picking up a piece of her toast and spreading it with marmalade. He still had the condescending attitude that Steve so hated. Steve wondered if he was English. He'd certainly gone to an English public school, and Sandhurst as well.

"Well, this is a mess, isn't it? It'd be a mess even if the Americans weren't involved. This Tourist Group are a rum lot. We can't find any of them."

While a rather bewildered Kelly looked to Steve for some explanation, Robinson continued smoothly:

"Alan Ready. He gave an address in Ascot; one of the best addresses in Brisbane. Trouble is; he doesn't live there. All we've got for him is an email address.

Danny Ridge. We don't even have an email address for him; just a post office box in Charters Towers. And his ticket on the tour was paid for by a well-known dealer in stolen fossils and antiquities.

Gina Bennett's parents bought the tickets for her and her boyfriend. The last they heard from her, she was going to spend some time on the beach. That means she could be anywhere between Port Douglas and the Gold Coast.

And - I've kept the best for last - the little old lady in the room next door... Forty years ago she was an urban terrorist. The Red Army Faction.. Kidnapping, bank robberies, you name it. The only reason she didn't spend the rest of her life in jail was because she did a deal. She isn't going to give up her marble without a fight."

Steve knew Robinson loved the sound of his own voice. He also knew that Robinson always worked on a strictly 'need to know' basis.

"So why are you telling us all this?"

Robinson put down the remains of his piece of toast and unfolded the suit carrier. He unzipped the front to reveal two identical, grey suits.

He opened the shoe compartment and took out a pair of shoes so highly polished that you could see your face in them. He also took out a package, unwrapped it and put it on the table. It was Steve's service pistol. The suits and shoes were also Steve's.

"Because old son, your sick leave is cancelled. You're being assigned to Ms McDonald as her bodyguard. You're going to find these people."

Steve wasn't upset by the news. This whole mystery was intriguing, and it wasn't likely he'd have to shoot anybody. He was sure the Americans wouldn't go that far.

Aware that Kelly had an expression on her face that suggested she'd been sucking on a lemon, Steve was careful not to show any enthusiasm. He picked up his pistol, checked its action, took out the magazine and started to load it. Obviously Robinson hadn't carried a loaded gun in his luggage.

"Why me?" Steve asked.

"Because you're the only one who knows what these people look like. You can start by making sure the Reinhardts get safely to the airport. We'll separate them from their marbles at Customs. No fuss, no witnesses, and straight on the plane back home."

Despite the look on her face, Kelly wasn't exactly upset by developments, either. She'd thought she was going to be taken off the case after stuffing up. She was anxious to see it through, but she recognized that Steve was probably more vital to the search than she was now; not that she was going to admit that.

"Who's in charge of the search?" she asked. "Me or Corporal Moss?"

"Oh you, dear lady," Robinson smiled. "The Corporal is just there to protect you."

Robinson opened the side compartment of the suit carrier and took out a few more items.

"A phone for you that the CIA hasn't had a look at and copies of everything we know about the people on the bus."

Robinson was careful to give a folder to both Kelly and Steve.

"I'll take the shell and the ball bearing thingee you have. Get the boffins at the Australian Aerospace Facility in Brisbane to look at it. The Reinhardts are on the noon flight. They've booked a taxi for nine-thirty. I want you two waiting in your vehicle outside when they leave. Make sure they get safely to the airport. And make sure they don't drop anything off or post anything on the way. Frau Reinhardt used drop boxes in her Urban Terrorist days, apparently. My man will watch them until they leave."

Robinson took the shell and the marble that Kelly handed over, dropped the see-through evidence bags into his overnight bag, and opened the door.

"Keep in touch."

"Tell your boffins to be careful," Kelly said. "The marble's programmed to protect itself using electric shock."

Steve looked surprised.

"I examined it while you were out shopping last night," Kelly explained casually and then returned to eating her breakfast as if what she'd said was the most normal thing in the world.

She wasn't going to let a couple of soldiers think they knew more about what was going on than she did; even if they were SAS.

On the screen in the room opposite they had a full shot of Robinson's bodyguard, standing outside Kelly's door, apparently staring straight at them. They watched as Robinson came out of Kelly's room and gave his bodyguard his instructions. Then the two men walked towards the lift. While Robinson rang for the lift, the bodyguard sat on the seat provided, which afforded him a clear view of the corridor right up to the Reinhardt's corner room.

The second man in the room opposite was already opening his overnight bag. He removed his tie and business shirt then took a rather garish Hawaiian shirt out of the bag; something that he hoped would make him look like a tourist. His partner started to follow suit.

"Do you think we can risk going out past the bodyguard?" he asked.

"I don't think we've got much choice."

The second man packed the screen into his overnight bag and removed the camera from the peephole on the door.

Shortly before nine-thirty, Steve and Kelly were sitting in his 4WD, parked outside the Shangri-La. Steve was wearing one of his grey suits from the suit carrier that Robinson had delivered. He'd also put his vehicle through the car wash, so it now looked like every other car parked under the shade of the hotel façade.

While they waited, Kelly read through the notes that Robinson had given her on Leda and Luc.

"I think this little old lady's laughing at us," she said. "She wasn't just an urban terrorist. She was a smuggler. She smuggled weapons and drugs from the Middle East. She's probably getting a buzz out of reliving her past. Only this time there's no penalty if she gets caught."

Steve's phone rang.

"They're on their way down. My man's in the lift with them. He won't let them out of his sight until they get into their taxi."

Robinson hung up without waiting for a reply.

Steve waited patiently, used to this sort of thing. Kelly, less patient, fiddled with her phone. They were taking a long time.

Eventually, Leda and Luc emerged from the foyer. They were dressed in almost matching outfits, as they had been when Steve first met them at Long Waterhole. Micro shorts over tanned legs. A khaki short-sleeved shirt over a white T-Shirt with a sign showing that it had been purchased at Uluru. Each was carrying a small backpack as cabin luggage. The only difference from the outfits they'd worn on the tour was a change of footwear. Instead of the heavy hiking boots, both were now wearing runners, not unlike those that Alan Ready had worn on the tour but in much better condition.

Behind them, a porter pushed their two outsized canvas rucksacks on a luggage trolley.

Kelly wondered how Leda had managed to hump her rucksack around Australia. It looked heavier than she was.

Leda got into the back of the taxi and the porter loaded the rucksacks into the boot.

Still Steve didn't move. Kelly looked at him anxiously but Steve waited until Luc had tipped the porter and was getting into the driver's side back seat before switching on his engine and engaging gear.

At exactly the same moment, an unmarked delivery van drove into the driveway and stopped just in front of Steve, effectively blocking him in.

And just as the Reinhardt's taxi pulled away from the

curb, the delivery driver jumped out of his van and ran into the foyer carrying a parcel. Steve called out to him, hit his horn, but the delivery driver just kept going.

Steve got out of his vehicle, walked around to the driver's seat of the delivery van and was almost run down by a nondescript hire-care that sounded its horn and drove past after the taxi.

Steve waved a couple of fingers at the unseen driver, then jumped into the delivery van and reversed it back, giving himself enough room to get his vehicle out. He pulled on the van's parking brake and got back into his own vehicle, pulled out into the driveway and set off after the taxi.

The whole incident had only taken a minute or so, but it was significant.

As Steve drove north along the Esplanade and turned right along the mangrove-flanked Airport Drive, he was suddenly confronted by a small traffic jam. Cars were backed up along the road. Steve still didn't panic; if they were stuck in traffic, he reasoned, so was Leda and Luc's taxi. But he was wrong. The taxi wasn't somewhere up ahead in the traffic jam. It was the cause of the traffic jam.

The driver of the nondescript hire-car who had sounded his horn at Steve wore a garish Hawaiian shirt, as did his passenger. After he'd driven past Steve, he had gunned the engine up The Esplanade so that by the time the Reinhardt's taxi reached Airport Drive the hire-car was sitting directly on its tail.

The Taxi Driver soon became aware of the idiot directly behind him, tailgating him. He deliberately slowed down to let the hire-car pass.

Half way along Airport Drive, where the road is

hidden from the main highway by the mangrove swamps, the hire-car pulled out to overtake the taxi.

Instead of continuing past, the car got in front of the taxi, then swerved violently left and braked, causing the taxi to also brake hard and swerve, so that when it came to a halt, it was in the drain separating the road from the mangrove swamps.

Before anybody in the taxi could react, the passenger of the hire car was out, pointing a gun at the head of the Taxi Driver and yelling for him to,

"Spring the trunk. Spring the trunk," then, remembering that he was in Australia, "Open the boot!"

The Taxi Driver was quick to comply.

The man then hurried to the boot of the taxi and relieved it of the two overstuffed rucksacks.

The driver of the hire car had also sprung the hire-car boot open before leaping out of the driver's seat, drawing a gun, like his companion, and hurtling down to the taxi and around to the back door on the passenger side.

He didn't seem to notice that this meant he was wading through brackish water in the drain. He opened the back door of the car and yelled at Luc and Leda:

"Give me your bags. Give me your bags".

Luc gave his up immediately but Leda instinctively grabbed her small backpack to her flat chest. She glowered at the man.

"No! No!"

The man in the Hawaiian shirt was in no mood to argue. Using his gun like a knuckle duster he hit Leda on the jaw, hard.

The effect was electric; literally.

A flash of blue light arced across from Leda to the man, causing him to leap back in pain.

He wasn't quite sure what had happened.

Had she bitten him? Stabbed him with some sort of device?

He checked his gun hand, which had received the shock. No stab wound. He looked down at Leda. The blow had knocked her unconscious; the backpack lay in her lap. The man grabbed it and clambered back up the bank to the hire-car, with both the smaller backpacks.

All this time, the traffic on the Drive was backing up. The hire-car was still on the road, but cars could get by if they tried; it was just the normal Australian reaction to help somebody in trouble that had caused various cars to stop and these were blocking the road.

The drivers were getting out and hurrying towards the taxi, which they assumed had simply run off the road.

The man, stuffing the large rucksacks into the boot of his car, saw them and turned to face the oncoming Good Samaritans, levelling a gun at them.

All thoughts of helping evaporated; they fled back to their cars.

The two men in Hawaiian shirts got into their hire-car, drove to the next roundabout and were already on the other side of the dual carriageway, heading back towards the Esplanade, when Steve and Kelly came abreast of the taxi and realized what had happened.

Kelly pushed her way through the small group that had gathered around the taxi,

"Could you move aside please, I'm a Doctor."

Steve hung back. One of the crowd was dialling on his phone,

"What happened?" Steve asked.

The man looked up.

"They stole their luggage. They had guns."

"Did you see where they went?"

"Up the Drive."

The man looked up the Drive towards the Airport just as the hire car was passing them on the other side, traveling at speed.

"That's them," the man pointed, and then started talking to Emergency Services, asking for an ambulance, police.

Meanwhile, Steve stepped onto the median strip that ran down the middle of the drive. He watched the hire car quickly disappearing while he talked on his phone to Robinson.

"They've stolen the Reinhardt's luggage. A yellow Toyota. Probably a hire-car. Two Caucasian Males, both dressed in Hawaiian shirts."

As he watched, the car turned left, heading south on the Esplanade. Steve gave Robinson the car's registration number then he pushed his way through the small throng to find Kelly leaning through the rear car door, checking Leda's pulse. Or lack of it.

"How is she?" Steve asked although the question was rhetorical. One look at Luc's distraught face told him that Leda was dead.

Kelly shook her head slightly, then turned to Luc.

"Was your wife carrying the marble on her?" she asked.

He exploded, immediately furious.

"My wife is dead, and you ask about a damned marble?"

Kelly began to say,

"I'm only trying to ascertain whether the marble was in your luggage," but half way through, Steve grabbed her arm and pulled her out of the car. She tried to shake her arm free.

"Let go of me."

Steve held her even tighter.

He was right next to her; he hissed in her ear.

"The Police'll be here any minute. When they find out it was a car-jacking, they'll call in Homicide. Everybody will be held for questioning. It could take all day. Come on."

They could already hear the wail of sirens approaching.

Steve turned and headed for his 4WD. Kelly had no option but to follow. They were already too late. As Steve opened his car door, a squad car pulled up behind them, and the siren's whine slowed and died.

Steve looked back to the policeman driving the car and smiled apologetically.

"Sorry," he called, "We'll get out of your way."

Steve got in and drove the 4WD slowly forward to allow the police car to park in his spot.

But Steve didn't stop. He drove slowly on, up over the median strip that separated the dual carriageway and back towards the city.

As he cruised past the crash site again, the policeman was already out of his squad car and watching him with a frown.

 Steve smiled again, waved, mouthed the word, "Sorry" and drove on.

"What are you saying sorry for?" Kelly asked, still annoyed.

"To confuse him," said Steve. "He should have insisted we stay there, give our names and addresses."

Steve switched on his hands-free and dialled Robinson.

"There was a white van at the Shangri-La," he said. "Cut me off, so we couldn't give the Reinhardts Close Protection. It was probably on purpose. Check out the driver; what he was delivering."

"We're on to it," said Robinson. "My man saw the whole thing. Get back here."

"He doesn't seem pleased," said Kelly.

But nothing could have been further from the truth. Robinson was in a surprisingly good mood when Steve and Kelly got back to the Shangri-La. As far as he was concerned the Americans had shown their hand. And the two idiots they'd hired to grab the luggage were a pair of complete fools. The car they'd used was a hire car, as Steve had thought, and they'd hired it in their names. It was just a matter of time before they were picked up. And even if they refused to talk, Robinson could use the men as bargaining chips with the Americans.

"Bargaining chips for what?" Kelly wanted to know.

"We want to know what they know," said Robinson.

Kelly objected: "But then they'll want to know what we know."

Robinson smiled the patronizing smile that so irritated Steve.

"Dear lady," he said. "They already know what we know. They've got the Reinhardt's marble. You should concentrate on finding the other marbles. You can start with Danny Ridge's crooked fossil-dealing friend. If he paid for Danny to go on the Ahearn Tour, he must have had a reason for doing so."

12 - *Buried Treasure.*

When Greg dropped Danny Ridge off at the long-term car park the previous evening, Danny hadn't driven straight home to his base in Charters Towers. Instead, he'd booked into the cheapest motel in Cairns. Even the cheapest motel bed was luxury to Danny, who was used to sleeping in his swag, laid out either in the back of his truck or on the hard ground.

Despite this, Danny was a relatively rich man; although this was less because he was hugely successful at finding gold and more because he hated spending money.

Nevertheless, had Steve and Kelly decided on the upmarket Steak Restaurant rather than the Chinese Restaurant in The Pier the previous evening, they would have found Danny dining on a huge rare steak and drinking a fine red wine. The reason was simple: Danny wasn't paying. The bill was being picked up by Doug Thatcher, the man who had paid for Danny's place on the Ahearn Bus Tour.

Thatcher was a large, overweight man who never went bush but who owned what he called an Indigenous Art Gallery, in the second block of buildings away from the

Harbour in Cairns. Bang in the middle of the backpacker accommodation and the food halls.

Although there were a couple of good examples of indigenous art in the gallery, they were just for show. Thatcher specialized in the cheap, modern, mass-produced versions of boomerangs and didgeridoos that backpackers buy for their parents to prove that they spent some of their time in Australia soaking up the culture, rather than just drinking and fornicating on the beach.

Backpackers are not known to have a lot of money. Although Thatcher bought the boomerangs and didgeridoos cheap, there still wasn't a sufficient profit margin to make a good living. But Thatcher could afford rare steak and fine wines because his real business was dealing in genuine but stolen indigenous art; or should we say indigenous art obtained in less than ethical ways. Getting an indigenous artist drunk, for example; or buying "no questions asked" from people who had no proof of ownership.

One of the sources of Thatcher's indigenous art was Danny Ridge.

Danny hung around the Outback and wasn't above occasionally swapping grog for works of art if the opportunity arose. Thatcher always paid Danny under the odds because, as he explained to Danny, he had to provide provenance for the art before he could sell it on. Mind you, providing provenance for a work of art that had been made by an unknown artist who was long dead, and whose birth had probably never been officially recorded in the first place, was a lot easier than providing provenance on a Picasso or a Rembrandt. So both Thatcher and Danny made a tidy profit, and only the indigenous artist missed out, which was how both Danny and Thatcher thought it should be.

It was natural therefore that when Thatcher heard about another rich source of treasure in the Outback, he should turn to Danny to see if they couldn't both make an even bigger profit.

Once upon a time all the prospectors in Queensland were like Danny; prospecting for gold and other minerals. Then they were joined by engineers searching for gas and oil. All over the Outback, huge mining companies took out mining leases, pushing the likes of Danny aside and spending millions on exploration.

The indigenous population didn't like the miners digging up their sacred land and poisoning the water and the farmers didn't like the miners digging up their grazing land and poisoning the water. It was all highly political, and the miners understood they had to tread carefully. Which is why, when they stumbled on an area rich in fossils, some of which were of animals thus far unknown to science, they decided to be good citizens and report the find and move their mining exploration team elsewhere.

The find was made in an area known as Fallon's Depression. Local legend had it that it was so named because a prospector named Fallon had committed suicide there.

It was, in fact, the site of a deep, ancient lake. The depression had been formed by a renting of the earth's crust back in the days when the area was primordial swamp. The movement in the earth's crust had created a lake nearly two hundred meters deep with no way for the water to run away. Thus, the bottom of the lake had become bereft of oxygen and bacteria. Anything that fell into the lake and dropped to the bottom remained there, undisturbed, for millions of years, joining the flora and fauna that was already building up on the lake floor.

By the Eocene Period when the swamp surrounding the lake was first beginning to dry out, volcanic activity deep under the lake had sent gas rushing to the surface in huge bubbles. Birds and bats flying overhead, even mammals drinking at the lake's edge, were overcome and sank into the lake, leaving a continuous record of evolution in Australia over more than a hundred million years.

The mining company had surveyed Fallon's Depression before and found brown coal. But the area was remote, and the price of brown coal was falling, so they decided that it wasn't worth pursuing. With the renewed interest in shale oil and natural gas, however, they had recently surveyed the area again, which is when they found the fossils. A quick look at the old samples from the previous exploratory dig revealed that they too were rich in fossils. The previous exploratory dig had been several hundred yards from the new survey. Clearly the fossil bed was massive and could be as large as the famous Messel Pits in Germany, which were declared a World Heritage Site.

While Fallon's Depression may have been an important find, the current Government had as much interest in investing millions in uncovering fossils as it did in saving the environment. The location of the find became a closely guarded secret while the archaeologists involved searched for ways to finance a major excavation.

But in the Bush closely guarded secrets have a way of getting out.

Because Thatcher was well-known in circles where stolen artefacts were bought and sold, it wasn't long before potential customers were contacting him, looking for rare fossils. Thatcher didn't know where the fossil site was. Danny Ridge didn't know where the fossil site was. But they had both heard rumours.

Greg Ahearn had happened across the exploration team at Fallon's Depression when they made the original fossil discovery. Greg was sworn to secrecy but in return he proposed a business deal. He would pay a substantial fee to take his tours to the edge of Fallon's Depression.

The fees would go towards the cost of a proposed dig at the site. The visits would be strictly controlled.

Greg wouldn't take his tours to the actual site, but to an area close-by with similar geological structures. Shale samples containing fossils would be kept under lock and key at the tourist site. Other shards would be piled near the samples, which the tourists could split for themselves. Almost every slate was likely to reveal a fossil. Until they discovered the crashed Ariane Rocket nose cone, the visit to Fallon's Depression was always the highlight of the Ahearn's tours.

To add to the excitement, and comply with his promise of security, Greg applied strict conditions to their visits there. All mobile phones had to be switched off and handed in, so nobody could get a GPS reading on the site. For the last half-hour off the sealed road, the truck drove with the curtains drawn, so that no one but the driver could see where they were going. The tour groups were so excited by the adventure that, as a rule, they didn't question Greg's conditions for visiting the site, nor concern themselves with where the real site might be.

Danny was the exception that proved the rule. He had smuggled a separate GPS in his bag and recorded coordinates, surreptitiously. He knew exactly where the fossil samples were stored, and the slate piled. He was also a professional prospector; not college trained, but he knew more about geology than most university graduates. He knew the slate the tourists were splitting open didn't come from that exact spot. A quick survey of the area revealed truck tracks leading off to a depression to the west. Danny was sure the tracks had been made by a truck bringing in the slate samples.

He knew exactly where he was, and he knew exactly where the fossils had originally been found. Not that this was information Danny was prepared to share with Doug Thatcher as they dined on rare steak and red wine followed by fruit and ice cream.

The deal had been that Thatcher would finance Danny to take the tour and provide him with a second GPS. In return, Danny would tell Thatcher where the find was, and they would share the proceeds. But Danny had changed the deal. He knew that if Thatcher learned where the fossils were, there was nothing to stop him from selling that information or going to the site himself and cutting Danny out. So Danny offered another deal as he finished off the last of his ice cream. He would return to the site alone and bring back a truckload of fossils, which Thatcher would sell.

Thatcher wasn't happy. Carrying the fossils in the back of a truck could damage them, he said. Danny might have an accident. Danny said Thatcher had better pray that he didn't. Because there was no way Danny was telling him the location of the site.

Thatcher had no option but to accept the new deal, but he was so angry he didn't leave the waiter his usual two dollar tip.

When Steve and Kelly turned up at Thatcher's Art Gallery, they found that questioning him was a bit like punching jelly. There was no resistance, but there was no satisfaction either.

Thatcher claimed, quite truthfully, that he had no idea where Danny was going. He'd only paid for Danny's holiday because Danny was an old friend, down on his luck and needing a break. Yes, he knew Danny had one of the osmium marbles. Now that Thatcher heard that Kelly was offering a reward of five hundred dollars to get it back, Thatcher wished he had bought it off Danny the previous night. Danny had offered to sell it, but to be honest, twenty-first-century marbles weren't really the business Thatcher was in.

"And what business is that?" Steve asked.

Thatcher spread his arms expansively indicating the merchandise around him.

"As you can see; cheap tourist tat."

As Steve and Kelly left the Art Gallery, Steve was thinking that Thatcher seemed to be making a very good living on cheap tourist tat. Kelly, however, had moved on. If Thatcher had paid for Danny to go on the tour, a cost of over three thousand dollars, then Thatcher must have expected Danny to bring something back or find something that was worth the expense. They were heading for Ahearn's Tour Depot. If anybody knew anything about hidden treasures visited on this tour, it would be Greg.

Greg knew exactly where Danny was heading as soon as Steve explained the situation. However, he was reluctant to give Kelly the location, even after she showed him her Australian Federal Police I.D.

Aimee suggested Greg call the Curator at the Queensland Museum.

Kelly suggested he tell the Curator that Danny was heading for the site with a bloody big truck. It might be in everybody's interest if they told her where the site was so that she could stop him.

The Curator immediately saw the logic of Kelly's argument and while Greg gave Steve and Kelly the coordinates for Fallon's Depression, the Curator was already on the phone to the Queensland Premier's Office suggesting that they erect "No Trespassing" signs and a gate on the Fallon's Depression Road. Not that any such signs would stop Danny, who had left Cairns earlier that morning. By the time Steve and Kelly discovered his intended destination, Danny had eight hours start on them. This wasn't a problem as far as Steve was concerned. Danny would have to collect supplies on the way, and there was no reason why he'd be in a hurry or drive through the night. If they left immediately, they could probably catch him before he reached Fallon's Depression.

Steve quickly packed his suit carrier and went along to Kelly's room.

She was just checking the room to make sure she hadn't left anything behind, a routine she always did at least twice, when Steve's phone rang.

It was Robinson. They had found the hire-car. It was parked in a motel on the main road through town. The two occupants had taken a room there. There was a police car watching the room, but the police had agreed to hang back and wait for Robinson and his bodyguard to arrive. If the occupants of the room were CIA, they didn't want to cause a diplomatic incident. Robinson wanted Steve at the motel for back-up before they confronted the two men inside.

The motel was easy to find. It was one of the many motels on the Cook Highway, which all seemed to have been built and designed by the same architect; if indeed they had employed an architect at all. A single storey structure built around a reception, which led to a square of small featureless rooms each facing inwards towards the car park. The sort of place people stay because they don't care where they sleep when they are on their way to a cruise out to the Barrier Reef or heading up to Port Douglas or south to home.

The police car wasn't exactly inconspicuous, parked as it was on the highway outside. But since all the rooms in the motel were off the road and, therefore, couldn't see the highway, this probably didn't matter.

Robinson was waiting in Reception checking the register. The two men had checked in a short while after they'd grabbed the luggage from Luc and Leda. It looked like they'd driven out to the main highway and turned into the first motel they could find, figuring that with the off-street parking; they could search the luggage at their leisure.

To explain the fact that they were checking in at ten in the morning they had said they were travelling from Port Douglas to Brisbane. They found it easier to drive at night so they would be sleeping all day, then moving on. They paid up front and told Reception they didn't want to be disturbed.

The Receptionist, who had shown them to their room, had seen them carry a fair amount of luggage into the room in backpacks.

Robinson's bodyguard returned from a circumference of the motel. He reported that while the rooms all opened inwards onto the courtyard and car park, they did have windows in the kitchenettes, against the back wall; windows that were big enough for somebody to climb out of if they removed the flywire frame. The frame to the kitchenette window of one particular unit was missing, presumably so that the men could make a quick escape if anybody came knocking. Robinson ordered his bodyguard to station himself around the back of the motel. He and Steve would take the front door. Kelly should keep well back.

They waited for the bodyguard to advise that he was in position then they checked and re-holstered their guns. Casually, they stepped into the carpark and strolled in opposite directions, heading for the corners at each end of the row of units where the hire-car was parked.

Once out of sight of anybody watching from the room's front window, they drew their guns and moved along the row of motel rooms, keeping as close to the wall as possible. When they reached their target, Steve had to duck down to pass under the window before they stood on either side of the doorway.

The motel was made of a prefabricated material that was so fragile the men inside the room could probably shoot holes through it. Steve, therefore, stood as far from the door as he could while still being able to reach out and knock on the door.

"This is the police. We know you're in there. Come out with your hands up."

Silence.

Nothing from the bodyguard watching the rear window, either.

Steve tentatively tried the door handle. It turned. The door swung open inwards.

In unison Steve and Robinson went through the door, guns raised.

The room was empty but spread across the bed, on the lounge and the table; the Reinhardt's clothes were laid out in neat piles. The remains of their backpacks lay on the floor, having been cut into pieces as somebody had searched each compartment, seam and lining in the luggage. There was also a single mobile phone on the table. Steve picked it up and checked the contact list. Leda's name was there. The phone belonged to Luc. Steve put it in his pocket.

After ensuring the bathroom was clear, Robinson invited Kelly into the room.

She stood, inspecting the piles of clothes, the shredded luggage.

"What do you make of it?" Robinson asked.

"They were searching for the marble, and they didn't find it," Kelly concluded. "Unless it was in the very last piece of the luggage they cut up, which seems pretty unlikely. They wouldn't have gone on cutting things up if they'd found what they were looking for."

Kelly picked up Leda's hiking boots. They had been cleaned and polished so that they looked brand new; unworn.

"Look at these; immaculate. Why would she wrap these in cling wrap to protect her clothes?"

She looked around the room.

"And where's the cling wrap?"

Kelly looked in the waste paper basket, under the piles of clothes. The cling wrap wasn't there.

"Maybe they took it with them," suggested Robinson.

"Why would they do that?

Kelly thought it was a lot more likely that it wasn't her boots that Leda had wrapped in cling wrap. She was a smuggler. She had smuggled drugs in condoms that she'd then swallowed, to get them through customs.

Kelly spoke to the police who were still waiting on the highway as back-up. She asked how many pathologists they had at the local morgue. One, she was told.

It was as Kelly had expected. Cairns was a small place. The pathologist probably worked nine to five, so he wouldn't have done the autopsy on Leda yet. He'd probably just queued her and put her in the freezer overnight. They could go to the morgue and check. Kelly was sure they would find the marble in Leda's stomach.

Robinson felt they should follow proper procedure. If they went cutting up bodies at the mortuary people were likely to start asking questions.

Kelly agreed. She went back to policemen. Did they know where the local pathologist lived or how she could find him?

The two policemen grinned at each other.

"I don't know where he lives," the more senior officer said, "but I know where you'll find him; where he is every night after work and every lunchtime: in the pub."

'Pathologists that drink' were a familiar phenomenon for Kelly. Many doctors, herself included, chose Pathology rather than Medicine because they couldn't handle the patient contact. Then they found that they couldn't handle the constant carnage a pathologist is faced with on a daily basis; People dying needlessly; bodies smashed up in car crashes or drunken brawls; murdered and butchered corpses. Kelly had some sympathy with the condition and it might even be useful in this case. If this pathologist was a drunk he was more likely to be compliant and agree to let her conduct the autopsy. The problem would be getting him out of the pub; she wanted to do the autopsy immediately.

The Pathologist was sitting on his usual bar stool, into his third or fourth drink when Steve and Kelly found him. Kelly showed him her Federal Police Pathology I.D. and explained the situation. At least she gave him a version of the situation.

He didn't make eye contact with her at all as he listened; staring down into his drink.

Kelly told him the woman whose body had been brought to the morgue earlier was part of a drug smuggling syndicate that the Federal Police had been following for some time. She had drugs hidden in her body. They were going to let her through and track her to Europe, but now she had died the other members of the syndicate would be able to flee the country and get away. Kelly wanted the drugs so they could arrest the woman's husband before he got on a plane.

The Pathologist waited until she was done, then said he was finished for the day; she should come back tomorrow.

Eight o'clock, at the morgue. He'd open up the old lady then.

Kelly wasn't giving up. She spoke a little more quietly, right into his ear.

"It would help your disciplinary case if you co-operated with us," she said.

He looked up at her now, for the first time.

"What disciplinary case?" he asked, with the touch of paranoia that usually accompanies alcoholism.

"There have been complaints about your drinking," Kelly said. "A case the police lost, because of the pathology? They say you stuffed up because you were drunk."

Kelly was winging it, but she felt she was on pretty safe ground. There was always a case that the police felt they'd lost because of the pathology. With a drinker like this guy, it was doubly certain he would often get the blame.

"It wasn't my fault," the Pathologist said. "I did everything by the book."

"Not what the police are saying, I'm afraid," continued Kelly." They say you were drunk. They say you're always drunk. How do you think we found you? The cops told us where you were; where you always are. The same cops who told us about the complaint."

The Pathologist drank deeply from his glass.

"Take us to the morgue now," Kelly continued. "That's all I'm asking. I'll do the autopsy. And I'll make a special note in the case files about the exceptional co-operation you've shown the Federal Police."

The Pathologist thought about it.

He got off his stool and stood up as straight as he could.

"I gotta pee," he said and walked off to the toilet, making a special effort to walk straight and appear sober.

"What if he hadn't fallen for all that?" Steve asked Kelly.

"Then you'd have had to twist his arm behind his back and march him out," said Kelly.

Steve nodded. "I think Robinson will be happier doing it this way," he concluded.

But none of them, including Robinson, would have been at all happy had they known where the two men in Hawaiian shirts were at that moment.

They were sitting in another hire car, on a side street next to the morgue. It was raining, and the last rays of the sun were hidden by the clouds.

They had watched the Pathologist head off to the pub earlier and waited for the day staff to lock up and leave.

They had decided to wait just a little longer.

It would be easier breaking into the Morgue un-noticed, once it was completely dark.

Luckily the new moon was just a couple of nights old.

13 - The Living Dead.

The two men in the Hawaiian shirts were a father and son team. Both were named David Armstrong, and both had been soldiers before they began working freelance for the CIA. Armstrong Senior first came into contact with the Agency during the Vietnam War. He had retired to Far North Queensland when the Coalition of the Willing's invasion of Iraq opened up a new career path: running a private security company, operating in Iraq. His son, Dave Junior, a veteran of the first Gulf War and Somalia, had been his partner in that.

It was a sign of how quickly events surrounding the osmium marbles had developed that the CIA had had to bring the Armstrongs out of their second retirement. They simply didn't have enough people on the ground in the area, and they were really scraping the bottom of the barrel with the Armstrongs. Neither of them had ever operated in a friendly country before, let alone their own country. They were used to operating in areas where the occasional dead body wasn't going to cause too much trouble, which is why they'd so badly botched the job of getting hold of the Reinhardt's luggage.

Their inclination, now that they'd worked out Leda had swallowed the marble, was to go to the Morgue, snatch Leda's body, and take it somewhere quiet where they could cut it up and dispose of it afterwards.

Their Controller in Pine Gap wasn't keen on this idea. They had already snatched the luggage; snatch a body as well and he doubted even the special relationship between the security organizations of the U.S. and Australia would save them. He preferred to gamble on the belief that the Australians hadn't realized that the CIA didn't have the marble and hadn't worked out that Leda had swallowed it. His instructions to the Armstrongs were to break into the morgue, preferably without leaving any signs of the break-in, then check the woman's belongings and make sure the marble wasn't there.

If it wasn't, they should find the woman's body and locate the marble in her abdomen. The woman was thin, so they could probably locate it by simply feeling around on the surface of her skin, but they were to take a metal detector with them just to be sure. Then they were to make a small keyhole incision where the marble was and pull it out with tweezers. There shouldn't be much blood because the woman had been dead for ten hours. They could remove the marble, clean up any blood, sew the incision up, put the old lady back into the freezer and hope nobody recognized the significance of the incision when the autopsy was eventually performed.

Junior thought this was all a waste of time, but he didn't have any qualms about cutting into a dead body. He had a scalpel, a metal detector, even a needle and thread, which he'd borrowed from his wife, and plenty of gauze to clean up the blood. He also had a very powerful torch.

His father had a torch as well, and a gun and a Swiss

army knife, with which he sprang the catch on a side window in the morgue.

The two men silently slipped into the darkened interior of the building before closing the window and switching on their torches, making sure to keep the beams pointed to the ground.

They were in the administration area of the morgue, which at this time was empty.

They did a quick reconnoitre of the building. There was only one Night Porter on duty. He was in his small office just off the arrival dock, which was situated at the back of the morgue.

The Armstrongs heard the noise of his television before they saw him. They switched off their torches and approached, guided only by the light coming from his office. They looked in.

The Porter was fast asleep. He had his feet up, and there was an empty beer can on the table beside him. He hated working nights; found the morgue creepy in the dark on his own and it didn't help that he was addicted to vampire and horror movies. So when he was on night duty, he habitually joined the Pathologist for a liquid lunch, had an afternoon nap and then took a slab of beer into work. He kept the beer in one of the empty freezers that normally held the bodies. Between dozing and watching TV, the slab usually lasted him until dawn.

Since they were supposed to get in and out of the morgue without leaving any signs of entry, Armstrong Senior decided to leave the Porter where he was.

They made their way by torchlight to the freezer room. They could have found it using only their noses. It had that butcher's storeroom smell of refrigerated meat. Armstrong Senior had been in a lot of morgues in his time and it always reminded him of the tropical jungle smell when he first got off the plane in Vietnam over forty years earlier.

He checked the wall of refrigerated compartments where they kept the dead bodies, and the Night Porter kept his beer. He quickly located Leda's body and pulled it out, on its tray.

A name tag was attached to its toe, which he checked to be sure. At the bottom of the tray was a clipboard with a list of the effects that were registered on her arrival. Next to it, were the effects themselves in a sealed see-through evidence bag.

Armstrong Junior was about to cut open the bag, but his father silently stopped him. He checked the list and stared through the see-through bag at its contents; a mobile phone, tissues and a pill dispenser.

Armstrong Senior was able to open the pill dispenser through the plastic. The contents rolled out; a myriad of different coloured small pills but no marble.

"Cut her. I'll watch the door," Armstrong Senior whispered to his son.

He positioned himself at the door where he could just see through to the open door leading to the arrival dock and still keep an eye on his son at the same time. They didn't know that Kelly had worked out where the marble was and was, at that moment, driving to the morgue, so they were in no hurry.

Junior placed his equipment on the floor with his torch standing on its base so that it threw a reflection up onto the ceiling and gave enough light to work by. He laid out his other equipment neatly on the floor before he undid Leda's shirt and pulled up her T-Shirt. He didn't need to touch her micro shorts, which were down on her hips anyway. He bent down and picked up the metal detector.

As he brought it close to Leda's body, there was another blue arc of electricity, a flash.

Junior dropped the metal detector in shock and pain and fell backwards.

As he did so, the metal detector dropped onto Leda's body, and she seemed to sit up, possibly as a reaction to the metal detector falling on her abdomen.

The noise woke the Night Porter, although he was still half asleep and half drunk; for a moment he didn't know where he was and what had woken him.

"What the hell are you doing, Junior?" Armstrong Senior hissed at Junior, and he flashed his torch across at his son sitting stunned on the floor.

"She's got some sort of stun gun," Junior said. "It went off when I tried to grab her bag before. I must've set it off again, with the metal detector."

"Bullshit," said his father," the machine probably just shorted."

Armstrong Senior crossed to the trolley, to investigate.

The trolley was empty. He stared at it for a moment, stunned.

"Where the fuck's the body?"

The metal detector was there, lying on what was now an empty trolley; body, evidence bag, the lot, were gone.

Armstrong Senior looked on the floor; nothing. Then he became aware of a blur in the periphery of his vision. He flashed his torch. Somebody was running through the exit door.

The Night Porter was sufficiently awake now to go and investigate the noise he had heard. He stepped from his brightly lit office into the darkened access bay. In the darkness, he saw a pale shape that looked very much like the body he had signed for earlier, carrying the bag of possessions that he had also signed for. It ran full-tilt into the access bay and almost bumped into him.

The body wailed. The Night Porter fainted.

The body charged for the access bay roller door; it was locked. It slammed against the door to no avail, turned and ran through the darkness, back the way it had come.

By now Armstrong Senior was in pursuit. Not at all sure what he was dealing with, he had tentatively approached the door that led from the morgue to the access bay. As he reached it, it swung open, smashing into him and sending him flying.

The shape charged through the door and seemed to pause as if wondering which way to go. There was a faint light coming from a plate glass window in the administration area. The shape headed for the light.

Despite his sixty odd years, Armstrong Senior was quick to react. He got up and gathered his gun and torch.

The shape ran out into the corridor towards the administration offices, looking one way then the other for a means of escape.

As Armstrong Senior burst into the corridor, the shape made up its mind.

It charged at the plate glass window as if it wasn't there.

The glass shattered with a cacophony of sound that mingled with the sound of Armstrong Senior's gun as he fired twice at the fleeing figure.

Armstrong rushed towards the window and peered out.

"I hit her."

Junior, somewhat shaken, had now picked up his torch and the metal detector and joined his father.

"Hit who?"

"The Reinhardt woman. It was her."

Junior used the metal detector to clear away the jagged remains of glass at the bottom of the window to give them an easy way out.

"She's dead, dad. Besides, she couldn't jump through this window. She must be ninety in the shade."

"Then where's the body?"

"Somebody beat us to it; somebody who hid in the freezer when they heard us coming and pretended to..."

"Don't be bloody stupid!" Senior said to his son.

Junior climbed out through the window. He checked the footprints in the damp earth.

"Whoever she was, she went that way."

He pointed his torch beam up the empty street. His father climbed out through the window.

"Let's get after her."

At that moment, Steve's 4WD pulled up at the front of the Morgue.

Nothing looked amiss as Steve and Kelly waited for the Pathologist to unlock the door. And they didn't take much notice of a car in the side street driving away.

Inside the morgue, it was a different matter. As the Pathologist switched on the lights, the first thing they saw was the shattered window. Then the Night Porter wandered into the corridor looking like he'd seen a ghost, which he thought he had.

"What happened?" the Pathologist demanded.

"She came after me," wailed the Night Porter.

"Who came after you?"

"The Zombie. The Zombie they brought in this afternoon."

The Pathologist stood close to the Night Porter and smelt his breath.

"You've been drinking," he said. "You're a bloody disgrace."

More quietly he whispered,

"Pull yourself together, man. They're Feds."

Kelly was too occupied inspecting the broken plate glass window to bother about them.

"Well, something happened here" she said. "Can we check the body?"

The Pathologist led the way.

As soon as he stepped into the freezer room and switched on the light, they could see the freezer door open and the empty trolley.

"They've beaten us to it," said Kelly.

While she hurried back into the corridor, Steve picked up the clipboard, which was the only thing left on the trolley. He checked the name was right and noted the contents of the missing bag: mobile phone, tissues, pill dispenser with assorted pills. He followed Kelly out.

Kelly was in the corridor. Here was something she understood; a crime scene. She put her white gloves on, took a sample bag from her pocket and picked up Armstrong Senior's two spent cartridges with a pair of tweezers. She dropped them into the bag, which she put in her pocket.

She flashed her torch on the sill of the window. There were smears of blood on the ground, both inside and outside the window. She took samples then stepped out through the window and examined the footprints on the wet ground,

"Why smash the window to carry her out?" Steve asked through the window.

"They didn't carry her out," wailed the Night Porter. "She ran."

"Will you shut up?" hissed the Pathologist.

"You're going to get us both sacked. Stop making a bloody fool of yourself."

"I'm not sure he is," said Kelly from outside the smashed window.

She directed her torch beam down onto the ground.

"There are three sets of footprints here. The deepest set is the smallest; a pair of small runners, like Leda was wearing."

"You're not telling me she jumped out of the window?" said the Pathologist.

"No, but they didn't carry her out, either. Their footprints would be a lot deeper if they were carrying a body. The porter did see somebody running around here."

"So where is she?"

"That, I don't know."

In fact, Leda wasn't far away at all. At least her body wasn't far away, and it was breathing, despite a bullet hole in the back of her shoulder.

She watched from a dark corner beside a shop further up the street as Kelly examined the footprints and declared that somebody had either cut themselves going through the window or had been shot.

Leda felt the bullet hole in the back of her shoulder, looked at the blood on her fingers and checked the front of her T-Shirt. There was no exit wound.

She wasn't dead, but she looked like she might die at any moment. Despite this, she showed no reaction to the pain from touching the open wound in her shoulder or to the pain the wound itself should have been causing.

She was holding her possessions in the evidence bag with her injured arm.

She ripped open the bag with her other hand, put the

mobile phone into her shorts pocket and retrieved the tissues.

She let the evidence bag, pill dispenser and pills fall to the ground, then pushed the tissues in under her T-shirt so that they covered the wound.

The blood quickly soaked the tissues, but it also stuck them to the wound, partially stemming the flow. Leda left the discarded bag on the floor and walked off purposefully.

She knew exactly what she was looking for. She just didn't know exactly where to find it; but it shouldn't be far.

14 - DIY Surgery.

The Petersen Street Medical Practice was on the edge of the small suburban shopping centre near the morgue. It was a quiet area at night when the shops were shut. The street lights were barely adequate to light the roads. The shop fronts were in semi-darkness.

The security system at the Practice consisted of a sign that read "No drugs are kept on these premises," and alarms on the doors and windows.

However, the alarms only sounded when the doors and windows were physically opened. So when Leda wrapped her elbow in her khaki shirt and knocked the glass out of one of the windows, the alarms remained silent.

Leda climbed through the window and went searching through the various rooms.

One of the Doctors obviously specialized in Paediatrics. There was a jar of jelly beans on the desk. Leda poured the jelly beans down her throat in one go.

In the kitchen behind Reception, she found a half full bottle of milk in the fridge, which she sculled without the milk touching the sides.

Leda knew she had to get high energy food into her system as quickly as possible.

There were also a couple of apples in the fridge, which she put on the table.

Refreshed by the intake of food and drink, Leda quickly found the medical supplies cupboard, which she again opened by virtue of smashing in the front glass.

She laid out sticking plaster, scissors, tweezers, antiseptic and bandages, and started to create a couple of pads from the bandages. She looked for a scalpel, but couldn't find one. She used the scissors to cut her T-Shirt away from her shoulder and threw it and the blood-soaked tissues into the bin. She wasn't wearing a bra, and it was a long time since she'd needed one. She inspected the wound in her back by looking in the mirror.

She then checked the front of her shoulder. The bullet was still there, so close to the surface that if she pressed hard with her bony finger she could feel it under the skin.

She covered the large pad with antiseptic and attached sticking plaster in large strips. She then repeated the process making a much smaller, but otherwise identical pad. Again using the mirror, she positioned the larger pad over the wound in the back of her shoulder and pressed it into place using the sticking plaster. Then she poured antiseptic over the scissors, poured more antiseptic over the front of her shoulder, and plunged the scissors into her shoulder until they reached the bullet. Ignoring the blood that was now pouring from her shoulder, she put down the scissors, picked up the tweezers and pulled out the bullet. She dropped the bullet and tweezers onto the table. Then, she pressed the smaller pad onto her shoulder and held it tight there until the plaster stuck.

Throughout the process, she showed no reaction to the pain because there was no pain. The messages that would normally be sent from the wound to her brain were being blocked by the osmium marble, which had attached itself to the nervous system on Leda's spine and was now controlling her entire body like a second brain; which is what it was.

The creators of the osmium marbles had gone through literally hundreds of scenarios trying to anticipate what conditions and circumstances the marbles might encounter on their journey. They'd chosen osmium as the outer coating for its hardness, and its high melting point, to give the marble the best chance of surviving entry into the atmosphere of any planet.

For added protection, they'd installed the ability to generate electric impulses when the marble felt threatened, much like an electric eel. The trigger for the electric shock was the proximity of metal; the creators considered that if anybody was going to try to damage the marble they would use a metal implement.

To survive the long journey, the marbles remained dormant until their outer coating came into direct contact with living tissue from a warm-blooded animal. Even then, the contact had to be of a certain duration - equal to ten Earth minutes, as it turned out - to give the brain time to thaw completely. The time delay would prevent the marble from activating when it was just being picked up or handed around.

After ten minutes, the marble had the ability to cut through any living tissue, disappear inside and repair the incision behind it.

This ability to regenerate living cells also applied to the whole of the host body because the creators had envisaged that the marble might come to rest in a body that was not in the best physical condition.

Certainly that was the case with Leda. Even though the cells in her body were constantly regenerating just like the cells in the body of any warm-blooded mammal, when the marble entered her body she was near death. By the time the marble was activated, she was already dead.

Put simply, there are two reasons why the constant regeneration of cells can't stop the aging process in humans.

Firstly the cells of the cerebral cortex don't renew, so the brain ages and the body follows. For the marbles, this wasn't a problem. The marble would work its way through the host body until it reached the spinal chord. There it would attach itself and tap into the nervous system. So if the host brain was old, malfunctioning, or even newly dead, it didn't matter. The marble was by-passing it anyway.

Secondly, although the cells of a human body regenerate, its DNA doesn't. The DNA degrades with each generation, so the regenerated cells are slowly degraded, and the body grows old. The creators had found a way to reverse this process by including an enzyme in the marbles' DNA that caused a Telomeres Activity similar to that which occurs naturally in crustaceans like lobsters. Lobsters replace their cells each time with new cells in prime condition, so that it is impossible to tell their age. Nor is it possible to tell when, or even if, they will ever die.

The effect the marble had on Leda's body was much the same. Once the marble was in place on her spinal chord, it sent an electrical impulse to restart the heart and injected telomerase into the DNA so that the repair could begin. The new cells generated by the body were therefore not old and degraded but equal to cells generated when the body was in its peak condition. Over time, Leda's whole body would attain that state.

In humans the cells on the surface of the skin are replaced completely every five days, so in five days Leda would look the way she did when she was twenty-five years old. In three weeks, her complete epidermis would be regenerated. But while Leda would appear youthful, the regeneration of her vital organs would take far longer; a year for a new liver and pancreas; ten years for a new skeleton; a lifetime for a new heart.

When Leda decided to smuggle the marble out of Australia by swallowing it, she didn't think she was exposing herself to any danger. She had smuggled lethal materials across Europe and the Middle East, inside her body. As long as the condom stopped the narcotics from coming into direct contact with her system, she was safe.

The same applied to the marble in the cling wrap. Covered in an inert substance the marble had no idea that it was cocooned in a living body. That is, until Junior stuck a gun in Leda's stomach to persuade her to let go of the backpack.

The marble was inside the stomach. The gun was right next to the stomach.

The defence mechanism automatically activated and the electric shock leapt through her body to the gun.

The current hadn't damaged Leda's living tissue, but it did cause a rift in the cling wrap that encased the marble. The cling wrap split, the marble sensed the living tissue; and lay dormant for ten minutes. Reassured that it was indeed inside a living body, after ten minutes the marble started to work slowly toward the spinal chord.

An hour later when Leda was pronounced dead at the hospital, the marble had reached the spinal chord. It found the brain dead; the body inert.

It methodically started an internal examination to check if the body could be re-activated. Was there a blood supply? Did the heart work? It was still in the middle of this process when the body was transported to the morgue.

The process was completed by the time the Morgue Attendant was registering the body's receipt and wheeling it off to the freezer. The marble had checked Leda's memory, her motor neuron system, her heart and her lungs. Everything could be re-activated, but the marble realized that Leda's body was weak, with a low energy supply. Rather than face a confrontation with the Morgue Attendant, it decided to wait until he left before activating the heart. However, the marble hadn't reckoned on being placed back into deep freeze. Leda's body had now been dead for several hours and had given up much of its warmth. The freezer completed the process. The cold reduced the marble's ability to function and it lay there, inert in an inert body.

All that changed again when Junior reappeared, albeit with a metal detector instead of a gun. This time the arc of electricity had re-activated the heart. Fear forced adrenalin into the body. Fight or Flight. The marble knew its energy supply was almost on empty and chose Flight. When Leda had escaped through the window, she was already running on empty. She had to rest in the darkness before she could go on. The discovery of the jelly beans had come just in time; otherwise the doctors would have found her inert body on the surgery floor when the practice opened in the morning.

Leda ate the two apples on the table, pips, core and all. She drank three large glasses of water and went looking to see what else the surgery had to offer.

One of the doctors was obviously a keen jogger.

Female, too, not that it would have mattered to Leda. A jogging kit was hanging on the back of the surgery door in a backpack. Leda took out the doctor's T-Shirt and pulled it over her head. She also took the rest of the jogging kit and the backpack.

In the general office, she forced open the drawers and rifled the cash box. Tapping into Leda's human memory, she counted over three hundred dollars; more than enough to refuel her system from something the same memory bank told her was a Convenience Store.

Finally she picked up her khaki shirt. There was a bullet hole in the back and it was blood stained but Leda decided to put it on. She needed the warmth until she had refuelled.

Leda left the surgery via the front door, which set off the burglar alarm. Leda was unconcerned. She knew from her days as an urban terrorist that the more casually you left the scene of a crime, the less likely anybody was to challenge you.

The creators of the Osmium Marbles had envisaged that the marbles might get separated on landing on an alien planet, so they'd given the marbles the ability to communicate with each other over relatively large distances. Well, not communicate, exactly; that would require the brains inside the marbles to be activated. They would still be cryogenically frozen on landing and it was more than likely that many, if not all, would remain in that state for some time. While still dormant however, they could simply sense each other and in that way, the creators reasoned, they would eventually be able to regroup.

Leda walked down to the Cook Highway and crossed to stand in the middle of the median strip.

With no building immediately nearby, she started to rotate just as Gina had done on the rock the day before.

As Leda faced south, she heard, or rather sensed, a single ping, followed by another and another, until she could pick up seven separate signals. All of the marbles had travelled south.

Leda then went looking for a Convenience Store. She found one that fitted the image in the memory bank quite easily, filled her backpack with fuel and water and returned to the Cook Highway.

Her memory told her how to hitch-hike, and her long legs and micro shorts quickly got her a lift in a passing truck.

As she clambered on board, however, the Truckie wasn't so sure he'd done the right thing. She had great legs, this one, and a slim figure... but her face! She looked ancient. And she had a disgusting habit of pushing food into her mouth and swigging from an energy drink while making the sort of noises that his dear old mum had drilled out of him when he was still a baby.

15 - Man's Best Friend.

Kelly was still at the morgue, carrying out a closer examination of the building and surrounds when she received a call from the police to go to Petersen Street Medical Centre.

What she found there, evidence of the do-it-yourself medical procedure, Leda's discarded T-shirt, the tissue and the bullet, confirmed her earlier suspicions. Nobody had carried Leda's body out of the morgue. She had jumped.

Leaving the local police to search for Leda or, more likely, Leda's body, since it seemed improbable that she would survive the shooting and her self-administered surgery, Kelly and Steve got into Steve's 4WD and headed back to the highway. As Robinson had instructed, they went south, in search of Danny Ridge.

As they drove, they discussed what they knew and what they thought they knew, and Kelly relayed what information they had to the AFP Laboratory set-up in the Australian Aerospace Facility at Brisbane Airport, where they were examining Greg Ahearn's marble.

It now seemed likely that Leda was alive, she told them, though maybe not for much longer.

There were a couple of possibilities, the first being that Leda never had been dead. That the marbles might contain a poison similar to the poison of the puffer fish, which causes the metabolic system to slow to such an extent that a casual examination would miss the occasional faint heartbeat. Kelly had given the body only the most rudimentary examination at the crash site and she had no faith that an overworked doctor at Cairns Hospital would have been any more diligent.

The Lab replied that they had checked the marble in their possession for any trace of the poison and found nothing. If it existed, it must be safely inside the marble, which they hadn't yet been able to penetrate.

The second possibility that Kelly suggested was a lot closer to the truth. Leda had died, but the attempt to cut open her body had triggered a defence mechanism in the marble. The electric shock had reactivated the heart and she'd run, purely on instinct and adrenalin. Because she had been dead for several hours there was bound to be brain damage. She'd been shot. She was in her seventies. She had pancreatic cancer. Kelly expected that sooner or later the local police would find Leda's body.

The Lab agreed with this assessment. They'd already encountered the electric shock phenomenon while examining the marble. They had found, however, that by constantly taunting the marble with a mechanical arm the shocks had quickly weakened and after a few minutes they had been able to examine the exterior of the marble with impunity. Unfortunately, they could find no way of looking inside the marble. X-rays and ultrasounds had proved useless. They were left with the prospect of either dissecting it with a laser or smashing it.

They had decided to wait until they had a second marble before embarking on any such drastic action.

Steve listened as Kelly assessed the situation in her cold and systematic way. His sympathies were with Leda. What must she be thinking? How must she be feeling? Dead, then brought back to life; somebody or something controlling her body. Something she couldn't possibly understand. The poor woman must be on the verge of insanity. And how was her husband feeling?

"What about Luc?" he asked when Kelly had hung up.

"Luc?"

Kelly's voice was blank as if she had no idea who Steve was talking about.

"Luc - the husband? What's happened to him? What have they told him?"

Kelly shrugged.

"As far as he's concerned the body's still in the morgue. It wouldn't be released anyway until the police have finished their investigations. There's no point telling him anything right now. He'd probably kick up a hell of a fuss."

"You think?" Steve asked.

Kelly could recognise a rhetorical question when she heard one. She ignored his sarcasm

Given Kelly's total lack of compassion, Steve didn't bother to continue the conversation either. Instead, he waited until it was her turn to drive. Then he took out Luc's phone and typed:

'If you need help, call me.'

Sitting in the truck travelling south, several hundred kilometres ahead of Steve, Leda heard the alert and checked her phone.

She smiled when she saw the name of the caller. It was Luc. He was worried about her.

Then she frowned. The message was in English. It was a trick. She switched off the phone. Phones can be traced, her memory told her.

Leda sat back, relaxed, and quietly passed wind. The massive intake of food and drink required to provide energy and to regenerate her body cells also generated a lot of by-products, initially in the form of gas. The Truckie winced. He'd heard that little old ladies smelled, but this was ridiculous.

When Leda asked how long it was to the next stop because she needed the bathroom, the Truckie saw his chance. He stopped at the first available all-night service station and pulled up at the diesel bowser.

Apparently getting out to refuel, he indicated to Leda where the ladies' toilets were. But as soon as Leda disappeared into the toilets the Truckie jumped back into his truck, gunned the engine and disappeared too, down the highway, making sure to wind down both windows on the way.

Leda didn't even notice. The effort of escaping and filling up with so much fuel had left her body exhausted. The marble was alert, but it knew the body needed rest. The marble shut the body down, only maintaining a slow, regular heartbeat.

The body slept sitting on the toilet seat and was still there when the marble was alerted by a knocking on the door. Somebody needed the toilet and had been waiting for some time.

Leda came out of the cubicle totally refreshed. She washed her hands, face and upper body in the sink. She looked into the mirror. If she had taken a course of

Botox, she couldn't have been more pleased. She didn't look sixteen, but she didn't look seventy-five any more, either. Maybe a well preserved fifty-five, and even her breasts were beginning to swell again.

She stepped out into the forecourt of the service station, which was now bathed in early morning sunlight. She silently checked the whereabouts of the other seven marbles. They were all still south of her, but the closest marble was now moving west. Leda risked switching on her phone for a few moments to check which road went west, maybe fifty miles south of her current position. It was the Townsville by-pass, heading up the escarpment to Charters Towers.

Charters Towers is one of the forgotten gems of the Queensland Outback. It's not flat and featureless like Winton or Hughenden. It's not even an old cattle or sheep town like so many others. Charters Towers was the location of one of the world's greatest gold discoveries in the nineteenth century. In those days it was the second largest city in Queensland.

Impressive Colonial buildings still stand in the centre of Mosman Street. The Stock Exchange Arcade, built in 1880, housed the town's own Stock Exchange and Assay Office.

The Australian Bank of Commerce building has now been converted into the World Theatre; so called because, in the nineteenth century, the town called itself, simply, "The World." People from every corner of the globe flocked there.

Henry's Café has a high vaulted glass roof and is decorated with original paintings based on Henry Lawson's stories, painted by his grandnephew, Peter Lawson.

It isn't just these buildings that attract visitors. Charters Towers is at the top of the escarpment, high above the coast. Its climate in summer is dryer and cooler than nearby Townsville, so it's a popular weekend destination for people fleeing the heat and humidity.

The area is amply supplied with accommodation, including well-appointed motels and caravan parks. The 1887-built Royal Private Hotel, also in Mosman Street, has been renovated to recapture its former glory. You can stay in a suite with a four-poster bed if it takes your fancy, with double doors opening out to a typical wraparound Queensland veranda.

Danny Ridge certainly didn't stay in anything as grand as the Royal Private Hotel or even any of the surrounding motels when he was in Charters Towers. He preferred a local pub made of breeze blocks with a tin roof. It was a building that would have looked more like a barn than a hotel if it weren't for the large satellite dish on the roof, the Forex sign and the sign reading: *Sports Bar and Counter Lunches Seven Days a Week.*

It was from this hotel that the sound of howling could be heard, coming from a dog, half blue heeler, half dingo that was tied up in the yard behind the pub.

The Publican yelled at the dog to shut up.

The Publican's Wife, who was one of the only two people in the world who could control the dog, was more sympathetic.

"Can you smell your master, boy?" she asked.

The dog who went by the name of Dog, wagged his tail enthusiastically.

Dog could indeed smell his master. Or at least somehow sense his master's presence even when he was still some miles away. And at that moment Danny Ridge was driving his truck off the highway, over the railway line, past the McDonald's and into town.

The Publican wasn't aware of Danny's presence until he walked into the bar. Greetings were exchanged with the usual Queensland understatement.

"About bloody time. Next time you can take the bloody dog with you on holiday; hasn't stopped barking since you left."

In fact, the dog had stopped barking.

"I can't hear him," said Danny, and walked through towards the yard where he knew Dog would be tethered.

"Wanna beer?" called the Publican's Wife as he passed.

"Just the one, gotta be on the road. Found somethin' real interestin' on the tour."

Danny had only driven as far as Townsville the previous day. He had a contact there in Army Ordinance who could always supply him with a bit of gelignite and a few caps. He'd also bought his general supplies in Townsville where they were cheaper than in Charters Towers. Even though his hometown was doing it tough, he didn't see why he should pay extra to support the local business community.

Danny untied Dog who wagged his tail furiously and tried to rub up against Danny's legs, almost tripping him over.

"Get out of it, you stupid mutt," said Danny.
But Dog just wagged his tail even harder and generally got in Danny's way as he walked back into the bar.

The Publican's Wife put a cold beer on the bar; so cold that the condensation was already gathering on the outside of the glass.

The Publican slapped a bill on the bar.

Danny sipped his beer, looked at the bill.

"Fifty dollars? What's this?"

"Dog food."

"Dog eats scraps."

"Not here he don't. The wife spoils him rotten."
Danny reluctantly pulled out a wad of money, muttering as he did so.

"Bloody dog. If I'd known, it was gonna cost me this much I'd have shot him before I went."

But Dog knew he didn't mean it. He wagged his tail and panted, watching Danny's every move with unconditional devotion.

In the meantime, Leda had reached Townsville and was now on the Flinders Highway heading west. She had found another lift with another truckie, and since she no longer smelled and now looked like everybody's mum rather than an ancient witch, she was engaging in a rather pleasant conversation with the driver.

She had a friend, she told him, who was also travelling west. Leda was trying to catch up with her.

The Flinders Highway went as far west as Mount Isa and on to The Northern Territory; where was Leda's friend heading?

Leda said she'd phone and check.

In fact, what she did was send out an impulse to Danny's marble, followed by another.

The time it took to get a response and the time between responses told her how far away the marble was and that it was no longer moving west. Correlating this with her GPS, Leda told the driver her friend was in Charters Towers and staying there at the moment.

Danny had finished his beer and was heading out to his

truck with Dog when the marble that he had in his shirt pocket, still wrapped in his dirty handkerchief, seemed to give him a slight electric shock. This was followed a moment later by another. It had happened a few times lately, and Danny assumed it was just static, but it was bloody irritating. He'd tried unsuccessfully to sell the marble to Thatcher and didn't really know why he was holding on to it.

He let Dog into the passenger seat in the front of the truck. As he went around to the driver's seat, he took the marble out of the handkerchief. He wiped his nose with the dirty handkerchief and stuffed it into his trouser pocket. The truck had no glove box, just a tray where Danny piled his rubbish, maps and sweets, and where he now tossed the marble before he started the engine and drove off.

As the truck moved, the marble rolled up the dashboard. Up and down, up and down.

Dog watched the marble back and forth, back and forth.

He looked at Danny as if he might explain this phenomenon, but Danny was too busy negotiating the roads out of town and back onto the Flinders Highway.

Once on the Highway with the almost deserted road stretching ahead of him, Danny could relax and turn his attention to his favourite pastime; teasing Dog.

"What is it Dog?" he asked. "What is it, eh? Food?"

Dog hadn't thought so, but if that's what Danny said… Dog lunged forward and swallowed the marble in a single gulp.

Danny brought the truck to a halt with a screech of brakes.

"You stupid bloody thing," he grabbed Dog by the jaw. "Cough it up. Cough it up."

Dog just looked confused.

Danny got out of the truck, pulled Dog out of the passenger seat and threw him into the back of the truck where he tied Dog to the roll bar with a rope kept there for the purpose.

"You stay there 'til you pass the bloody thing,"

Danny yelled at Dog, who cowered in the bottom of the tray wondering what he had done wrong.

Danny got back into the truck, started the engine and roared on down the road.

Dog lay in the bottom of the tray for ten minutes, not moving. Then he stood up and looked around. He felt the wind blowing against his face. He put his front paws up on the roll bar and stood bracing himself against the wind, luxuriating in the sensation of the air rushing past him.

The wind blew back his cheeks, revealing his fine, strong teeth.

It looked for all the world like Dog was grinning.

16 - *A Friend of the Earth.*

Steve and Kelly had driven until quite late the previous evening. Eventually they'd stopped at an all-night service station to eat and sleep for six hours in two of the small motel rooms behind the service station.

They made an early start and stopped further down the road for breakfast.

They were having breakfast, still an hour or so north of Townsville when Steve received a call from Greg Ahearn. Greg and Aimee had just arrived at the depot to start work. Somebody had broken in overnight. Nothing was missing except a copy of the Ahearn Outback Itinerary including the location of Fallon's Depression. And somebody had got into the computer and printed off copies of contact details for all the people on the last tour. Could it have something to do with the marbles?

Steve was sure it did. He also knew the CIA already had people on the ground in Winton. It would be late in the day before he and Kelly could get there. He phoned Bill Maher at the Winton Police Station.

While he waited for a reply, Kelly whispered, "Don't tell him anything you don't have to."

Steve had already decided how he was going to handle it.

He asked Bill if he'd heard about a huge fossil find they'd made at Fallon's Depression? It was supposed to be a secret.

As far as Bill was concerned, it was a secret. He'd never heard of it. But his partner Carl had.

Steve explained that Danny Ridge, one of the people on the last Ahearn Tour was a wildcat prospector. He was heading to Fallon's Depression with some dynamite to blow up some of the bedrock and collect a truckload of fossils. Steve wanted Bill to go out to Fallon's Depression and arrest Danny.

Bill couldn't care less about fossils and he didn't much fancy driving out to Fallon's Depression, which was up the dirt Jundah Road, over the Tully Range and down into the depression where the first tributaries of the Diamantina River appear: A hell of a drive.

He wanted to know by what authority Steve was asking him to do this.

Kelly offered to call Brisbane and get authority if necessary, but Carl said it wasn't necessary. There were sacred sites out around Fallon's Depression. Carl didn't want Danny blowing up bits of it any more than the archaeologists did. He'd go out there and arrest Danny; alone, if necessary.

Bill shrugged. They were due in court that morning. It shouldn't take long. They'd head out there afterwards around lunchtime. If Danny Ridge was driving back from Cairns, they would probably get to Fallon's Depression before he did.

In fact, Danny had made better progress than they had imagined. If they'd looked out of the courthouse shortly after midday, when they were due to give evidence, they would have seen Danny drive through town, with Dog still standing with his paws on the roll bar.

Leda had also made good progress. She didn't know who had the marble or where it was heading, but she did have the advantage of being able to track the marble and to call on the entire memory bank of her host body. Before the truck reached Charters Towers, she re-checked the location of the marble and found that it was travelling west again. Knowing the marble was with one of the tour party, she assumed they were retracing their footsteps back to somewhere on the tour; probably the crash site.

She took a punt and after checking the GPS on her phone again, she announced that her friend had got a lift to Winton.

This suited the truck driver admirably; he was going to pick up a load in Winton. He was happy to take Leda all the way. It was a pleasant change having somebody to talk to, and his passenger was a nice lady; German, but she knew more about the Outback and its flora and fauna than most Australians. And she shared her sandwiches and soft drinks with him.

In the end, he was rather sorry to see her go when he dropped her off just before the turn-off to the Winton Cattle Yards. Although, on consideration, it was probably just as well. He was a happily married man, but he was sure she just got more and more attractive as they drove along. If he'd stayed with her much longer, he might have made a fool of himself.

Leda was, of course, completely oblivious to the effect she had on the truck driver. As soon as he dropped her off she checked the direction of the marble and started walking towards the Jundah Road. The marble was further south; too far south to be going to the crash site. Leda guessed its destination was Lark Quarry a couple of hours down the road, or the secret fossil site the tour party had visited somewhere off to the south-west. She hoped she could get a lift from somebody heading for the Quarry but it was now early afternoon, and most visitors made the trip from Winton to Lark Quarry in the morning, so they could get back by nightfall. She might have a long walk ahead of her. Still, the marble now had her body working at maximum efficiency and she strode out purposefully, comforted by the fact that if the marble she was tracking was visiting Lark Quarry or the secret fossil site, it would probably come back the way it went and inevitably meet up with her.

If Bill and Carl had got straight onto the road when they left the courthouse, they would have caught Leda before the bitumen road finished, a few kilometres out of Winton. But Bill had insisted on getting lunch, so Leda was well onto the dirt road and climbing the ridge east of the Tully Ranges when she heard a vehicle behind her. She recognized the police vehicle before they saw her. Her memory told her the authorities wanted the marble. She resisted the temptation to hitch a lift and hid in the scrub on the side of the road as the paddy wagon sped past. Then she continued walking, purposefully and tirelessly, down the road.

The road to Lark Quarry is regularly graded. Even so, parts of it are so heavily corrugated that vehicles shudder on their way up and down, and vehicles pulling caravans are advised not to make the journey at all. The side tracks running off to the west towards the Tully Range start off smooth and well-kept because they are private roads leading to outback station homesteads. Past the homesteads and over the mountain range, however, the tracks deteriorate quickly and are only suitable for heavy duty 4WDs.

The state of the road didn't slow Danny, who was used to travelling on trackless wastes. He pressed on at speed even when the road virtually disappeared. Soon he was following just a set of wheel tracks heading to the GPS location where Greg had shown the tour party the fossils from Fallon's Depression. Danny had been inside the bus, with the curtains drawn, on that occasion, so he had no memory of the terrain but when he got to the location where Greg had stopped and they'd all got out, he recognized it immediately. The fossil samples that Greg showed the tourists were there, locked in their heavy duty box. Alongside was the pile of slates which almost certainly contained more fossils. The samples and slates were probably worth a few thousand dollars, but Danny resisted the temptation to take them. To do so would reveal that he'd been on the site, and he wanted to keep his visits secret.

So, unaware that Steve and Kelly, the Winton Police, ASIO and the CIA all knew where he was, he followed the tracks away from the samples and over the ridge to Fallon's Depression. Here he quickly found evidence of an exploratory dig.

Danny checked a few of the slates lying on the ground and split a couple open. He found his first fossil within minutes. Convinced that he was at the right place, he parked his truck at what he thought was a safe distance from the dig.

His plan was simple. He would put a series of small charges along a fault line in the rock a few meters from the edge of the dig. This should blow a section of the rock-face away in a clean cut. Danny then just had to load the loose slate onto his truck and drive back to Cairns to make his fortune.

Danny got Dog out of the back of the truck and inspected the tray for signs that Dog had passed a motion.

"Haven't you shit yet? Useless animal."

Danny tied Dog to the bumper and set out a dish of water and a dish of dog food for him; only because he thought they might help the process along. He then gathered up some gelignite, caps, a drill and a pickaxe, and headed for the rock-face.

Dog didn't move as he watched him from the safety of the truck.

He watched Danny drill holes in the rock.

He watched Danny load gelignite into the holes, cap them and crouch well back behind some rocks.

Dog still didn't move until Danny set off the charge.

Suddenly Dog leapt into the air, barking, growling, pulling so hard on the rope that it seemed he was trying to pull the truck all the way to where Danny was still crouching behind the rock.

As the dust settled, Danny called back to Dog,

"Shut up, you mongrel,"

He went to inspect the blast.

The charge had been too small. A crack had appeared in the rock, but not big enough to enable Danny to pull it apart with his pickaxe.

He had to be careful. Too small a charge and the rock held firm. Too large and the rock would be blown to smithereens and Danny would have nothing. He inspected the crack in the rock. Another equally small set of charges set along the same fault line and he was sure the rock face would come away almost intact. He started drilling again. Meanwhile, the explosion had triggered a response in Dog that he had never experienced before.

When the young girl had warned the United Nations that the marbles must protect any planet they might happen to land on, the scientists had taken her suggestion very seriously, but it was a surprisingly difficult imperative to install. Finally, they settled on saturating the marbles with a simple but chilling set of memories, designed to play on a loop of subliminal flashes:

An animal carcass rotting in the sun; a tree being felled; a man shot; a city bombed; an open-cut mine blasted; toxic clouds from the explosions; clouds of pollution; industrial chimneys belching smoke; smoke hiding the sun; desert; dust storms; dying plants; starving children; an animal carcass rotting in the sun; a tree being felled...and so on and so on.

Dog locked on to the image of the open-cut mine blast, which melded into a vision of Danny blowing up the cliff face. And now Danny was preparing to do it all over again.

He had to stop Danny. He pulled at the rope then, realizing that that didn't work he started chewing on the rope, trying to bite through it before Danny could reset the explosions.

Dog chewed furiously, pulling at the same time with such force that the rope separated with the last few strands just snapping.

Dog charged towards Danny, who was so engrossed in setting the fuses that he was totally unaware of Dog's approach until he was almost upon him.

Danny had no time to react before Dog leapt at him,

seized him by the throat and forced him over the rock face to the ground below.

When Danny hit the ground, he was already dead.

Dog stood up, shook himself and stared down at his master.

He had no idea how he had got where he was. He couldn't tell you this, but his last memory was of being tied to the back of the truck.

He nuzzled Danny, licked the blood from his neck, tried to bring him back to life. And when he failed, Dog lay down beside his master and whimpered.

Carl and Bill were on the side track leading towards Fallon's Depression when they were overtaken by a helicopter, travelling in the same direction. At first Carl didn't recognize the helicopter. It was too large to be used for cattle mustering. Maybe it belonged to one of the mining companies that were still exploring the area?

Then, as it came closer, he recognized it. Carl immediately realized why Steve was so interested in Danny. It wasn't the fossils; it was the ball bearings.

Carl was right. The two passengers in the helicopter were Ramirez and Bamberger, and the pilot was a former Gulf War veteran, who would ask no questions.

When the Armstrongs had broken into Greg's office and got the contact details for the tour party, the Controller in Pine Gap had assigned different teams to find the tourists. All they had for Danny was a Post Office Box in Charters Towers. Ramirez and Bamberger in Winton were the closest Agents the CIA had near there so they'd driven to Charters Towers to find him.

They didn't have much trouble. Charters Towers is a pretty small place and the Post Office Manager knew

Danny by sight. He was pretty sure he had a room in one of the local pubs.

The Publican had been quite chatty and seemed pleased with the prospect of Danny getting into trouble. He was happy to give Ramirez and Bamberger details of Danny's truck, Dog, and the fact that Danny had said he was going to check on something interesting that he'd found on the tour.

Ramirez and Bamberger assumed that he meant the crash site. They got the helicopter that had collected the nose cone from the site and flew back there. No sign of Danny or his truck, so they retraced the tour in reverse order; Long Waterhole, Lark Quarry, and Fallon's Depression.

Ramirez saw the truck first. Then as they flew in they could see Dog, lying beside Danny. They ordered the pilot to put them down near the man and the dog.

Although the helicopter threw up a cloud of dust that looked like a mini dust storm, it elicited no response from Dog, who still lay next to Danny. However, as Ramirez and Bamberger approached, Dog stood up and snarled, hackles raised, protecting his helpless master from these intruders.

Bamberger was used to handling dogs; he'd used them to get confessions out of suspects in Abu Ghraib, but there was something about Dog that caused him to pause. His fangs were red with blood. The man lying there, presumably Danny Ridge, had his throat ripped out, and his life's blood was seeping into the ground.

But Ramirez had noticed something else. Dog's tongue wasn't red with blood; it was black. A tell tale sign of that Osmium Oxide thing.

The dog had obviously swallowed the marble. That's why it had attacked its master. Bamberger and Ramirez both drew their guns.

At that moment, the paddy wagon appeared over the horizon, heading towards them.

No time to waste. Bamberger and Ramirez shot in unison. Dog lifted slightly in the air then fell down, dead, across Danny's body. Ramirez holstered his gun, picked up Dog and carried him to the helicopter. Bamberger held open the rear door, and Ramirez clambered in, still holding Dog. Bamberger climbed in beside the pilot, and the helicopter was up and gaining height before the Police reached Danny's truck.

The helicopter flew off cross-country so that the paddy wagon couldn't follow. Ramirez checked Dog's dead body with a metal detector. They were getting a response.

From the paddy wagon, Carl and Bill thought the men in the helicopter had shot Danny. A closer examination revealed no bullet holes in his body. They'd just shot the dog and carried it away. Why?

Bill called in the killings to the Police Station in Winton. He was lucky to find anybody there; they were only open from Monday to Thursday between 8.30 am and 3.00pm. Even then Bill had to wait while Winton contacted Brisbane for instructions.

Carl called Steve and got immediate instructions from Kelly. She and Steve were still a few hours north of Winton. Carl was to bag up Danny's body and all his equipment. Take him and his truck to the Winton Hospital. Kelly would examine the body there.

Bill said he wasn't taking instructions from Kelly. He waited and then got exactly the same instructions from

Winton. He wasn't pleased. He didn't want a smelly body in the back of his paddy wagon.

Carl suggested they wrap the body in one of Danny's tarpaulins and put it in the back of Danny's truck. Bill could drive the paddy wagon; Carl would drive the truck.

Carl quickly gathered Danny's equipment and carried it to the truck. He took his instructions from Kelly very seriously, even loading Dog's water and food onto the tray. Then he drove the truck over to where Danny's body lay, already collecting flies in the heat.

Bill was too squeamish to help until the body was safely wrapped in the tarpaulin. Then they loaded the body onto the truck and headed back to Winton, with Bill leading the way.

Ramirez and Bamberger had no time to waste on being squeamish.

Far out in the semi-desert, west of Fallon's Depression, the pilot brought the helicopter to rest, and Ramirez carried Dog's body out and put it on the ground.

Bamberger ran the metal detector over the dog. They got a strong response near the entry wounds. They cut deeply into the wounds and removed two metal shells. Then they tried the metal detector again; nothing. They searched around with their hands for the marble; nothing.

The marble wasn't in the dog.

Of course, if they'd had all the facts they would have known that. When they shot Dog, he'd died. The Armstrongs hadn't told them that when they shot Leda, she had just kept running.

Ramirez and Bamberger discussed the situation. There had been traces of the osmium on the dog's teeth and tongue. If it hadn't swallowed the marble, maybe it had regurgitated it as it bit Danny.

Maybe it was in Danny's body?

Ramirez and Bamberger returned to Fallon's Depression, but there was no sign of the police or of Danny's body.

Bamberger wasn't a genius, but it didn't take a genius to figure out that the police would take Danny's body to Winton; it was the only town within two hundred kilometres.

He decided they would fly directly to Winton and land at the airport. They'd be there long before the local cops; more than enough time to arrange a suitable reception and grab the body.

17 - The Gathering.

Leda hadn't managed to hitch a lift before she reached the turn-off from the Jundah Road that led in the direction of the last signal from Danny's marble.

Thankfully, she didn't need to set off down the side track. When she checked the signal again, the marble was getting closer. The marble was coming to her.

Leda stood and waited.

The Police paddy wagon and Danny's truck approached from the west. The marble was in one of the vehicles but at this distance Leda couldn't tell which one. The distance between them was so small that separate signals couldn't establish coordinates. She just knew it was in one of the vehicles. She stepped out into the road and signalled, just like any other hitchhiker.

Bill saw her first. With her micro shorts, tanned legs and long, blonde hair she looked like the hitchhiker of Bill's dreams, and dreaming was all Bill ever did. He was far too fat and lazy ever to chase girls, but he liked to look.

He pulled up to offer Leda a lift.

At close quarters, she wasn't quite the sweet young thing he'd imagined, but he'd stopped now. He could hardly refuse her a lift.

This close, Leda could tell the marble wasn't in the paddy wagon. She suggested that perhaps she would get the policeman into trouble getting a lift in a police wagon. Perhaps she should try the truck behind?

"The truck behind is evidence in a killing," Bill said. "You can't ride in there. Get in."

Obviously the two vehicles were travelling in convoy, so Leda clambered into the paddy wagon, and Bill drove on.

"There was a killing?" Leda asked.

"Yeah, bloody dog ripped its master's throat out," said Bill.

"How horrible."

The lady looked so upset that Bill wished he hadn't mentioned it.

"What happened to the dog?"

"He was shot."

"Is he in the truck, too?"

"No."

Leda now knew the marble wasn't in the dog.

As the convoy approached the outskirts of Winton, Bill asked the lady where she'd like to be dropped off. She asked where he was going.

"To the hospital."

The lady said she would like to go to the hospital too.

"They have an emergency department, yes?"

Bill confirmed that they did; asked if there was something wrong with the lady.

She shrugged.

"Just women's business."

Since Bill had no idea what women's business was, and didn't want to know either, he let the matter rest there.

At the hospital, Carl parked alongside Bill. Leda got out of the police wagon, smiled at Carl, thanked Bill and hurried toward the door marked Emergency.

"Women's business," Bill explained to Carl. "You find out where they want the body. I'll call Steve."

Carl went into Reception to see where they should stow Danny's body. He didn't notice that the lady was nowhere to be seen.

Bill was on the phone, telling Steve that they had reached the hospital. They would just leave the truck and the body there. Kelly insisted they stay with the truck and the body until she and Steve got there.

She also wanted to know whether the police had seen anything more of the helicopter. They hadn't.

Steve and Kelly were now just a few miles north of Winton when Steve hung up. They'd been delayed by the usual road works on the Kennedy Developmental Road from Hughenden to Winton. It was still just single lane bitumen for much of the way, with no room for passing unless one or both vehicles took to the dirt edge. The road works were meant to improve that but in the meantime made things worse.

Kelly didn't know if it was good news or bad news that the helicopter hadn't been sighted again.

It probably meant they already had the marble and were no longer interested in Danny's body.

If they'd stayed on the phone just a little longer, her query would have been answered.

As Bill switched off his phone, he felt a gun stuck into his back.

"Don't make any sudden moves," said an American voice, "just act natural. Open up the back of the wagon."

It was Bamberger, holding the gun.

Beside him, Ramirez also had a gun, which he held down by his side. In the other hand, he held the metal detector.

As Bill led Ramirez and Bamberger around to the back of the paddy wagon, Leda quietly reappeared from nowhere and walked quickly past the front of the vehicle to the truck, parked beside it. Keeping the truck between herself and the paddy wagon, she bent double, moved alongside the truck and slithered over the side and into the tray, where she came to rest next to Danny's body.

The Americans had discovered that the rear of the paddy wagon was empty. Bamberger stuck his gun in Bill's face. He pulled Bill's gun from its holster and threw it on the ground.

"Where's the body?"

Bill was thinking fast; having a gun pointed at him had that effect.

"We took it into the hospital."

Bill might have got away with it if, just at that moment, Carl hadn't appeared around the side of the wagon with an Orderly and a trolley.

"We've got to store it in Pathology...whoa!" Carl stopped, mid-sentence, as he came face to face with both Bamberger and Ramirez, pointing their guns at him.

The Orderly, shielded from the guns by Carl and the trolley, took his chance and turned and ran for the hospital entrance.

"Call the cops! Somebody call the cops!" he yelled, at the top of his voice.

Then he fell silent, realising that the only cops within

a hundred kilometres were standing behind him.

Although his silence may have been due to the fact that he reached the hospital's automatic doors before they had a chance to open. He hit them hard; then, as the doors shuddered and slid open, he staggered, dazed and bruised, into the safety of the hospital.

Meanwhile, Leda had pulled away the tarpaulin covering Danny's head and shoulders. The wound in his neck was covered in congealed blood that was already starting to turn black. Without hesitating, Leda plunged her hand into the wound and pulled out the blood-covered marble. Giving it a perfunctory wipe with her clean hand, she popped it into her mouth and swallowed it.

She was just wiping her blood-stained hand and arm clean on Danny's shirt front when she heard Bill say the body was in the truck. She slid back over the side of the truck and crouched there as she heard a new voice join the conversation; a loud voice, yelling from a distance.

Steve and Kelly hadn't had to drive all the way into Winton to get to the hospital. It was located north of the town off the Kennedy Development Road.

As they'd pulled into the car park, Kelly had spotted Ramirez and Bamberger holding Bill and Carl at gunpoint behind the paddy wagon. Steve stopped the car, got out and drew his gun and hurried towards the paddy wagon.

Kelly phoned the Winton Police Station, which was pretty much a waste of time because there was only a civilian receptionist there.

When Steve got close enough, he yelled,

"Put down your guns."

Bamberger and Ramirez turned in unison, pointing their guns at Steve. Bamberger smiled.

"Two against one," he said.

"That won't help you," Steve dropped to one knee and took a two-handed shooting position that told them they weren't dealing with an amateur. "You'll be dead."

Ramirez backed away towards the truck; gun raised in the air to show he wasn't a threat.

"Take it easy. Take it easy."

Ramirez could have almost touched Leda if he'd known she was there, crouched behind the truck. Instead, he waved the metal detector, which he still held, over Danny's body. He looked across at Bamberger and shook his head, indicating that there was no metal in Danny's body; no marble.

At the same time, the helicopter suddenly appeared overhead and descended noisily into the car park.

Using the confusion as cover, Leda silently backed away from the truck and disappeared around the back of the hospital.

Bamberger and Ramirez backed away to the helicopter, all the time keeping their guns trained on Steve. As they clambered aboard, the helicopter took off.

Steve lowered his gun, but Bill was scrambling for his police revolver.

"Shoot the bastards. Shoot the bastards," he yelled.

"And have a helicopter crash on the town? Forget it. They didn't get what they were after."

Steve holstered his gun as Kelly rushed to inspect the body.

Kelly took in the fact that the tarpaulin was pulled away; the wound was re-opened; the shirt, freshly bloodstained.

Was Steve sure they hadn't got the marble?

Steve was sure. The guy closest to the truck had his

gun in one hand, the metal detector in the other. He never put either of them down.

Bill suggested maybe some vermin had got into the back of the truck at the mining site; helped itself to lunch on the way back.

"And wiped its hands on his shirt?" Kelly asked sarcastically, pulling up the front of Danny's shirt to show the marks where Leda had wiped her hands.

"Has anybody else been near the truck?

"No."

"There was the hitchhiker you picked up on the way back." said Carl.

"Hitchhiker?"

"Yeah," said Bill defensively. "Nice lady. She was on the Jundah Road.

"Don't tell me," said Steve, "German, long blonde hair, long legs, micro shorts and a white T-Shirt."

The look on Bill's face told him he was right.

"That's the other party looking for the marbles."

"Well, how was I supposed to know?" Bill snapped.

"You weren't," said Steve. "But you know what she looks like now. Search the hospital. We'll check the bus terminal. If we don't find her, we'll meet up in the main street. She'll probably try to get lost in the crowd. If she's on foot, she can't get far at her age."

Steve and Kelly were already heading back to his vehicle when Bill called out,

"What d'you mean her age? She was younger than me."

As they got into the vehicle, Kelly wondered aloud if it really was Leda:

"If she was younger than Bill?"

"Who else could it be?" asked Steve.

"Somebody wearing exactly the same clothes, who's interested in the marbles? It's a bloody big coincidence."

"No harder to believe than that she's growing younger," Kelly muttered.

While Steve drove back onto the Kennedy Development Road and turned right into town and the bus depot, Kelly called the Federal Police in Brisbane. She carefully omitted to mention that the mystery woman might be Leda.

Meanwhile Leda hadn't headed for the bus depot. She didn't even know where the bus depot was. There was nothing in her host's memory bank about that. Instead, she sprinted the several blocks south to Elderslie Street and the tourist area. She slowed to a walk; blending in like any other tourist, as long as you didn't look too closely at her blood-stained right arm.

At the Royal Open Air Theatre and Museum, she stepped off the busy tourist thoroughfare, up a laneway and around to the back of the North Gregory Hotel.

The hotel car park was just a red-dirt open space surrounded by the backs of commercial buildings. Leda searched around until she found a rather old Landrover with no roof. She wasn't sure how one hot-wired a modern car with computers, but this was more her vintage.

She sat in the driver's seat, reached under the dashboard and pulled out two wires leading to and from the ignition. She stripped them and twisted them together ignoring the slight electric shock it gave her. The engine immediately coughed into life.

She put the lap seatbelt on and reversed out of the parking space, drove down the lane and turned left on Elderslie Street heading for Longreach. She knew all the other marbles were in that direction, but where they were, exactly, she couldn't tell, because the battery on her phone was flat. She rummaged in the glove box and found a phone charger that fitted into the vehicle's cigarette lighter and also fitted Leda's phone. She left her phone switched off as she drove so that it would recharge more quickly.

As Steve searched the hotels and cafes along Elderslie Street, shortly after Leda had left the area, he got a call from Robinson. Robinson was a lot chattier than usual, almost excited. The CIA had really shown their hand this time, he said. The cops had arrested the Armstrongs in Cairns. Now the CIA had used the same helicopter they'd used to transport the nose cone to Brisbane, to try and snatch a body from Police custody. They were obviously making it up as they went along. The CIA spook at the American Embassy in Canberra had almost sounded relieved when Robinson suggested they talk. Robinson was flying to Canberra. At last the Americans would have to come clean and tell Robinson what they knew.

Steve wasn't convinced the CIA would tell Robinson anything, but he didn't share his misgivings with Robinson. Instead, he asked if the cops had found Leda's body in Cairns. He wasn't surprised to learn they hadn't, although Robinson was sure it was just a matter of time. They'd checked the blood samples at the Funeral Parlour and the Medical Centre. Both belonged to Leda. She must have been in a bad way. Robinson assumed she was lying in a ditch somewhere, and they'd find her, sooner or later.

Steve didn't bother to disillusion him. Instead, after he'd finished the call, he used Luc's phone to text Leda:

'I know u r alive. I just don't know how.'

Then he thought about it and sent a second text:

'This is Steve, the guy who showed u the stars. If I meant u harm, I wld have told them abt your phone. They cld have traced u.'

He waited for a moment to see if there was an immediate response, then pocketed the phone and went to find Kelly.

Together they decided to leave Bill and Carl to search for Leda and head for Longreach, themselves. They had no idea Leda was already well on her way there, but like Leda, they were turning their attention to the other marbles. From Longreach, they could catch a plane direct to Brisbane and be there before nightfall. Alan Ready was next on Kelly's list. No one seemed to know where Gina and David had drifted off to but they knew, at least, that Alan lived somewhere in the State's capital.

As they drove south, Steve told Kelly about the call from Robinson; she wasn't pleased. She didn't trust the Americans; didn't believe they would share their information.

Kelly was right. They'd agreed to talk to Robinson, but they didn't intend to tell him anything the Australians didn't already know. And they kept their covert teams searching for Alan, Gina and Dave. Like everybody else, the Americans were playing their cards very close to their chests.

Robinson, for his part, wasn't going to tell the Americans that they didn't have either Leda's or Danny's marble. Rather, he expected to use the claim that the Australians had more information than the Americans as a bargaining chip.

And Steve wasn't telling anybody, not even Kelly, that he had Luc's telephone and was trying to call Leda.

Leda drove into Longreach and parked near the Tourist

Information Centre. She disconnected the hot wiring and unplugged her phone. The charger also had a USB connection. Leda put the charger in her bag along with a pair of sunglasses and a scarf from the glove box.

Leda's body still needed regular refuelling; over a late lunch, she checked her phone. She found the two texts from Steve and considered their implications as she finished eating.

It was true; Steve could have reported that she had her phone. They could be closing in on her now, but it seemed unlikely. She would have seen somebody following her. Or the Police would have been alerted to her presence in which case why had they given her a lift, not all that long ago?

It seemed that Steve was protecting her. But why would he do that? More likely he was trying to protect her host body; the little old lady he knew as Leda.

But surely he understood she was dead? It looked like sentimentality, and it surprised her. She hadn't realised the locals were sentimental. She'd seen no evidence of it. The memory bank of the old lady displayed no sentimentality In fact, it was frighteningly violent. The little old lady had killed members of her own species; something Leda could never do.

Leda decided that if she had a potential ally in Steve she should cultivate him. Not tell him the whole truth but perhaps lead him gently to an awareness. Intrigue him. Guide him.

Leda found the way to do this in the old lady's memory bank. She sent a reply to Luc's phone.

Steve heard the alert. He took out his phone. Nothing. It must be Luc's phone. Despite the fact that he was driving, he pulled the second phone out of his pocket.

Kelly was sitting next to Steve. She registered that he

had two phones.

"Robinson gave me one for official business," Steve explained, without even thinking about it.

The message on Luc's phone made him think, though:
'Mike, the Chicken.'
What the hell did that mean?

Kelly was listing all the addresses of people named Ready on the electoral roll in South-East Queensland. There was nobody called Alan Ready. In fact, there were only half a dozen Readys listed for the whole of South-East Queensland. Kelly had decided it was worth visiting every one of them. They might all be related.

"Mike the Chicken," said Steve.
Kelly, now transposing addresses, was working out the most efficient way to visit them all.

"What about him?"

"You know who he is?"

"I know what he was. He was a chicken. He lived for months, maybe a couple of years after his head was cut off.

"How?"

"Apparently most of the brain stem leading to his spine was still intact. His heart was still beating, He could walk around. They fed him with a dropper through the top of his neck. Why are you asking me this?

"Oh, somebody just sent me a joke."
Steve didn't elaborate. Kelly suspected that they had given her a halfwit for a bodyguard. She returned to her address list.

After a while Steve messaged:
'A body without a brain?'
Leda received the text as she was paying her bill at the café. She needed to be careful.

She didn't want to tell Steve the body was brain dead.

The memory bank had told her about Zombies. If Steve thought the body was a Zombie, he'd tell the authorities for sure.

Instead, she sent:

'Very good. But not without a brain, with a by-pass neurologische.' (The memory couldn't recall the English for Neurological)

'The body is controlled without the brain's consent.'

Leda hesitated before sending. Would it terrify Steve? Would it panic him? She thought he was not a man to panic.

She pressed *Send* and, to her surprise, the phone indicated an almost immediate response via e-mail.

But it wasn't an email from Steve; it was an email from Alan Ready.

18 - *Superspy.*

Alan Ready's real name wasn't Alan Ready, and that was his father's fault. Alan's father had been a refugee from the Communists in Eastern Europe after the Second World War. He had eventually made it to Australia to work on the Snowy Mountains Hydro-Electric Scheme. It was hard work, often bitterly cold and workers on the tunnels died in their dozens. But Alan's father was ready for anything which is why, when his fellow workers and bosses couldn't even pronounce his name, let alone spell it; he changed it by deed poll to Ready.

Of course, he didn't know that most Australians spelt their name Reddy, which is why Kelly had found so few "Readys" to check out. Nor did he know that Australian kids have a habit of shortening names and giving nicknames that are often cruel and unthinking. So he named his son Neville. And Neville quickly became Never, and Alan became Never Ready, and his life as the butt of schoolboy bullying had begun.

As soon as he left school Neville changed his name to Alan but he didn't bother to do it by deed poll.

So everybody knew him as Alan but his name on official documents, on his birth certificate, on the electoral roll, was Neville.

Alan liked having two names. It was like having an alias; a spy name. Alan was a dreamer. He couldn't make friends at school, and he didn't make friends as an adult. He withdrew into a world of Science Fiction and Video Games. After his father died, he continued to live at home with his mother in Logan, a relatively new, characterless suburb between Brisbane and the Gold Coast. Close to both big cities but belonging to neither, its council was trying hard to disprove its reputation as a cultural desert; but it didn't bother either Alan or his mother whether the place they lived in was a cultural desert or not. Neither of them ever ventured outside of the house except to go shopping at the supermarket or go to work.

In his dream life, however, Alan was a huge success. He lived on the river in the best suburb in Brisbane. He carried out impressive financial coups and repelled alien invasions. Had Alan known what the three marbles were that he kept in his bedroom beside his Star Wars figurines and video games, he would have realized that he was living his dream. The knowledge wouldn't have helped. It would have terrified him.

As it was, he thought he had just struck it lucky at last; finding something that somebody else wanted enough to pay him a lot of money.

First he got an email from Kelly offering him five hundred dollars for each and every marble he had.

A day later he received an email from NASA offering him five thousand dollars for just one of the marbles.

Alan may have been a dreamer, but he wasn't stupid. He figured out that he had a bidding war on his hands, and maybe he could build up the price. What he didn't want was for somebody else on the tour to sell their marble at the going price and ruin everything.

At the end of the tour, everybody had exchanged email addresses. Nobody actually expected to keep in touch, but it was a nice gesture. Now it came in useful. He emailed Gina and David, Leda and Luc, telling them about the offers and suggesting that they band together and try to force up the price. Almost immediately he got a reply from Leda and Luc, which surprised him because he thought they had already flown back to Germany.

'Dearest Alan,' the reply began, *'So glad to hear from you. We too, have received the offers and have had the same idea as you, you clever boy. We are coming to Brisbane. Give us your address and we will come and visit you.'*

Alan was flattered. He was also in a dilemma. He couldn't let the Reinhardts see where he lived.

So he wrote back:

'Very busy next few days. How about we meet somewhere in the city?'

The reply came back,

'Fine. We'll be there by tomorrow lunchtime. Name a time and place. And keep your marble with you at all times. Somebody tried to steal ours.'

Alan didn't want his marbles stolen, so he kept them hidden inside a toy rocket that sat on the shelf next to his Star Wars figurines. He thought they were safe there.

On the other hand, if he turned up at the meeting without a marble, it could affect his negotiations with the Reinhardts.

Super Spy Alan Ready decided on an elegant solution. He would take just one marble to the rendezvous with the Germans.

Then if they tried to double cross him, he would still

have two marbles. However, he was sure he could handle the elderly couple. Maybe even relieve them of their marble. No point in sharing if you didn't have to.

Alan's mother knocked on his bedroom door to tell him his dinner was ready. She worried about the way he locked himself away in his bedroom. She suspected he spent his time and energy on Internet porn. Why didn't he get himself a girlfriend?

"Actually, I met somebody on the trip." Alan told her, over grilled chops and two veg. "She's coming to Brisbane to see me. I'm meeting her tomorrow for lunch."

This was a novel turn of events for Alan's mother. Maybe the trip to the Outback had done him some good after all. Then again, maybe her son was lying.

"Who is she?"

"Her name's Leda," Alan told her. "She's tall, blonde."

"Blonde, huh?" said his mother, who had a very low opinion of blondes.

"She's smart," her son said. "She's a University Lecturer."

Now Alan's mother knew he was lying; a University Lecturer? What could she possibly see in her son? She knew she was destined never to have grandchildren.

For Steve and Kelly, the flight from Longreach to Brisbane was practically silent. Both were engrossed in their thoughts.

Kelly was at a disadvantage because she wasn't in touch with Leda, but even so she was beginning to come to the same conclusions as Steve. Leda almost certainly was alive, and had been dead. Something was keeping her alive. The dead astronaut had had foreign DNA in his body. Something might have been keeping him alive until the spacecraft burnt up during re-entry.

What if the marbles were some sort of implant; a second brain or a parasitic species that invaded the body and took over the nervous system? If so, where had they come from? And why? What was their purpose? Were they some new, sophisticated weapon that the Chinese or Russians had developed? Were they from outer space? That seemed too preposterous to be possible. Certainly it wasn't a theory she wanted to share with Robinson. And there was no point discussing it with Steve; he was swapping jokes with somebody about Mike the Chicken, for god's sake.

Mike was sending and receiving texts throughout the journey and all through dinner at the hotel, but he wasn't swapping jokes. He was trying to get answers to the questions that Kelly was asking herself. Only he was texting the source.

'Who are you?'

'Not who? What? We are a higher intelligence come to warn you.'

'Warn us of what?'

'You are destroying your planet. We know because our planet was your planet in a hundred years time. It is now lifeless.'

When the scientists had run through the many scenarios the marbles might encounter the first thing they considered was how, should they find an environment that already had a dominant species, would they replace that species?

If they arrived before the emergence of a dominant humanoid species, the solution was simple. They would look for the most advanced ape-like creature they could find, and imbue it with knowledge only they possessed. Within a few generations, the creatures would be the dominant species and controlled by the Osmia.

If there was a sentient species on the planet, the solution was rather more complex.

Osmium history was full of wars of conquest. They were always bloody and often disastrous. Violence simply begot violence.

However, throughout its history, there was one type of conquest that despite the violence it so frequently generated, seemed to continue forever, in a way that defied logic. All it required was a species that had come to believe that it was the most important thing in the Universe; that it had a special purpose, that it was the One chosen by God.

In such a case, the Osmia could just take the beliefs and prophecies of the planet's current religions and fulfil them.

If they expected a Second Coming, they would provide a Second Coming.

If they needed a Great Prophet, they would provide a Great Prophet.

And if they needed a miracle or two, like bringing Leda back to life, making the lame walk, have their prophets live until they were nine hundred years old, all this was possible for the Osmia.

Searching through the old lady's brain, Leda realized that this approach would still work for the large majority of Earth's population but for a significant minority, many of whom were in power, the Osmia were a couple of hundred years too late.

Industrial and scientific advancements meant yesterday's miracle was today's medical procedure.

They had looked to the Stars, these humans. They

knew there was no benevolent God or at least no special place in God's cosmos for them. Some of them paid lip service to the religions to please the masses, but the Osmia would need to take a more drastic course of action with this important section of the species if they were to succeed. They would need to tell the truth.

Leda had come to the conclusion that this was the case after she had trawled through the entire memory bank of the old lady.

The old lady had worked out the problem fifty years earlier. The problem was a Capitalist System that could only survive with growth. Hence more production, more profit, more people, more use of the Earth's finite resources, more pollution, more global warming: Disaster.

In the 1960s, Leda had attempted to destroy this system by force through the Red Army Faction and Baader Meinhof. Then she realized that force simply created a larger, reactive force. She switched to persuasion; she joined the peace movement and engaged in environmental activism. Eventually, she realized that the struggle would outlive her ageing body and gave up.

Now the Osmium Leda could draw on all that knowledge and continue the struggle to save the planet.

Much of this, Leda was able to explain to Steve in an abbreviated fashion, but there was one part of the Osmium plan Leda would never divulge. The inevitable consequence of following the Osmia and saving the planet was that when it was saved, the Osmia would have control.

Throughout the journey to Brisbane and into the night Leda gently worked on Steve's attitude to the Osmium cause. As with all good religious conversions, Leda concentrated on telling Steve what he wanted to hear. War was futile. Everybody must work together for the common good. The vested interest of the few cannot be allowed to destroy the lives of the many. There is still time if the World acts now. If all eight Osmia were brought together, combined, they would have the knowledge to save the planet.

Steve wanted to believe, but he had heard a lot of politicians in his time, and this sounded like a politician's promise. There was something else that bothered him. If the plan was to save the Earth, why hadn't they made the plan clear? And why had they sent just eight marbles?

Leda reminded Steve that, years earlier, his planet had sent a probe out beyond the limits of their solar system; into deep space. What had the probe carried? A very basic map showing the location of Earth in the Universe, some elementary algebra, a child's voice, some recorded music.

Why hadn't they sent more? Because that was the limit of their technical capability.

The marbles were at the limit of Osmian capability, Leda said.

Steve found her answers rather comforting. They made sense. Now in his big, comfortable bed in the big, comfortable hotel that Kelly had booked in Brisbane, he imagined what it would be like if Earthlings were to attempt to reach a far planet; how vulnerable that mission would be. Maybe the marbles weren't to be feared. Maybe the Osmia were to be pitied; alone as they were, and homeless, in a vast Universe.

It was late, and Steve was about to doze off with that thought when Luc's phone indicated that it had received another message. Steve checked the texts; there was nothing there.

Then he realized that Luc had received an email.

Alan had been negotiating with Leda to meet up in Brisbane, but she was a frail little old lady; she could easily forget or lose the message. To be on the safe side, Alan sent the final email to both Leda and Luc, just as he'd sent his original message.

Steve checked Luc's mail; there were two messages there. The first explained about the two offers Alan had received and suggested that they band together.

The second simply read:

City Gardens Café, City Botanical Gardens. 12.30.

19 - *When Worlds Collide.*

Over breakfast at the hotel, which was called The Royal on the Park and, conveniently for Steve, overlooked the City Botanical Gardens, Steve tried to find an excuse to get away from Kelly. He intended to be at the rendezvous with Leda and Alan at 12.30.

He asked to look at Kelly's list of potential Alan Readys. They were split almost fifty-fifty between addresses to the south of the Brisbane River, down through Logan to the Gold Coast, and north of the River, up as far as the Sunshine Coast. Kelly wasn't keen on phoning around because she didn't want to give Alan any warning of their arrival. Steve thought it could take a couple of days to get around to all the addresses if they were planning to turn up physically at each one. He suggested they split up. He'd take one half, Kelly the other.

Kelly liked the idea of going it alone for a while. Privately, she was growing increasingly suspicious of Steve and his constant texting. Was he reporting on her to Robinson? Was he reporting to the CIA? Presumably he'd worked with them in Iraq and Afghanistan.

Maybe he was working with them now? She agreed to take the south of the river.

When they went to Reception, to arrange two hire cars, Steve 'suddenly realised' that he'd left his wallet and driver's licence in his room. Leaving Kelly to hire a car for herself, he returned to his room and stood at the window, watching, until he saw Kelly leave the hotel and drive south on Alice Street. He noted how she took care to move to the inside lane so that she could turn left at the end of the street, onto the freeway and over the bridge heading towards the Gold Coast.

Then Steve went back to Reception; but instead of hiring a car he took a stroll across the road and into the Botanical Gardens, to check out the lie of the land.

From his seventh-floor hotel room the Gardens seemed to be covered in fifty foot high trees and looked almost impenetrable. This was an optical illusion. The trees bordering Alice Street, opposite the hotel, were indeed fifty foot high and closely planted to prevent traffic pollution from entering the Gardens. But although the trees appeared to stretch all the way to the river bend a few hundred yards south, the land between the street and the river fell away into a deep depression.

In times of heavy tropical rainfall, this central area was often flooded. As Steve followed the pathway through the trees and into the relatively sparsely vegetated depression, he came across a series of poles with plaques showing where the floodwaters had peaked in various years: 1893, 1974, 2011. The marker for the 2011 flood was higher than Steve's head, but he saw no reason to panic. The weather forecast was good; it was hardly likely to be flooded by lunchtime.

Steve had visited the Garden Cafe some years earlier but when he saw it again, he hardly recognised it. It used to sit in open gardens, with a heavily wooded slope running down to the river behind it on one side, and a natural amphitheatre on the other. The amphitheatre, which was just open grassland in those days, with blocks of stone for seating, was reminiscent of some ancient Roman ruin. Now it was surrounded by a three-metre high fence and had been converted into an open-air stadium, complete with a grandstand, lights and a sound system.

The open gardens that ran from the café along the river bank to old Parliament House had been taken over by the Queensland University of Technology. Their buildings extended along the riverfront and were now only separated from the café and the stadium fence by a wide pathway. An almost continuous stream of office workers and students ran up and down the pathway in their running shorts or strolled up and down in their jeans.

All this did nothing for the aesthetics of the café, which now called itself the Botanical Gardens Club and Café.

It looked like it hadn't done much for business either. The QUTS complex included a Food Court, not a hundred metres away, and students either ate there or picked up Subways and sat on the grass to eat.

While this didn't help the café, it certainly made life easier for Steve. He could sit on the grass, unnoticed, amongst the students, and keep watch. Furthermore, there were now essentially only two ways to approach and leave the Café. Either across the park from the entrance, the way Steve had come, or down the pathway running between the QUTS and the stadium fence.

Steve checked out the pathway. It led down to the Friendship Bridge, a footbridge that crossed the river to the South Bank Precinct in a wide, graceful arch. People walking over the bridge had nowhere to hide.

Of course if Leda and Alan arrived and left in opposite directions, Steve couldn't follow them both, but that didn't matter. He was only interested in Leda. He decided that if he sat on the grass, under a Golden Palm grove some way from the Café, he could watch which way she went and easily catch up with her after Alan had left.

Alan worked in a City Department Store selling menswear so his appearance was always very important. That morning he had taken even more care than usual in choosing his clothes, and he'd found an old pair of his father's cufflinks. Not that he wanted to wear them. He took the cufflinks out of their velvet-covered box, put them down next to the toy rocket and set one of the marbles into the box, like a precious jewel or an engagement ring.

Then he headed off to work with his mother's voice ringing in his ears,

"Say hello to Leda for me. You can invite her home if you want to. Call me if you decide."

"As if that's going to happen," Alan thought as he waited for the bus to the city.

Leda also made special preparations for the meeting in the Botanical Gardens. She applied some make-up; not to make herself look more beautiful but to make herself look older. She lightly drew back in some of the lines that had disappeared in the last couple of days. Then she put on the scarf she'd taken from the Landrover. She put up her hair, covered it with the scarf, and then wrapped the scarf around her neck in the way that women of a certain age do to hide their ageing necks. But Leda wasn't trying to hide her wrinkles; she was trying to hide her lack of wrinkles.

She'd bought a slightly too large and shapeless dress from an Op. Shop, and although she still wore her trendy, upmarket runners, with sunglasses on she thought she'd get away with it. Her brain didn't have a very high opinion of Alan, and she doubted he would be too interested in her. He was just interested in the money.

The CIA too had made preparations. They had decided on another method of tracing Alan. They didn't have his address or his real name, but they did have his email address; at least one of them. Fortunately for them, this was the address he'd used to contact Leda.

Their first inclination was to wait until Alan met the Reinhardts at the café and then surround them. The problem was the Garden Café was a very public place. They didn't want more trouble with the Australians, and they certainly didn't want to tell Robinson about the rendezvous. They decided on a scattering of agents around the park, to cut off any escape and support Bamberger and Ramirez.

Bamberger and Ramirez would wait for Alan and the Reinhardts to finish their meeting and grab them as they went their separate ways. In fact, they probably wouldn't even grab them. They would just offer them the five thousand dollars reward.

At twenty past twelve Alan left for lunch a little early, telling his workmate he had a date. He walked the two blocks down from where he worked to the park, and was sitting in the Garden Club and Café by twelve thirty.

Steve, a little way off, sitting on the grass under the Golden Palms, eating his sandwiches along with the other office workers and students, saw him arrive. Everything seemed normal.

Steve didn't recognize Leda until she approached Alan. The Leda he remembered had been fit and spritely, despite her years, and seemed to live in short khaki shorts. This Leda was dressed like an old lady, moved like an old lady; but it must have been Leda because she sat opposite Alan.

There was a sign telling cafe patrons to order their meals at the counter, then sit at a table and wait to be served. But business was slow, and a waiter arrived at Alan's table as soon as Leda sat down.

It wasn't an extensive menu and Leda quickly decided on an Avocado Melt on Sourdough, with coffee. Alan took forever to settle on a Ham and Cheese Toastie and tea, mainly because it was described as Bangalow Ham, from a town near Byron Bay, just south of the New South Wales border. Alan was convinced that they had only added the word Bangalow so that they could put a few extra dollars onto the price. In the end though, since almost everything else on the menu was vegetarian, he had no choice.

Leda waited patiently for Alan to order before explaining that the trip had tired Luc out. He was still back at the hotel. She waved her hand vaguely in the direction of the row of hotels that faced the Gardens, even though she'd approached the café from the footbridge.

"But you brought your marble?" Alan asked.

That was all he cared about, really. He wasn't interested in Luc.

"Of course. I never let it out of my sight. And you brought yours?"

"Yes."

"Can I see it?"

Alan hesitated.

"We'll swap."

Leda produced a marble in a see-through sandwich bag and casually placed it on the table. Alan pushed across the cufflink box.

They each examined the marbles while the waiter delivered their lunches. Alan looked up in time to see Leda holding the marble up to her face as if she were about to put it in her mouth.

"What are you doing?"

Alan's voice came out a lot shriller than he intended.

"Just seeing if it smells," said Leda. "I'm sure ours smells of something."

Alan sniffed at the marble in his hand while Leda put his marble back into its box. He could smell nothing. Leda put the little box back on the table but she didn't take her hand off it until Alan pushed her marble back across to her.

Then they both put away their marbles and waited for the other to speak.

Leda sipped her coffee, which as usual in Australia, she found weak.

"How much are you thinking of asking?" she asked.

Alan had thought about it.

"Twenty thousand".

"Twenty thousand for two marbles?"

"Twenty thousand each. Eighty thousand altogether."

Leda assumed Alan had found Gina and David and was acting for them as well?

"No," he said, and smiled.

"Ah," Leda understood. Alan had three marbles.

"Alan, you are very crafty," she smiled. "I think we can leave you to do the negotiations. Email us when you have fixed a price."

From their vantage point, Bamberger and Ramirez heard everything on their directional mikes. They wanted to move in, but the café was filling up quickly. Too busy, they decided.

They didn't have to wait long. Leda and Alan engaged in a little small talk and then he said he had to go back to the Stock Exchange; as if he were a stockbroker. Leda had to get back to "poor Luc". And in fifteen minutes they'd finished and went their separate ways; Alan back towards the city, Leda towards the stadium and the river.

Steve got up and wandered after Leda.

Bamberger and Ramirez moved a little more urgently.

Bamberger followed Alan down the path leading away from the café and back to the city, trying not to make it obvious that he was hurrying to catch up.

Alan himself was in no hurry. He was reliving the scene where Superspy Alan had met with the Beautiful German Spy to plot the sale of Vital Secrets.

Near the bottom of the depression, he followed the pathway as it passed between two thick groves of Golden Palms. Suddenly, he became aware of a burly man waiting at the other end of the grove, effectively barring his way. Alan didn't truly think the man was a CIA Agent but in his world of make-believe, the world where he was a superspy, he decided not to risk getting caught between the groves of Golden Palm. He turned to retrace his steps, but his way was blocked by Bamberger, who stood there breathing heavily.

Bamberger smiled.

"Mr. Ready. I think we agreed five thousand dollars."

Alan wanted to pretend he didn't know what Bamberger was talking about, wanted to turn and run, but as he looked back, he could see the burly man slowly approaching ever nearer. He felt trapped. Maybe he could bluff it out? Maybe he could run?

But as Bamberger pulled his coat back to put his hand in his pocket for the money, he made a point of showing Alan that he was carrying a gun.

Alan's knees turned to jelly. All thoughts of fight or flight disappeared.

"Five thousand dollars, fine," he croaked.

The exchange took just seconds and Alan walked back to work with the five thousand dollars, wondering whether he could still get twenty thousand for each of his other marbles. He doubted it. He'd probably have to settle for five, now.

When Alan left the table, Leda had started to walk towards the footbridge and the river, unaware that Ramirez was waiting on the pathway that ran between the Stadium fence and the QUTS Buildings.

However, she stopped before she got onto the pathway, and turned to watch Alan walking away across the park.

Alan lived in a world of make-believe but in a previous life Leda had been a secret agent; a warrior in the battle between the People and the Military Industrial Complex. Old habits die hard. She wanted to be sure that Alan wasn't a plant; part of a plan to trap her. So she watched him as he walked away.

She saw him stop just short of the Golden Palm grove. She saw Bamberger hurry after him and talk to him.

From that distance, Leda couldn't tell whether the two men were working together or whether Alan was being arrested. Either way she recognised a trap.

She turned to go, but instead of heading down the pathway towards Ramirez, she ran into the narrow laneway between the back of the café and the stadium fence.

From his vantage point thirty metres away Steve could see that the laneway must lead to the steeply wooded slope behind the café. Instead of chasing after Leda he ran around the front of the café, hoping to cut her off before she reached the woods. He was disappointed.

Steve reached the back of the café where a set of stone steps wound down through the thickly wooded slope. But this was the second set of steps leading down through the trees. Leda had taken the first set. Steve could see flashes of her dress through the foliage as she hurtled down the slope.

He charged down the stone steps. At the bottom, they led to a pathway that ran through the mangroves lining the bank of the river. He expected to reach the pathway no more than thirty metres behind Leda.

Ramirez had been more direct. He had been waiting near the QUTS Building for Leda to approach. When she stopped; he stopped and waited. When she ran, he didn't bother about stone steps; he just crashed straight down through the trees so that he came out onto the pathway below at almost the same time and place as Leda.

Students and City Workers, using the pathway for jogging during their lunch break, scattered as Ramirez emerged unexpectedly in their midst and came to a halt, panting, in front of Leda. Then they politely ran around the two people confronting each other and jogged on.

It took a few seconds for Ramirez to regain his breath. Had he been thinking more clearly he might have wondered why he was panting but Leda, who was in her seventies, had pancreatic cancer, and had been shot recently, was not. She stood before him completely composed and breathing evenly. He should have wondered, but he was too pre-occupied with retrieving the marble.

"Mrs. Reinhardt," he said between deep breaths, "I'm from NASA. You have something that belongs to us. We agreed to pay five thousand dollars."

Leda didn't hesitate. She smiled at Ramirez.

"Wonderful," she said, and pulled the marble in its see-through bag out of her pocket.

They completed the swap, and Leda was just putting the money into her bag when Steve hit Ramirez across the back of the neck. He went down like a sack of potatoes. Steve bent over him and retrieved the marble.

Leda was aghast.

"What are you doing?"

"Retrieving the marble."

"It's a fake. I brought two of them. I didn't know how many marbles Alan would have."

At that moment, Agents descended on them from all directions. People who were office workers a minute earlier now levelled guns at Steve.

"Don't move!" they were all yelling.

Leda ran like hell.

Another burly Agent stepped out from the trees to grab her. He extended a meaty hand. She grabbed it, twisted it and threw the Agent to the ground. At the same time, she dropped onto him with her bony knee and administered a Coup de Grace to his throat. He grunted with the impact of the knee and then he went silent.

She was up again and running before anybody could react; plunging off the pathway and into the mangroves below.

People everywhere were on radios.

"She's in the mangroves."

"She's running towards the bridge."

"Maybe heading for Parliament House."

"Close in on her. She can't get far."

Two Agents levelled guns at Steve while a third tried to revive Ramirez. Startled joggers pulled up and stood, gaping, not knowing whether to run on, or turn back.

"It's okay," yelled one of the CIA men, waving his gun in the general direction of the joggers. "We're Police. Nothing to see here. Move on."

The joggers gratefully ran on, and the CIA Man redirected his gun back onto Steve. Steve ignored him and reached for his phone.

"Fuck off," he said eloquently. "I'm SAS on assignment. You're just fucking, fuck-ups!"

He called Robinson and told him the CIA were all over the Botanical Gardens. They had Alan Ready's marble. They were searching for Leda.

Robinson didn't seem concerned.

"Leda? The little old lady? She won't get far."

But Robinson was wrong.

Agents scoured the area, looking for the little old lady. Steve sat and waited for Robinson to arrive, marvelling at the chaos around him as a dozen Agents searched for one little old lady.

After a few minutes, Steve noticed something in the river. Something the colour of the dress Leda had been wearing.

At first Steve thought it was Leda, swimming away.

Then he saw that it was just a dress, a piece of discarded clothing.

He looked up the river to the footbridge that crossed to South Bank. Even though the CIA were searching the area, they hadn't closed it off. Joggers were still running across from the Gardens.

On the other side of the river was Griffith University and students from there crossed the bridge each day to exercise and jog in the Gardens. Now, with lunchtime over, a lot of fit young students were literally racing back to their studies.

Among them was a tall blonde in micro shorts and T-shirt, striding out powerfully.

Hiding in clear view, Leda looked like any other Phys. Ed. Student; but not to Steve. He watched her as she ran up to the crest of the bridge then disappeared down the other side into the crowd.

A short while later, an attractive woman in a head scarf and sunglasses knocked on the door of the Ready household in Logan. Mrs. Ready answered the door.

The woman smiled.

"Mrs. Ready. Is Alan home?"

"No, he's at work."

"Oh, we were supposed to meet today."

"You're Leda?"

"Yes."

"He went to meet you for lunch."

The woman smiled.

Alan's mother couldn't believe it. This woman wasn't one of her son's fantasies after all. Then the woman said *she* couldn't believe it. They must have got their wires crossed, she said. She thought she was to come to Alan's home. She had arranged to buy some rocks from Alan;

interesting rocks that he had found on the trip.

So the woman wasn't Alan's girlfriend. Mrs. Ready was disappointed, but she wasn't surprised. And she didn't bother to protest when the woman gently pushed her way in and asked to see Alan's room. Perhaps the rocks were still there, the woman said.

The two women stood at the doorway of Alan's room and stared in as if it were the first time that either of them had seen inside.

It was a child's room: SF posters, Star Wars toys, video games and a pair of antique cuff links. The woman was immediately attracted to the cuff links because they looked out of place.

The shelf beneath the cuff links was wiped clean; elsewhere there was a light covering of dust. The woman picked up the toy rocket that also sat on the cleaned portion of the shelf. She shook it. It rattled. She opened it up and poured out two rocks or marbles, or some such thing.

"Ah here they are," she said and put the items into her bag.

Mrs. Ready wasn't sure that Alan would be happy if she let the woman take the rocks, and said so.

"Don't worry," said the woman. "We agreed a price."

And she took a large wad of one hundred dollar banknotes out of her large shoulder bag and counted ten of them into Mrs. Ready's greedy hands.

By the time Robinson could speak to the Americans, the CIA had their story down pat. They'd come across the arrangements for a meeting between Alan and the Reinhardts in an email. They didn't tell Robinson because they suspected that Steve couldn't be trusted.

The fact that he'd turned up at the Gardens without telling Robinson was proof that he was freelancing. If Robinson wanted co-operation from the Americans, they wanted Steve off the case.

Robinson was quick to comply.

Steve didn't object, although he insisted that he still get his expenses at the hotel covered for another night.

An hour or so later, when Kelly returned, Steve was having a relaxing drink in the bar.

Robinson had filled Kelly in on what had happened. She wasn't pleased. Not because Steve hadn't told Robinson what he knew, but because he hadn't told her.

Steve was unapologetic. If he told her, she might tell Robinson and Robinson might tell the Americans. Nobody could be trusted.

"Including you," snapped Kelly.

Steve grinned.

"Hey, lighten up. You're getting rid of me now. Let's have a drink. I've got a going-away present for you."

He placed the marble in the see-through bag onto the bar. Kelly grabbed at it.

"Where did you get this?"

"Don't get too excited," said Steve. "It's a fake. Leda gave it to me. And from what she said, the marble the Americans got from Alan was a fake as well. She switched it. They've still got nothing."

His grin widened.

"So, what are you drinking?"

Kelly didn't answer immediately. She fished her metal car keys out of her bag and brought them close to the marble.

Nothing. No flash; nothing.

The marble was a fake. She put it into her bag.

"Not just at the moment," she said, and stood up.

" I've got to go somewhere. I'll be back about four, okay?"

Steve shrugged. He didn't intend going anywhere.

He watched Kelly walk out. He was right. She did have good legs; but not as long as Leda's.

Had Steve followed Kelly out he might have got the chance to do a direct comparison on the relative merits of Kelly's legs versus Leda's, because Leda was waiting just across the street.

Kelly walked off in the direction of the city.

Leda followed at a distance, waiting her chance. Because it wasn't Leda who had visited Mrs. Ready, it was Kelly. And Kelly now had three marbles in her bag, two real and one fake, and she had a problem. She could trust nobody. If she handed the marbles over to the Federal Police, they would share them with the Americans. She still didn't know what had set the Americans off on this massive operation to recover the marbles. From the start, they'd known more than they'd let on, and it was still the same. Kelly was determined to crack this thing herself and share her knowledge with nobody.

A couple of blocks up Adelaide Street Kelly found what she was looking for: a large bank.

She went in, showed her Federal Police ID and asked to see whoever was in charge of safety deposit boxes. She was told the relevant bank officer was the Branch Accountant, Jeff Friedman, and he'd be with her shortly.

Leda had taken the risk of coming into the bank. She waited until Friedman appeared, to answer Kelly's query, and then she quietly left before Kelly looked in her direction and possibly recognized her.

Kelly explained to Friedman that she was working on

a case. She had vital evidence. It must be kept safe, but she had to continue working in the field.

She wanted a safety deposit box. She was a client of the bank in Canberra. She had her Federal Police ID. He could check with the Canberra branch of the Bank.

Jeff told her that the big commercial banks no longer provided safety deposit boxes, but he could provide her with a safety deposit envelope, which they would keep in a locked cupboard in the strong room.

He assured her that it would be quite safe. She would be shown to a customer's room where she would be left alone to put whatever she wanted in the envelope, seal it with a seal and sign over the flap. Then he would return, take the envelope and put it in the cupboard.

The cupboard had two locks so two bank employees would be needed to open it. Nobody would be allowed to tamper with the envelope. Nobody could tamper with the contents of the envelope without breaking the seal.

Kelly would have preferred a safety deposit box to which she held the key, but she had no alternative but to accept this arrangement. Jeff assured her again that it was perfectly safe. Nobody had ever lost an envelope. And, of course, there was no key for Kelly to lose.

Satisfied, Kelly allowed herself to be led off to the customer's room.

Kelly came out of the bank fifteen minutes later, still in plenty of time to get back to the hotel by four o'clock for a drink with Steve.

Leda watched her go. She didn't follow her because she knew she was no longer carrying the real marbles. She had left them in the bank. Leda entered the bank.

Jeff Friedman didn't normally work as a teller, he was too senior. Leda waited until he was walking past the counter in the business section of the bank and called to him. Could he help her? Her parents were sending money out to her from Germany. She wondered what would be the best way for them to do this.

A junior teller stepped forward to assist but the woman smiled so warmly at Jeff that he felt, in the interests of Bank PR that just this once he could answer a counter query.

Steve was still drinking in the hotel bar when Kelly got back from the Bank. She asked how many drinks he'd had. He assured her he was pacing himself. It was his last night in Brisbane. He intended to enjoy it. He sounded expansive; he sounded drunk. Kelly suggested maybe he needed a rest.

"Okay," he shrugged. "If you don't want to hear what I know."

Kelly did want to hear what he knew. And she wanted to be sober when she heard it. She suggested a walk in the park.

"Maybe we can have dinner later. Seeing as it's your last night."

Steve nodded. He shouldn't get drunk. He had too many secrets. He drained his glass and stood up.

"Let's go."

20 - *Strange Bedfellows.*

Kelly had worn sensible shoes for her sortie around the suburbs looking for Alan, so she found walking in the park very easy. Being Kelly, though, she couldn't help turning the stroll into a forensic examination of a Crime Scene.

Not that Steve seemed to mind. He was keen to talk.

The park was nearly empty now; the café shut. Steve showed Kelly where Leda and Alan had sat; where he'd sat and watched; where the CIA, disguised as office workers at lunch, had waited.

He showed Kelly the direction in which Alan had walked, and where Leda had run off, through the trees.

They walked down to the spot where Ramirez had confronted Leda, and he'd knocked Ramirez out. He described the eruption of action, people coming from all directions, Leda disabling a sixteen-stone CIA Agent and running into the mangroves and away.

This was the part Kelly found hard to believe; a little old lady had outrun the CIA and knocked one of them senseless?

"She was Red Army Faction, remember?" Steve said.

"She would have been taught unarmed combat; assassination without weapons."

"That was fifty years ago," Kelly scoffed, "I doubt she could even remember it, let alone do it."

"Oh, she'd remember it," said Steve. "At least the marble inside her would remember it. It can tap every memory she's ever had."

It was at that moment that Kelly realized that Steve knew a hell of a lot more than he'd been sharing with her. Now she was determined to hear it all; even if it took all night; which effectively it did. It took the walk, a candlelit dinner, and a post-coital conversation in her bed, before Kelly was sure that she knew everything that he knew and just what she was going to do about it.

She had started tentatively, as they walked along to the footbridge and stood watching the Brisbane River.

"You say the marble can remember? What is it; a computer?"

"I suppose it could be called a computer. It's a living intelligence; a brain enclosed in an osmium exoskeleton. It has no body. It has to attach itself to a warm-blooded creature to get energy and mobility."

"It's a parasite."

"It's parasitic, but it doesn't harm its host. Look at Leda. She was practically dead before she swallowed the marble. Now she's knocking out CIA Agents and running marathons."

Kelly couldn't deny that.

"Does she know she's got the marble inside her?"

"I don't know. Sometimes when I talk to her, I think it's her who's answering. Sometimes I think it's the marble. Sometimes they seem to merge."

"You talk to them?"

Steve pulled out Luc's phone,

"It's Luc's. I took it from the motel room in Cairns. I noticed Leda's phone wasn't in the morgue; I texted her on the off chance."

"And the marble answered."

"Yes."

"How do you know it was the marble?"

"Because she told me things; where she - it - came from; why it's here."

"Why is it here?"

Steve stared out at the water. Kelly said impatiently,

"You can't stop there."

"I'm afraid you'll think I'm nuts."

That made Kelly laugh, albeit rather nervously.

"Steve, we're standing on a bridge talking about an alien marble that invades humans and controls their behaviour. It's a bit late to worry about our sanity. Where did it come from? Why is it here?"

"To save the world."

"A sort of alien Jesus in a marble?"

Steve grinned.

"Not quite. It comes from a planet it describes as Earth a hundred years from now. The planet's dying. Probably dead by now. The marble's got no idea how long they've been traveling. Or where in the universe their planet is."

He looked around him at the wooded slopes of the Gardens and the river glinting in the late afternoon sunlight.

"In the end," he continued "when global warming had made their planet uninhabitable, they found a way to save it, but they were too late. Or maybe they weren't too late. Maybe it was just too hard politically to get anything done. Anyway, they decided to leave the planet.

Move out and look for another habitable planet and, if necessary, stop them from making the same mistakes."

"By why come in a marble without a body? Why a bunch of..." Kelly searched for another word and could find nothing more appropriate, "...marbles?"

"What would we do in the same situation? What will we do when the Earth threatens to become uninhabitable? Will we have the technology to solve the problem? Will we have the common will? Will it be only the rich and powerful that get away? And if they do, how would they survive the journey over possibly hundreds of years, possibly even hundreds of light-years? The Osmia were cryogenically frozen. They come to life when they engage with the warmth of a warm-blooded creature; a woman like Leda who swallowed her marble to smuggle it out, remember? Or, in Danny's case, his dog; who wouldn't have known any better."

Kelly began to suspect she was as mad as Steve because it was all making sense. Then he said something that brought her sceptical scientist's brain back to life.

"When they're all activated and together again, they can show us the technology that can save the world."

"Oh yeah, which is?"

"Nuclear Fusion; limitless clean energy for everyone. No more pollution; the deserts can bloom, the seas cool, and life can thrive."

"Ok, so, what's stopping them showing us right now? What are they worried about?"

"Roswell, Area 51."

Kelly laughed, genuinely amused this time.

"The UFO site? That's just a myth, Steve. All those Aliens they're supposed to have incarcerated there? There's no proof they've ever found any UFOs or Aliens, whatever the babble from conspiracy theorists."

"That's not the point. Papers have been leaked about the CIA and the American Military secretly investigating hundreds of possible UFO sightings. Why did they keep them secret?"

"To stop people panicking."

"Why would people panic if they've found nothing? Quite the opposite, I'd say."

Kelly shrugged.

"And if they found something, if they did, would they tell us, d'you think? What happened when you found DNA on the dead astronaut?"

He could see by her frown that he was getting through.

"These creatures, if they exist, if it's not some strange hallucination I'm having, possess technology that we can only dream of. Do you think the Americans are going to share it with us? With the rest of the world?"

It was the mention of the DNA that Kelly had found on the astronaut that swayed her. She wasn't convinced that these marbles really were from another planet or that they had the answer to the world's problems or that their intentions were good. What she was sure of was that they shouldn't fall into the hands of the CIA.

The question was, how could she stop this from happening?

The sun was dipping below the horizon now. The tall city buildings threw shadows over the footbridge and Kelly felt a chill. Steve took off his jacket and put it around her shoulders.

"They say some of the best restaurants in Brisbane are down on the river here," he said, "Maybe we should have dinner and think on it. I'm still on expenses until tomorrow."

Kelly agreed. She needed to eat. And she needed a drink. In fact, she needed a lot of drinks if she was going to figure this one out.

No more than a few city blocks away, Jeff Friedman was also thinking about dinner but he wasn't aiming quite so high. He was standing in an arcade that ran off Adelaide Street, looking at the menu of a cheap Noodle House and wondering whether to eat there or get takeaway.

It was a place that specialised in quick meals for city workers or students, and takeaway meals for busy urban singles who couldn't be bothered to cook. And this was a description that fitted Jeff exactly.

Depending on your point of view, Jeff was either a successful young man, achieving the position of Branch Accountant at a major Brisbane Bank before the age of thirty, or he was a complete disaster. Because outside of work he had virtually no interests whatsoever.

He left school at eighteen and went straight into the bank. His promotion meant he had to study nights and work days. Within ten years, he had bought a high rise apartment on the Brisbane River, in a building that was part private apartments and part apartment hotel. It gave him the best of both worlds; the convenience of living in a hotel and the privacy of having his own place.

He did have a live-in girlfriend for some years, who worked in the bank alongside him. But she'd got bored. She wanted to marry, have kids. He wanted to gain more qualifications, move higher in the bank.

In the end, she applied for a position at another branch and moved out. It wasn't even a proper breakup; more a lapse in interest through lack of commitment.

The only thing Jeff missed about her leaving was having home-cooked meals. Not that he was such a chauvinist as to let her do all the cooking. He was a better cook than she was; at least he thought so. The problem was that it was such a bother to cook just for oneself. So on most nights Jeff dined alone at one of the small arcade cafes or got takeaway. And tonight he was trying to decide which he would do when he heard a voice beside him.

"Is this place good?"

He turned to see the attractive young woman from the bank; the one who had wanted advice on getting money from Germany. He felt himself blush and hoped that, in the half-light of the arcade, she wouldn't notice.

"Oh, I don't normally eat here," he said. "Just working late tonight."

"I have to have takeaway until my money arrives from Germany," she said cheerfully. "It's either here or MacDonald's."

"Oh, this is much better than MacDonald's," Jeff said.

"Good. What do you recommend? Perhaps we can choose together."

She stood beside him as he looked at the menu again, totally distracted by the fact that she was standing so close that they occasionally brushed together, and he could feel the warmth of her body on his arm.

He couldn't help noticing that she wasn't wearing a bra under her T-shirt. He had noticed, earlier in the day, that her shorts were very short and her legs very brown. He was almost surprised to hear himself saying:

"Perhaps I could buy you dinner... in a restaurant?"

She smiled.

"Oh, I couldn't let you pay."

He smiled back and said,

"Well you can pay me back when your money arrives."

Then wished he hadn't. She smiled even more broadly.

"Well then, that would be lovely," she said.

He settled on a small Italian Restaurant at the end of the arcade. In fact, it was a large Italian Restaurant but it was divided into several smaller areas, each specialising in something different; Pizzas, Pastas and A La Carte. A La Carte had white tablecloths and little cups of olive oil and balsamic vinegar to dip your bread into.

He used to eat there a lot with his girlfriend but hadn't frequented the place lately. Still the waiter remembered him and nodded approvingly at his new dining companion.

The meal went swimmingly: antipasti followed by lasagne, washed down with a bottle of Chianti, which was finished before the meal even though they were only there for an hour or so.

She was beautiful. Smart too, apparently, as she was at University studying Political Science. But she wasted a lot of time, travelled a lot instead of studying. She wasn't like Jeff, she said; so industrious and a Bank Manager when he was still so young.

Jeff thought he should probably tell her that he wasn't a Bank Manager, but a second later decided it didn't matter.

The conversation had now moved on to how beautiful Brisbane was. The view over the river at night with the lights was like something in a fairy tale. Did Jeff live in the city?

Yes, he did, on the fifteenth floor with a fabulous view of the river all the way down towards Morton Bay.

"I'd love to see it," she said.

How could he refuse?

He showed her into his apartment, moving around quickly to hide any signs of a mess, the odd magazine and this morning's newspapers. Nothing really; Jeff was pretty fastidious. In any case, the woman, whose name was Leda, was far too busy rushing to the balcony, opening the sliding doors and staring down onto the Brisbane River.

When Jeff carried a couple of glasses of wine out to the balcony, Leda suddenly kissed him.

Jeff felt quite awkward standing there with a glass in each hand, unable to return her embrace. Then suddenly he almost choked as she unexpectedly put her tongue down his throat.

It felt like there was something still in his throat even after Leda broke off from the kiss and took both of the glasses to prevent him dropping them. She apologized and then laughed as he coughed again.

He didn't like that. He began to think she had been laughing at him all along; that she'd only spoken to him to get a free meal. He decided that as soon as they'd finished their drinks he would make his excuses, say he had to have an early night and ask her to leave.

Unfortunately for Jeff the drinks took ten minutes to finish.

After that he couldn't remember anything until he woke up in bed, alone and naked, with the bed-clothes and pillows scattered all over the floor. There was a piece of paper on the bedside table with the message:

Thank you! L. x

He sat up. Apart from a slight tenderness around the throat he felt tremendously relaxed. He assumed he must have had a good time, but his mouth tasted like the bottom of a birdcage.

He went to the bathroom, stared at his bedraggled countenance in the mirror, stuck his tongue out, and got a terrible fright.

It was black.

Where the hell had he been putting it?

He put toothpaste on his brush, brushed his teeth, brushed his tongue.

Then a horrible thought struck him. He spat a mouthful of toothpaste into the basin and rushed back into the bedroom and checked his wallet.

His money was there. His credit cards were there. Everything was intact.

He let out a big sigh. He had had a good time.

21 - Bad News.

Alan Ready hadn't had a good time.

The shop where he worked didn't close until six, so Jeff and Leda were already sharing their Lasagne and Chianti before he finished the long commute home.

All afternoon he'd been jumpy, afraid NASA or whoever it was would come after him. Then, when nobody arrived, the cunning Alan started to replace the cowardly Alan.

He'd quickly handed over the first marble when he saw the gun. From a distance, however, his courage returned. He congratulated himself on having made a "Swift Operational Decision" that had got the "Enemy Agents" off his back.

He thought if he could hide the other two marbles somewhere safe he could negotiate a better price. Maybe the twenty thousand dollars he'd originally intended asking for. At worst he might have to settle for five thousand dollars each. That would be a total of fifteen thousand.

Not bad, but that wouldn't happen. No. He'd phone the newspapers and tell them about the marbles.

Once he was a celebrity, they wouldn't dare take the final two marbles off him at the point of a gun.

He arrived home in a better mood. Things were going well. His mother had even cooked him his favourite dinner: Hungarian goulash. She was smiling, told him he should go and wash his hands. Dinner would be on the table soon. It was a special occasion.

Alan stopped on his way to the bathroom.

"What special occasion?"

His mother explained that Leda had been there. His mother had given her the rocks.

"What the hell do you mean?"

He was so angry he yelled at his mother. She just smiled.

"Don't worry. She paid me for them."

She took the ten one hundred dollars bills from the pocket of her dress and beamed at him.

"A thousand dollars."

He was too shocked to speak. He took the money from her and went into his bedroom.

Mrs. Ready thought he must be upset because he had missed Leda. She was a very beautiful woman, after all.

Alan must have cared for her because when she went to his bedroom door a little later to tell him that dinner was getting cold, she could hear him through the door, crying.

"He must have cared for her very much," she thought.

About the same time, Kelly got some bad news as well.

She and Steve had found a restaurant that was built on the river bank and sloped down to the water over several levels and balconies so that it looked like a boat. The place was busy; some of the clientele, pretty boisterous.

Their voices resonated off the hard surfaces of the restaurant. But It didn't bother either Kelly or Steve. They had picked the quietest table, and the ambient noise meant nobody would overhear their conversation.

In fact, Kelly almost didn't hear her phone.

It was the Assistant Director of ASIO. The one who had guaranteed that Kelly would get first crack at any space junk landing in Australia.

Kelly knew immediately that it was bad news because the Assistant Director said:

"It's bad news, I'm afraid. The Government and the Americans have decided to pool resources on this one. Two man teams. One Australian, one American."

"You're telling me I'm going to have to work with an American?"

Kelly wasn't pleased. But it was only getting worse.

"No, you're off the case. They think you're too close to Steven Moss."

Kelly glowered across at Steve.

"That's not my fault! I didn't ask for a bodyguard."

Her voice was raised. Steve knew she was talking about him.

The Assistant Director just continued talking in a level, reasonable voice.

"I know you didn't, Kelly. None of this is your fault. Come back to Canberra. We'll debrief you here and maybe I can get you on the team when they start laboratory tests on the two marbles we've got."

Kelly was so angry, she just hung up.

Then she switched off her phone so that the Assistant Director couldn't call back and ruin her evening even further.

And that was a mistake.

When Kelly had sent out emails offering to buy the marbles, she had attached her mobile phone number with an invitation for the recipients to call her. She'd now worked out why Alan hadn't called her. He was a sneaky little toe rag. She didn't understand why Gina and David hadn't responded.

The truth was they hadn't read their emails since they'd left the Ahearn tour bus, in Cairns.

The relationship between Gina and David was complicated. They were both Marine Biology students at Wollongong University; in the same year, getting the same high grades. There, the similarities ended.

David was a boy from the working-class Western Suburbs of Sydney, worried about his grades, worried about the HECS Loan he'd taken out to pay for University.

Gina was a girl from Sydney's North Shore, who seemed to achieve excellent marks with no effort at all. And she never worried about paying for University Fees or anything else much. She had two very doting, very rich parents. Her main worry was getting away from them because they were unbearably overprotective.

David understood Gina's need to get away from her parents occasionally, but he was worried that they would think that he was irresponsible and a bad influence on their daughter. And since David had long ago decided he wanted to marry Gina, that wasn't a good thing. Throughout their trip north David had regularly communicated with Gina's parents.

On the Ahearn trip there had been daily emails and, of course, Gina's parents would mention things to her that David had told them in their emails. Eventually, Gina became convinced that her parents were spying on her, and that David was the spy.

It had to come to a head on the bus trip back to Cairns. David was horrified at Gina's interpretation of what he saw as merely a demonstration that he could be relied on to keep her safe.

To prove that he was not in collusion with Gina's parents, David had been forced to agree that he wouldn't contact them for the rest of the holiday. There wasn't much of the holiday left to go so David was hoping Gina's parents wouldn't get too alarmed by the sudden radio silence.

To ensure David kept his word, Gina had insisted that he switch off his iPad and stow it in her backpack. Gina then put the whole affair out of her mind completely, and the two of them made their way at a leisurely pace down the coast from Cairns.

They intended finishing their holiday with a visit to the marine park at Tangalooma Island where visitors had up close and personal contact with wild dolphins. For Gina and David it was a sort of busman's holiday; part holiday, part study for their course.

On the day that the CIA tried to relieve Leda and Alan of their marbles, Gina and David had reached Townsville.

They had spent the day taking the ferry out to Magnetic Island where they'd hired a boat and explored the uninhabited coastline around the National Park at the north-west tip of the island. They'd finished with a swim at Horseshoe Bay and a bus ride back to the Ferry Terminal just in time to return to Townsville in the dark.

By the time they got back to the backpackers hostel where they were staying, they were hungry and dirty. Not only were they dirty, but they also had no clean clothes to change into because they hadn't done the laundry for a week.

They decided to play rock, paper, scissors.

Winner goes and buys takeaway fresh prawns, chips, salad and crusty bread; loser does the laundry in the communal laundry in the Hostel.

Gina lost the first game of rock, paper, scissors, and insisted they play again, which suited David because he wanted to lose. There was a computer in the laundry and Wi-Fi throughout the Hostel. David intended to send Gina's parents a quick message, just to stop them worrying and to impress on them what a responsible, future son-in-law he would make.

After the best of three, and then the best of five, Gina eventually won and went off to get supper.

David took their combined dirty washing to the laundry where he stuffed everything into one machine and used the spare change to get onto the Internet.

He realized that he wasn't a moment too soon. He and Gina had only been out of contact for a few days but already there were nearly a dozen emails. Most were from Gina's parents. David sent off a quick reply.

'iPad broken. Using Hostel computer in Townsville. All well. Moving on to Tangalooma tomorrow. Love David and Gina.'

That should reassure them and explain why they wouldn't hear from him again during the last few days of the trip.

David then looked at the other messages; two from the woman who had phoned the bus asking them to return the marbles, one from NASA and one from Alan Ready.

David couldn't believe his eyes. He read them in chronological order.

The first offered five hundred dollars each for the return of the marbles.

David had forgotten all about the marbles; they were

in Gina's backpack along with his iPad.

But if they were worth five hundred dollars, maybe they should be taking more care of them?

He read on.

NASA was offering five thousand. He started jumping up and down. Five thousand dollars was a lot of money to him.

Then he read the final email, from Kelly. It read:

'We'll match any offer you get from elsewhere. Call me.'

David looked at the bottom of the email for the telephone number. There was a mobile number there and a fixed line number from Canberra, along with a digital signature from Kelly and her job description: *Forensic Pathologist. Australian Federal Police.*

David was so excited he didn't even bother to read Alan's email.

When he'd calmed down a little, David realised he had a problem. It wasn't the fact that Kelly was a Forensic Pathologist, although if he'd thought about it, it should have bothered him. David's problem was that he desperately wanted to claim the five thousand dollars, but he couldn't tell Gina he'd contacted her parents.

After a while, he thought of a solution.

As soon as the washing cycle was finished, he put the whole load into a dryer and set the cycle on warm for ninety minutes. It would take at least that long to dry.

He then deleted the message he'd sent to Gina's parents and returned to the room.

He opened Gina's pack, took out his iPad and plugged it into a charger. He checked the side pocket of the backpack to make sure the marbles were still there then he lay back on the bed, pretending to be asleep.

The first thing Gina saw when she entered the room was

the iPad, and, as David had predicted, she wasn't pleased. He quickly assured her that he hadn't contacted her parents. She could check the iPad if she didn't believe him. He'd just been checking to see if there were any messages. And it was lucky he did.

Leaving her to simmer, he switched on the iPad, opened his email and let her read the correspondence for herself.

As he had hoped, Gina instantly forgot her suspicions regarding David's loyalty - or lack of it. She immediately checked that the marbles were still in the rucksack. She pulled them out and stared at them.

"These things are worth ten thousand dollars?"

She couldn't believe it. She examined the marbles minutely, wondering what was so special about them, then wiped the black smudges off of her fingers.

"What are we going to do?" asked David.

The answer seemed too obvious to Gina.

"Sell them of course."

"Who to?"

"I don't care."

David did care. His world was filled with a lot more imagined dangers than Gina's carefree existence. He had been thinking it through as he lay on the bed, waiting for Gina to return.

"This Kelly McDonald woman, she's Federal Police. Perhaps we should sell them to her. It might be safer."

"Okay. I'll phone her now."

Gina took out her phone and turned it on. There was a list of messages that she ignored, knowing who they were from. She dialled the number on Kelly's email.

Kelly, however, was deep in conversation with Steve over dinner, with her phone switched off.

Gina received a *"The number you have called...."* message.

She waited for the tone and then spoke clearly and evenly into the phone.

"This is Gina Bennett. I'm with David. We'll accept fifteen thousand for the marbles. If I don't hear from you, I'll contact NASA."

She hung up and grinned. David was apoplectic.

"They said ten thousand."

Gina shrugged.

"So? If they offered ten, they'll pay fifteen. Did you finish the washing?"

"It's still in the dryer."

Gina was already breaking open the prawns and chips. She stuffed a chip into her mouth.

"I suppose we ought to keep the marbles somewhere safe. Just stuck in the pack like that, anybody could take them."

That night, after David had recovered the washing, they slept as they normally did; David, wearing his pyjama shorts; Gina, wearing his pyjama top, which she always insisted looked better on her than on him because men in pyjamas looked dorky.

Tonight, however, Gina had another reason for wearing the top. It had a pocket with a flap and a button. Security in the Hostel wasn't good. Anybody could get into their room. To be on the safe side she put the marbles into the pyjama top pocket.

As they lay there discussing what they would do with fifteen thousand dollars, the marbles very slowly began to take warmth from her body.

And as Gina and David wrapped their arms around each other, the marbles between them very slowly heated up to body temperature.

Kelly and Steve were still in the Restaurant talking and arguing when Gina and David went to sleep.

The cause of the argument was no longer whether they were dealing with an alien intelligence. The American reaction when Kelly found DNA on the Astronaut; Leda's death and resuscitation, not to mention her growing younger by the day; even the episode with Danny's dog, had now convinced both of them that they were.

Nor did they disagree that this knowledge should not be left solely with the Military, who would surely keep any possible technical advancements to themselves in the name of National Security.

The cause of the argument was the motives of the Osmia, as Steve had christened them.

Steve was pretty much sold on the story that Leda had told him. After destroying their world, the Osmia were here to save this world from the same fate.

Kelly hadn't the benefit, or the disadvantage, of one-on-one contact with the alien intelligence. She, therefore, saw it in far more human terms.

What would humans do if the positions were reversed? Would they spread out across the Universe saving other species while their own perished? Or would they do what they had done with every new voyage of discovery, every new exploration and every new conquest? The Spanish in South America, the French in Africa, the Dutch in the East Indies, the British just about everywhere? Attack, conquer, subjugate, exploit and enslave.

With just eight marbles, Steve thought that was unlikely.

Even allowing for the fact that Pizarro with just a handful of men had conquered and subjugated the entire Inca Empire under Atahualpa, it was hard to see how eight marbles could conquer the earth.

Steve saw it more as a religious conversion than an invasion and quite often in such cases the converted fared better than the prophet. For example, Jesus was Jewish but the Christians had done much better out of his teachings than the Jews. Buddha was Indian, yet Buddhism isn't even one of the four major religions of India, despite the fact that there are millions of Buddhists living elsewhere in Asia.

The Osmia would bring the knowledge; humans would benefit from it.

It was a possibility that Kelly was reluctant to embrace without knowing a lot more, and ensuring there were safeguards if Steve happened to be wrong. The question was; how could this be achieved?

Kelly thought they should keep the Osmia apart, negotiate with Leda while keeping the other Osmia as hostages.

Steve thought this was barbaric, which was when Kelly yelled,

"Steve, we're talking about some fucking marbles."

Kelly already had two of the real marbles, she told Steve. She had found Alan Ready's home, persuaded his mother to hand over the marbles for a thousand dollars. They were somewhere safe; somewhere where neither the Americans, the Government, nor Leda could get at them. What Kelly needed now was the chance to talk to Leda face to face.

Steve thought he could arrange that. He would use Luc's phone to text Leda. Nobody had traced that he had been texting Leda because nobody knew about the phones.

There was still one problem.

There were still other marbles out there. Gina and

David had two and ASIO had one.

"And the Americans," Kelly reminded him.

"It's a fake, I told you," said Steve. "Leda switched it on Alan. And I wouldn't be surprised if she has Gina and David's marbles, too. The Osmia have some way of communicating, or at least sending a signal, giving their location. The problem is Greg Ahearn's marble."

It was then, as Kelly recalled later, that Steve suggested she should become a criminal. And she, being so intent on frustrating the Americans and ASIO, both of whom had betrayed her, thought it was a great idea.

Greg Ahearn's marble was under lock and key at the Australian Aerospace Laboratory at Brisbane Airport. Leda couldn't get to it. Neither could Steve. But Kelly could. She could arrange to examine the marble under some pretext then switch it for the fake marble Steve had given her earlier.

Kelly was just drunk enough to think this was a brilliant idea. She would then have three of the marbles. Leda would have to talk to her. The CIA and ASIO would have nothing and would just be running around like chooks with their heads cut off; like Mike the Chicken.

Kelly and Steve were so pleased with themselves that when they got back to the hotel they ordered another bottle of wine from room service and indulged in some very physical, passionate, but not exactly romantic sex.

22 - The Morning After.

Kelly woke with a dry mouth and a headache. Steve was still asleep on the other side of the king-sized bed. They hadn't slept in an embrace like Gina and David. Rather, they had coupled, admittedly to their mutual satisfaction, then Steve had retreated to the far side of the bed.

When she woke, Kelly wished he had retreated to his own room. She went to the bathroom, drank two glasses of cold water and took a couple of Panadol.

She filled the glass a third time and walked back into the bedroom.

Steve was awake. He pulled the sheet up to his waist.

Realising she was naked, Kelly handed Steve the glass of water and headed for the bathroom to find her dressing gown, leaving Steve with a very enticing view of her rear, although at that moment it did little for him. He was too busy running through what they had discussed the previous night.

Kelly came back wearing a hotel bathrobe and threw a second one onto the bed.

"You'd better get dressed and get back to your room before anybody's awake," she said.

Steve detected a certain chill in the air.

"Have you changed your mind?" he asked.

"About what?"

"About swapping the marbles."

"No. You just call Leda. Tell her from now on she has to deal with me."

Kelly sounded more self-assured than she felt. Like Steve, she was off the case.

The first thing she had to do was get permission to enter the Aerospace Laboratory.

It was still only 6.30 in Queensland, but Queensland didn't have daylight saving and Canberra did. The Assistant Director of ASIO was bound to be up. Kelly got her phone from her handbag and switched it on. A message alert immediately came on from a mobile number she didn't recognize.

Kelly thought the message might be from the Assistant Director, so she opened it first.

It was from Gina, offering to sell the remaining two marbles for fifteen thousand dollars. This complicated matters. She hesitated, wondering what to do next.

Steve had just returned from relieving himself in the bathroom when he saw Kelly standing there, seemingly transfixed, deep in thought.

"Something wrong?"

"No... No. Gina Bennett's sent me a message, offering to sell the other two marbles for fifteen thousand dollars."

"That's great," said Steve. "Can you raise the money? I've got a five thousand dollar a day limit on my account, but I could put in ten grand in two days."

"You mean buy the marbles ourselves?"

"Of course."

Kelly thought about it. She'd have five marbles out of eight. Leda couldn't refuse to deal with her then.

"It's still only six-thirty, but it's seven- thirty in Canberra. I'll call ASIO first. Get permission to visit the lab."

Kelly had the Assistant Director on her speed dial, so Steve had to talk quickly.

"Don't mention Gina's message."

"Of course not," Kelly snapped.

How dare he think she didn't know what she was doing?

The Assistant Director came on the phone and Kelly's voice became warm and conciliatory.

"It's Kelly MacDonald; sorry I was a bit short last night. You're right of course. I'm a Pathologist, not an Agent. I'll be back in Canberra in a couple of days. In the meantime, I'd like to ask a favour. I'd like to examine the marble at the Aerospace Laboratory."

"Kelly, you're off the case."

The Assistant Director was about to say it was out of the question, but Kelly just kept talking.

"I've got a theory that whatever's inside these marbles is living tissue. If I'm right, I have a way of checking it. The marbles give off an electrical charge when they're threatened by a metal object. The charge weakens quite quickly and stops."

"I know this. I've read the report."

Kelly didn't let that stop her.

"The thing is, if it is living tissue it will recharge its batteries, regain its charge, like an electric eel. I'd like to test my theory. It would be something we know that the Americans don't."

Kelly guessed, correctly, that the Assistant Director

wasn't any keener on being forced to co-operate with the CIA than she was. The prospect of knowing something the Americans didn't tipped the balance.

"Okay, I'll get you authorization for one visit. A technician will be with you at all times."

"Of course, just make sure there aren't any Americans there,"

By the time Kelly got off the phone from the Assistant Director, she was in an ebullient mood. The Assistant Director was arranging Kelly's access to the laboratory that very morning. She made coffee for Steve and herself.

"Black or white?"

"Black. Two sugars."

Kelly looked at her watch. A quarter to seven.

"Do you think it's too early to call Gina?"

Steve sipped his coffee.

"It's never too early to call someone to tell them you're giving them fifteen thousand dollars," he said.

But he was wrong.

Life in the Townsville Backpackers' Hostel started early. Backpackers were moving on, taking day trips out to Magnetic Island, or heading to low paid jobs where they could earn just enough to keep travelling around Australia.

David and Gina had no urgent plans. It was their last day in Townsville. They just had to phone ahead to make arrangements with the Eco Rangers at the Tangalooma Dolphin Reserve, and then catch the overnight train.

David woke with Gina sleeping peacefully beside him. Her hair spread across the pillow and over her face. He did love her. He was also feeling very randy. Talk of the marbles had dominated the conversation the previous night and in the end they had just fallen asleep dreaming of being rich. He reached forward, brushed the hair gently from her face. She smiled, still half asleep. He reached his hand down under her pyjama top, or rather his pyjama top.

She was awake in an instant.

"Hey, it's rude not to ask."

"Oh come on."

She was always teasing him, showing him who was boss.

She smiled then kissed him. He kissed her back, snuggled his face in between her breasts and, very unromantically got his nose caught in a tear in her pyjama top. He pulled his head away.

"What happened to your top?"

Gina looked down. There was a neat hole in the pyjamas, just on the pocket. She poked her finger into the hole and frowned.

"It goes all the way through."

Then it dawned on her.

"The marbles. The marbles have fallen out."

She jumped up so quickly, she hit his face with her backside as she turned and pulled back the sheets, searching for the marbles.

"They're gone."

She got down on her knees; looked under the bed.

"They're gone. Somebody's stolen them."

"How could anybody steal them?" David asked and took the sheets right off the bed, shook them and threw them to the floor. He checked under the pillows. They looked around.

It wasn't a big room, and sparsely furnished; it didn't take long to ascertain that the marbles weren't anywhere there.

"Those bastards," Gina yelled. "They've stolen our marbles."

"Who?" asked David.

"How the hell should I know?" Gina yelled again.

Gina and David were at the Reception Area in the Hostel when Kelly called. She had barely identified herself before Gina told her she was wasting her time. Somebody had stolen the marbles.

"Who?"

Gina was more polite answering the question from Kelly.

"I don't know. We're at Reception now reporting the theft. The Manager's going to ask everybody if they've seen them, but they're not going to tell us if they stole them, are they?"

Kelly thought quickly. She didn't want everybody to know Gina's marbles had been stolen. Nor did she want to lose them. She decided to play Federal Police Officer.

"Have you reported this to the local police?"

"No."

"Don't. They're not going to take the theft of a couple of marbles seriously."

"But if they're worth ten thousand dollars..." Gina began.

Kelly noted that she'd dropped her price.

"They won't know that," said Kelly, "and we don't want to tell them. The more people who know, the less likely it is that we'll get them back, and the less likely you'll get your money. What are your plans today?"

"Nothing. We're catching the train to Brisbane this afternoon."

"Okay, I'll send somebody up there. Tell the manager to make sure he has the names, telephone numbers and forwarding addresses of everybody who stayed there last night. And get their passport numbers."

"I'm not sure he'll do that," said Gina.

"Just put him on the phone. I'll tell him," said Kelly.

She put her hand over her phone while she waited for the Hostel Manager to come onto the phone.

Steve was listening anxiously. Kelly confirmed his fears.

"We're going to have to go up to Townsville. Somebody stole the marbles."

"Let's just hope it's some kid looking for a souvenir of Australia," said Steve.

"You think it's Leda?" asked Kelly.

Steve shrugged.

"Maybe she's in Townsville. She gets about."

The Manager came onto the phone, identifying himself as Peter Hepworth.

Kelly moved smoothly into police officer mode.

"Peter, this is Kelly MacDonald of the Australian Federal Police. Has Gina explained the situation to you?"

As Kelly spoke to the Manager, Steve took out his two phones. First he turned on Luc's phone.

No messages. He tried to dial. Leda's phone was switched off, as he'd expected.

He sent: *Gina's marbles stolen. Do you have them?*

Then he switched off Luc's phone.

On his own phone, he looked up flights from Brisbane to Townsville.

There was a flight at midday. That gave them plenty of time to check out of the hotel and travel to the airport together.

Steve could drop Kelly off at the Australian Aerospace Facility, which was also at the airport but still several miles from the Domestic Terminal.

He would then go on to the terminal, pick up the tickets and wait for Kelly there, although Steve was beginning to think the trip to Townsville might well be a complete waste of time. Leda had probably beaten them to it.

He shouldn't have worried. He was never going to get to Townsville.

23 - Change Partners.

Brisbane was initially established as a penal colony on the coast at Redcliff Point in 1824. The following year the settlement was moved several kilometres up the Brisbane River to its present site. The move was to be of great benefit a hundred and sixty-three years later, when Brisbane Airport was built to commemorate the same Australian Bi-Centenary that had brought sealed roads to Alice Springs.

Between Brisbane and the coast were kilometres of flat swampland, regularly flooded at high tide and uninhabitable, except for a small residential suburb on Cribb Island. When the city wanted to build a new airport, it simply had to move a few people off Cribb Island and pump billions of litres of sand out of Moreton Bay to raise the swamp above the high tide mark.

The result was probably the most convenient airport to any major city in the world, situated just a few kilometres from the CBD. As a consequence, it took Kelly and Steve's taxi less time to drive down the motorway to the outskirts of the airport than it did to find the Australian Aerospace Facility.

The swamp on which the airport is built covers nearly fifty square kilometres. The distance from one end to the other is greater than the distance from the airport to the city, and the taxi driver must have covered every inch of it before dropping Kelly at the gates of the Facility.

Steve offered to wait but Kelly insisted he go ahead and get the tickets to Townsville. She was sure somebody from the Facility would drive her to the airport or get her a taxi, hopefully with a driver who knew where he was going. She added this last bit for the benefit of the Taxi Driver, who had taken the scenic route. It was very likely a waste of time, however, because Kelly was doubtful the driver even spoke English. And even if he did, he certainly wouldn't appreciate the subtle art of sarcasm.

Kelly was met at the main gates by a Royal Australian Air Force Officer and an Engineer. The facility specialized in developing and building aircraft and helicopters for the Australian Military, and they had extensive laboratories. But these were set up to test the stress levels of metals and wing constructions. So after initially testing the marble and finding it attempted to protect itself with an electrical charge, they had taken a few samples from the surface of the marble and then locked it away for safe keeping.

The samples had revealed that the object, at least on the surface, was made of osmium. X-rays hadn't managed to penetrate the marble suggesting some manner of shield, installed inside the osmium. They had also discovered that the marble had a high level of radiation, suggesting exposure to cosmic rays. However, the level wasn't so high as to suggest long-term exposure and, therefore, the marble must have been in orbit for only a few days. The Aerospace Engineers estimated that it had been launched from earth only a week or so before.

Kelly agreed that it had been in orbit around the earth for only a few days but privately disagreed about how it got there. She thought it must have arrived from deep space in a vehicle of some sort that had protected it from the effects of the cosmic wind. As far as she knew, nobody on earth had the ability to construct such a vehicle. It strengthened her conviction that the marble was alien; a conviction she didn't share with the RAAF Officer or the Engineer.

Using rubber gloves and a dental probe, she repeated her test on the marble that had initially caused the electric arcing effect.

The RAAF Officer wasn't impressed. They had already conducted this experiment; what did it prove, doing it again? Kelly explained that it may prove the marble could regenerate an electrical supply like an electric eel; that it was possibly living tissue.

Kelly emphasized this point by waving her dental probe around so that it flashed in the light; an occurrence noticed by both the RAAF Officer and the Engineer.

Distracted, neither of them noticed that Kelly already had a second marble in her other gloved hand, and that it was this marble that she subsequently took between her finger and thumb and carefully "returned" to the lead-lined box where the marble was normally kept.

While the marble was being placed back in secure storage, Kelly asked if they could call her a taxi; going to the Domestic Terminal

Both the RAAF Officer and the Engineer thought Kelly was a bit of a flake. Who would send living tissue into orbit in an osmium-coated marble? They were both more than happy to leave her at the front gates when she said she would wait on her own for the taxi.

When she'd pulled off her rubber gloves in the laboratory she had wrapped them around the real marble and put them back into her bag. Now, making sure she kept her back to the Facility, she took out the marble, placed it inside the finger of one of the gloves and tied a knot in the glove to secure it. As she put the marble back into her bag, she noticed for the first time that her heart was racing. She had remained calm throughout the operation, but now she felt almost faint.

She took a deep breath and wondered who she should call first; the Assistant Director of ASIO or Steve. Not knowing who might be listening, she decided not to call Steve and instead used her speed dial to call Canberra. But before the Assistant Director had even answered her call, everything suddenly went black.

It was the Taxi Driver who found her. He called security, and the RAAF Officer and Engineer came running. At first they thought she had fainted but as she came to, Kelly complained of a pounding pain in the back of her neck.

The RAAF Officer examined the wound, or rather the bruise because the skin hadn't been broken. Kelly had been karate chopped by someone who knew what they were doing; somebody expert in the martial arts.

Somebody like an SAS soldier, Kelly thought. Suddenly it was all blindingly clear.

Steve and Leda were in it together. She had been taken for a ride, used to get the marble.

"The bastard," she yelled; then in a voice only slightly less angry ordered the RAAF Officer to instruct Security at the Airport to arrest Steve Moss, who was on a flight to Townsville.

The RAAF Officer just looked at her open mouthed.

"Arrest him for what?"

"Stealing the marble."

Kelly realized it was going to take too long to explain.

"Oh never mind," she said and picked up her phone, which had fallen beside her.

Still sitting on the ground, holding her neck, Kelly called the Assistant Director of ASIO. She didn't mess around with any preamble; there was no time.

"I've found out why Steven Moss has been acting so strangely. He and Leda are in it together. They've both swallowed marbles. Now he's got the Ahearn marble. He's the only person who knew I was at the Aerospace Facility."

The RAAF Officer and the Engineer exchanged frowns; wasn't the Ahearn Marble their marble? Surely it was still safely locked away?

The Assistant Director was also having difficulty following Kelly.

"How did he get the Ahearn marble?" she asked.

"It's a long story. I haven't got time to explain," Kelly said brusquely. "Look, he saved Leda from the CIA; he followed me to the Aerospace Facility. He has the marble. He's on a flight to Townsville. At least he should be. Get Airport Security to arrest him if he tries to fly out. Oh and another thing. You're not taking me off this case, now. Neither are the bloody Americans. I'm going to nail that bastard."

Kelly hung up, looked up at the RAAF Officer.

"Do you have any security here?"

"Of course."

"I need some muscle," she looked at the Taxi Driver. "You can take us to the Domestic Terminal."

"Let's get you some first aid, first," said the RAAF Officer in soothing tones.

He still wasn't sure whether the woman had been affected by the bang on the head or quite what was happening.

"There isn't time," Kelly insisted.

But the RAAF Officer and the Security Guard gently lifted her to her feet and led her into the facility.

The Taxi Driver watched them go.

"Should I wait?" he called.

"Yes," Kelly yelled back as she was led away.

"No," yelled the RAAF Officer.

Steve was already at the Terminal, but he wasn't on the run. He had no idea what was going on a few kilometres away. He was having coffee at a kiosk positioned just outside the entrance to the Domestic Departures Terminal and wondering whether it was time to get the tickets. He was just finishing his coffee when he saw Kelly enter the Domestic Terminal. He drained his paper cup, threw it into the bin and chased after her.

When he got into the terminal building, he saw Kelly immediately. Her mass of red hair was impossible to miss. She was standing some way back from the check-in counter, looking around, presumably for Steve.

Steve walked up behind her and whispered in her ear,

"Did you get it?"

Kelly turned and faced Steve but the eyes he gazed straight into weren't green, like Kelly's eyes. They were blue, like Leda's.

"If you try to get on that plane," she said, "They'll arrest you."

She ushered him away to a quiet corner of the Concourse.

"The Ahearn Marble, as you call it, has been stolen," she said.

"By you."

It wasn't a question. Steve knew it was her. She didn't bother to deny it.

"They think you did it. There is a general order out from ASIO to arrest you if you try to board that plane. You should come with me."

Steve didn't move.

"Why? Why don't I just grab you? That'll fix everything."

Leda didn't bat an eyelid.

"I came to warn you, Steven," she said. "I could have just let you be arrested."

She looked quickly around the Concourse. Then turned back to him with a smile

"Besides if you try to grab me, I could break your neck."

Steve looked at her. She was as tall as he was, but twenty kilos lighter at least. On the other hand, who knows what extra power the marble had given her? In any case, she seemed completely unconcerned as she pulled an ID wallet out of her handbag. She handed it to Steve.

"Take this, flash it to the security guard standing next to the Townsville Check-In. Ask him if he has a photo of Steve Moss. If he doesn't know what you are talking about, you're home free. If he does, you'd better come with me."

Steve looked inside the wallet. There was a picture of a slightly overweight but tough looking man named John Busselton, and it identified him as CIA.

"Where did you get this?" Steve asked.

"I took it from him... at the Gardens... when I knocked him out."

Steve thought about it.

Could Leda knock him out as well?

Were the authorities after him? One way to find out.

Steve walked up to the Security Guard standing near the Check-In Counter. He flashed him the I.D. just long enough to establish the CIA, not long enough to get a good look at the picture. He stood watching the crowd alongside the Security Guard.

"Do you have a picture of this Moss guy?" he asked in his best attempt at an American accent.

"No," said the Guard, "We're just supposed to wait and see if he tries to check in."

Steve nodded, still not looking at the Guard.

"I'll cover the entrance," he said and walked back to where Leda was waiting with five of the fifty one-hundred dollar bills that Ramirez had given her, in her hand.

"Now what?" asked Steve.

"You are going to hire a car for us, Mr. Busselton," Leda said. "I'm sure they'll accept your American Driving Licence."

"They'll probably accept my American credit cards for security, too," Steve pointed out. "That is if they haven't already been reported as stolen, in which case they'll arrest us as we pick up the hire car. We'll get a taxi."

Shortly after Steve and Leda drove off in the taxi, Kelly arrived at the Domestic Departures Terminal in the RAAF Officer's car.

She was met by Ramirez and Bamberger who had driven straight from the city. They told her Steve hadn't tried to board the Townsville flight as yet, and it was due to close any minute.

"What do we do now?" Ramirez asked.

He'd been told to afford Kelly every courtesy. It worked. Kelly was flattered by his tone of respect. Maybe she'd been wrong all along. She should have been helping the Americans, not Steve. In any case, they were now taking instructions from her. Obviously everybody realized she knew more about what was going on than they did.

"Is there an all points look out for Steve?" she asked, then corrected herself, "For Moss?"

Ramirez said there was, and with him being SAS they had plenty of ways to track him. They had his driving licence, credit cards, photo ID. He wouldn't get far.

Satisfied, Kelly said she should go after the other two marbles. Twelve hours ago they were in Townsville. She would catch the flight she had intended taking with Steve.

"If you don't mind, Ma'am," said Ramirez, "we'll tag along with you."

"Mind?" said Kelly, "I'm insisting on it."

Bamberger made a call and was surprised to learn there was no such thing as a First Class flight, Brisbane to Townsville. He had to accept that the three of them would be put on the flight in Premium Economy.

As they walked through the departure gate and out to the waiting plane, Ramirez couldn't resist asking,

"So you think we really are dealing with aliens?"

Kelly shrugged.

"There doesn't seem to be any other logical explanation."

Ramirez shook his head.

"Twenty years I've been chasing UFOs," he said.

"Area 51?" Kelly asked.

"Yeah," said Ramirez and he smiled. "We never found a damn thing. I'm retiring soon. It'd be nice to find one... just once."

Since Gina and David's train to Brisbane left Townsville just ninety minutes after Kelly, Ramirez and Bamberger touched down there, the CIA had arranged to meet them at Townsville Airport to save time. As agreed, they'd brought along the list that the Hostel Manager had prepared of all the staff and guests who had stayed at the hostel the previous night.

As they sat in the café, and Ramirez and Bamberger got stuck into their hamburgers with the same enthusiasm that David showed, Kelly sipped her coffee and questioned Gina. How long had they been staying at the hostel?

"Just one night."

"How many people at the hostel knew about the marbles?"

"Nobody."

Gina and David had arrived on the morning train from Cairns, checked in and left their bags there, then headed to Magnetic Island for the day.

"So you left the marbles at the hostel all day?" Kelly asked.

"No, they were in my pack. I took that with me," said Gina.

Kelly was beginning to think it had to have been Leda who took the marbles.

"Have you seen anything of Leda Reinhardt since you got off the tour bus?" she asked.

Gina seemed a little thrown by the question.

"No, she caught a plane home, didn't she? Why do you ask?"

It seemed such a left-field question.

Kelly pushed on regardless.

"What about any of her relatives? Say, her daughter?"

"There was that woman on the ferry coming back from Magnetic last night," David cut in between mouthfuls of hamburger and sips of coke.

"What woman?"

Ramirez put down his hamburger and took out his electronic notepad.

"She was on the ferry. She looked like Leda, only heaps younger. Could've been her daughter. Remember, Gina?"

Gina nodded.

"Did you show anybody the marble on the ferry?" Ramirez asked.

"Yeah, we were showing it around. But nobody believed it was from a rocket."

Ramirez nodded,

"This woman, did she have a name?

"I guess so," laughed David.

"Don't be stupid, David," said Gina, then to Ramirez: "Her name was Helen. I remember because it seemed such an English name and she had an accent."

"Did she give a second name?"

"Troy I think; yes, Troy."

Kelly had heard enough. She stood up.

"Okay guys," she said to Gina and David, "we won't keep you any longer. Will fifty dollars cover your cab here and to the railway station?"

"We came by bus," said David, then tailed off as Gina stared at him to shut up.

"Fifty dollars will be fine," she said.

"Pay them," Kelly told Bamberger; then she got up to look around for the ticket desk. It wasn't hard to find. Townsville Airport was very small.

As she walked towards the ticket desk, Ramirez caught up with her.

"What's going on?" he asked.

"I guess they don't teach you Greek mythology in Langley, Virginia," Kelly said.

"Helen Troy; Helen of Troy. She was Leda's daughter. Her father was the God, Zeus, who screwed Leda, disguised as a swan. Helen was born in an egg; just like a marble."

She gritted her teeth.

"That bitch is laughing at us. At least that bloody marble's laughing at us, which is worse. We've got to get back to Brisbane to get the last two marbles."

"How do you know they're there?" asked Ramirez.

"Because I've got them," said Kelly.

Ramirez stared.

"Don't worry, they're safe; as long as Leda and Moss don't know how to break open a bank strong room, that is."

Later, as Kelly and Ramirez stood around waiting while Bamberger arranged seats on the first flight back to Brisbane, Ramirez said:

"I still don't get it. If this Leda is an alien, how would she know about Greek mythology?"

"Steve says the marble can recall every memory the old lady ever had," Kelly explained.

"Shit," said Ramirez. "That'd be embarrassing. There's a few things I'd much rather forget. Do you think she can recall every memory Steve Moss has had?"

Kelly thought about their rather athletic lovemaking the previous night.

"I hope not," she said. But she was pretty sure she could, and it made Kelly's mood even darker and her sense of Steve's betrayal stronger still.

24 - *All Together Now.*

Leda and Steve had booked into a three-star hotel on the edge of the Brisbane CBD. The only stipulation Leda had insisted on was that that Steve paid in cash.

It wasn't the sort of place where the staff showed you to your room, which suited them both just fine. While Steve put the burglar chain on the door and checked the bathroom, Leda stood in front of the mirror and took off her blouse. She still hadn't taken to wearing a bra.

As Steve came back into the room, she fluffed up her mass of red hair and watched him in the mirror.

"Do you like my hair like this?" she asked. "It's just like Kelly, I think."

"Why did you do that? Why did you choose that style and colour?"

"I had my reasons. Why? Does it bother you?"

"Why should it?"

"It might remind you of Kelly."

She turned and faced him. He was aware of her breasts, which, while not large, certainly didn't look seventy-five years old. As if reading his thoughts, she moved closer.

"Would you like to kiss me?"

"No, thanks," said Steve, moving away.

Leda had a playful smile on her lips.

"Are you frightened?"

"Of course I'm frightened," said Steve. "I don't want you stuffing a marble down my throat."

"Don't worry," she said. "I don't need you to carry the marbles. I can carry them myself."

This thought hadn't occurred to Steve.

"How many marbles have you got?" he asked.

"Four, half a band," she again moved forward towards him, teasing.

"Would you like to join us?"

Again he moved until he was backed up against the wall.

"Look, I want to help you. I think you deserve to survive. I think you can help the world. But I'm not turning myself into a bloody zombie to do it."

Leda shrugged, moved to the bed and stepped out of her skirt. She pulled off her pants.

"I've got to shower and change," she said. "There's somewhere I have to be."

She moved towards the bathroom.

At the door, she paused and looked over her shoulder at Steve.

She knew what he could see: tight ass, slim figure, long legs, nipples that almost pointed upwards.

"If you change your mind..." she said.

"I won't."

She laughed and went into the bathroom. He moved to the bathroom door, which she had left open on purpose.

"You Osmia, or whatever you call yourselves, you have a strange sense of humour," he said.

She switched on the taps of the shower to adjust the temperature.

"No," she said. "It isn't us. It's Leda. That old lady has a wicked sense of humour. She loves to tease."

For some reason that made Steve feel even more uncomfortable. Although why the idea of being teased by a seventy-five-year-old woman was worse than being teased by an alien, he had no idea.

Half an hour later Leda came out of the bathroom wrapped in a towel, which she pulled off and used to dry her hair. Even though Steve was lounging on the bed watching her, she seemed totally unaware of her nudity. Not that it affected Steve now, either. He was too aware that he was dealing with an alien being... or was he?

"Can Leda control what you do?" he asked.

"Of course not," Leda dried her hair vigorously, then threw away the towel and started putting on her jogging outfit.

"So how come you say she loves to tease?"

"Because she does. We know her every memory, every pleasure. She has always enjoyed teasing men; even now she is old and dying. And we thought you might like it. She finds danger sexy. Being an urban terrorist was a great aphrodisiac... Do you find killing and violence an aphrodisiac?"

"No. I've done my killing in Iraq and Afghanistan. There's nothing very sexy about blood, sweat, sand... and the smell of it. It's ..." Steve searched for the word, "nauseating."

Leda nodded approvingly.

"I'm glad. That is what we feel, too. As we've occupied other bodies, we've discovered that Leda is not very typical."

"So you have Gina and David now?"

Leda nodded.

"They are wonderful people. They care for the environment, other species, everything."

"They're young," said Steve. "They care because they're going to inherit the mess."

Leda put her scarf back over her hair. It was impossible to tell now whether she was a blonde or a redhead.

"Yes, when the young ones take over, things will be easier. We can be accepted, then," she said.

"I wouldn't count on it," said Steve. "People change. And those with power and money never seem to want to let go."

"If they don't," said Leda putting on her running shoes, "you will suffer the same fate that we did."

"Did you have power struggles on your planet? Wars?"

"Oh yes, and it got much worse towards the end, as food became scarce."

Steve was now more convinced than ever that he was dealing with a small, desperate band, not an alien invasion.

"It's surprising any of you got away."

Leda didn't disagree with him.

"It is surprising; more surprising than you think. Because even at the end the many Governments couldn't come together, even to save themselves," she said. "It was an eccentric entrepreneur who financed the Osmia. Ironic, huh? Capitalism destroyed us, and Capitalism saved us… Well, some of us."

There was silence for a while. Steve was thinking what the end of the Osmian World must have been like.

The reality was that Leda couldn't have told him. Her memory of the end of her world was imprinted on her brain very late, and then only in the form of a set of facts, not an experience.

She was first to break the silence. Having finished dressing, she picked up her backpack and headed for the door.

"Don't wait up for me," she said." I won't be back until late. I'll try not to wake you."

"Don't worry," said Steve. "I won't be asleep."

Leda smiled.

"You're afraid we'll slip a marble into your mouth."

Steve didn't deny it.

"We don't want to make you one of us, Steven," Leda said. "We have a far more important task for you."

And she walked out; making it even less likely that Steve would go to sleep.

What the hell was this important task?

He felt trapped. He felt he had to do something; to put himself back in control. He leapt off the bed, picked up his room key and headed for the door.

The lift doors had already closed, and Leda had disappeared. They were only on the fourth floor. He rushed to the fire stairs and starting descending, two at a time. He wasn't going to just sit there while Leda managed everything.

He reached Reception just as Leda was disappearing out the front doors onto the street. He waited until she was out of sight before following her.

On the street, Leda immediately fell into "aimless backpacker" mode.

She walked around casually, looked in shop windows, bought an ice cream.

Steve kept his distance. Even so, he wondered if Leda had spotted him.

If she had, she didn't react in any way.

She just gradually made her way across town until she went into a large residential and hotel apartment building.

Steve hurried to get to the door; he needed to see where she was going, or at least which floor of the building she was heading for.

As he got to the glass front doors, he had to screech to a halt.

Leda was in the foyer, chatting to the Doorman. Obviously they knew each other. Was he an Osmium?

Steve moved back far enough to be hidden while he still had a view of the foyer.

Leda finished her brief chat with the Doorman, moved to the lift and pressed the button.

From the shadows, Steve watched her take out a room key from her backpack, she walked into the lift, pushed her room key into the slot to access the lift.

As the lift door closed, Steve moved quickly but calmly to the lifts and watched to see which floor the lift stopped on. He also kept an eye on the Doorman to see if he was being watched. The Doorman had disappeared behind the reception desk and seemed to have no interest in Steve

The lift stopped at the twelfth floor, then the thirteenth floor, then the fifteenth floor.

It seemed Leda had spotted him. There was no way he could tell which floor she had got off on. Nor could he access all the floors without a room key. He wandered back out onto the street.

Leda watched from Jeff's balcony as Steve walked away.

She went back into the room, took two frozen takeaway meals from the freezer and put them on the kitchen counter to thaw out.

Then she stretched out on Jeff's bed, set the alarm clock and lay back and closed her eyes.

Her breathing became shallow, her heartbeat slowed to a couple of beats a minute. She fell into a deep sleep. Her skin had rejuvenated in just a few days but her vital organs, her skeleton, her heart, still belonged to a seventy-something woman. She had to rest; the next twenty-four hours would be vital to the survival of her band.

Now out on the street, alone, Steve started thinking about his own safety. He didn't know this part of Brisbane, but it couldn't be far from the railway station.

He walked a couple of blocks west and found it. He looked at the timetable and caught a local commuter train south, over the river.

He got out at the third suburban station, crossed over the railway lines and waited for the next train heading north.

When the station indicator showed the next train was just three minutes away, he risked switching on Luc's phone. He was sure his own would be tapped by now. Maybe they had missed the second phone.

They hadn't. As soon as he switched it on, the police were tracing his co-ordinates.

Still, it took him just a few seconds to text:

'It wasn't me. It was Leda. She has Townsville marbles too. You'd better hang on to the last two. I'll try to arrange meeting between you'

He had thought carefully about what he would say.

He assumed that ASIO and the CIA would think the last two marbles he was referring to were the one at the Aerospace Laboratory and the one the CIA had taken from Alan Ready. Kelly knew these were now both fake and, therefore would know he was referring to the two marbles she had stashed away somewhere. He was trying to warn her without betraying her.

Whether she'd appreciate this, he didn't know. He certainly wasn't leaving Luc's phone on long enough for her reply. He switched it off and jumped on the next train north, back towards Brisbane.

Kelly, Ramirez and Bamberger were at Townsville Airport halfway through a two-hour wait for the next plane back to Brisbane when she received Steve's message. She relayed its contents to the CIA Men.

Bamberger was keen for her to set up a meeting that same night; Ramirez was more circumspect. Moss must know Kelly's phone was being bugged. He wasn't going to turn up to a pre-arranged meeting again. He'd want something spur of the moment so they couldn't make any plans to stake the place out. Kelly felt at least she had to try. If she made the location cryptic, something only she and Steve would know, maybe he'd respond. She sent:

'On plane back to Brisbane. How about the place we ate before? 8. p.m.'

Steve picked up the message at Brisbane Station and replied immediately:

'No can do. Leda not here. Call u tomorrow.'

And again he quickly switched off.

Ramirez wasn't surprised. He was sure Steve would use multiple calls to arrange any meeting; with instructions for Kelly to follow that would ensure she would be alone. They would just have to wait for Steve to call again.

Steve walked out of the Brisbane station. He was still a long way from his hotel, but to be doubly careful he walked off in the opposite direction down to the river to find somewhere to eat alone. After that, he went back to the hotel and worked out in the hotel gym, which was just a small room with a running machine and an exercise bike. He watched some television and despite his best efforts eventually fell asleep.

It was the small hours of the morning when Leda returned. She quietly locked the door and attached the burglar chain. She sat in the darkness watching him with a strange mixture of curiosity and affection.

There were now five marbles inside her. The other four marbles discussed whether they would help an alien if one were to invade their land. They decided four votes to nothing that they wouldn't, but it didn't matter anyway.

Leda was just that; the Leader. The others had no free will; they had to follow her, and she had decided she would trust him. If she were to put a marble inside him now, he would be more compliant; but when the time came to remove the marble and call on his help without it, he might be resentful. Certainly he would feel they had betrayed his trust.

Although ultimately in their group all decisions were made by the dominant female, the others weren't happy that they were being put at risk. Leda assured them they were at no risk. She had found them a haven. She would deliver them there. Steve's job was to deliver her there, too. And if she didn't make it, one of them would take over.

The sun had already risen when Leda shook Steve awake. He was still dressed. The television was on although the sound was almost subliminal. It was the normal early morning ABC show; a mixture of news headlines, promotions, gossip, and weather forecasts.

Leda told him to shower and change. She had ordered room service. Steve wondered if that was wise.

"Better than being seen in the dining room," said Leda. "I've been watching the News. No mention of us but they must have people everywhere, looking."

As Steve headed for the bathroom, Leda asked,

"What did Kelly say?"

He turned to face her. She smiled.

"You must have called her. She is your friend. You would worry about her."

For a brief instant, Steve wondered if she had slipped a marble into him and knew what he was thinking. But if she did, why would she ask?

"She wants to meet," he said.

"Yes," Leda agreed. "You must tell her to go to Rydges Hotel, Southbank at 11 o'clock. And tell her to bring our two marbles."

"So you can take them?" Steve asked.

Leda looked at him thoughtfully for a moment before answering.

"You know Steve; we had a discussion about you early this morning."

"We?"

"The other Osmia; they don't trust you. I do. Am I wrong?"

"How can I trust you, when you don't tell me anything?"

Leda hesitated.

"I'll tell you when the time is right. I don't tell you now for your own protection. If things go wrong and you are caught, you can't tell them anything."

"If I 'm caught, you'll probably be caught as well."

"Why? They are looking for an old lady with white hair. Even at the Gardens I was still an old lady."

"Kelly knows you've changed."

"She will be looking for a blonde. If you are recognized, I can just walk away unnoticed."

Steve could see the sense in this, but he still didn't like it. He didn't like blindly following instructions from an Alien, or indeed anyone else. He tried one last time to get her to tell him exactly what their plan was.

"So, you're not not telling me for my protection," he said. "You're not telling me for *your* protection."

"No," said Leda, with Teutonic seriousness. "It is for your protection. If you betray me, the other Osmia have decided to kill you."

"Nice," said Steve.

Leda put her arms around him with genuine affection.

"I 'm sure it won't come to that."

She smiled and kissed him gently on the cheek. It didn't make Steve feel any more comfortable.

Leda and Steve checked out of the hotel a little before nine am. The timing was important because Leda wanted Steve to text Kelly before the banks opened.

Leda told the driver the first stop was any of the banks in Adelaide Street; they needed an ATM. The taxi drove the couple of blocks to Adelaide Street and parked illegally while Steve jumped out of the taxi and headed for an ATM. He didn't use the machine. Instead, he took out Luc's phone and texted Kelly:

Be at Rydges South Bank at eleven. Bring the marbles with you.'

Steve immediately switched off the phone and hurried back and jumped in the taxi.

"Holt Street Wharf," Leda said.

And the taxi pulled away.

They had tracked Luc's phone almost as quickly as Kelly had picked up the text. Steve was in the Brisbane CBD; near the Bank.

By the time the police responded and sent cars to Adelaide Street, the taxi was already halfway down Kingsford Smith Drive and under the Gateway Motorway Overpass.

And by the time Kelly responded to the message, the taxi had already deposited Leda and Steve at the Holt Street Wharf to catch the ferry to Moreton Island and the Tangalooma Resort.

Not that it mattered. Steve wasn't checking his messages anyway.

As Kelly read out the text, sitting with Ramirez and Bamberger in the Royal on the Park having breakfast, she was thinking there were two possible scenarios.

Steve and Leda intended to make the meeting and try to steal her marbles; or they knew where the marbles were and they wanted Kelly out of the way while they robbed the Bank.

Ramirez thought that was a bit far-fetched until Kelly pointed out that, under the Osmium influence, they had made a seventy-five-year-old woman jump through a plate glass window, and knock out a CIA Agent. Who knows what they could do with a trained SAS killer; especially one who was armed, courtesy of ASIO?

She wanted an armed guard placed on the Bank. She wanted to be assured there had been no break-ins. Then she'd get wired up and make the meeting at South Bank. And she wanted a gun.

Ramirez had met a lot of single-minded people in the CIA, but none of them compared with Kelly. He wasn't sure he liked her, but he'd been told to follow her instructions, at least until he had his hands on the two marbles. He acted as if she were in complete control. Armed men were sent to the Bank. A stakeout was set up at Rydges on South Bank. Kelly was wired up and given a small derringer that fitted neatly into a holster, which in turn fitted neatly to the inside of her thigh. Kelly had had gun training with the Federal Police; she hadn't handled anything this small, but she had no doubt that she'd soon got the hang of it.

The report came back from the Bank that all was well. Armed guards were placed inside and outside the building. Marksmen were stationed around Southbank together with three-man teams in fast cars, to follow in the event that Kelly had to move on to a second or even a third location. And, finally, they had two helicopters standing by.

The CIA and ASIO had managed to elicit all this support from the Queensland Police by telling them that the marbles were highly radio-active and that Leda and Steve were Terrorists intent on making a dirty bomb.

At eleven o'clock Kelly got out of her taxi at Rydges on South Bank. The derringer strapped to her thigh rubbed against her other leg and initially she found it a bit difficult to walk normally, but she quickly got the hang of that, too. She found herself a place to sit in the foyer of the hotel, and checked that her phone was switched on and her wire was working. Then she ordered a coffee while she waited.

It was destined to be a forlorn wait.

Leda and Steve were already enjoying an exhilarating ride on a high-speed catamaran ferry out to the Tangalooma Island Resort, and they'd met up with a couple of old friends.

The train from Cairns via Townsville had arrived at Brisbane Station on time that morning, at nine a.m., and Gina and David had joined the throng heading for the Taxi rank. They were too excited to be tired even though they'd slept sitting up all night. They were travelling third class and didn't have a sleeper.

The next few days were to be the highlight of the trip, which is not to say the trip hadn't a few highlights already: visiting the secret fossil site at Fallon's Depression; finding a crashed rocket nose cone and the marbles; and finally, having the marbles stolen.

But none of this, they felt, could compare with what was to come. As part of their University course in Wollongong, they had arranged to spend a few days with the Eco Rangers at the Dolphin Reserve on Tangalooma Island.

Under very strict supervision, the public is allowed to feed the wild dolphins there each evening, but Gina and David would do so much more. They would temporarily become Eco Rangers themselves. They would not only feed the dolphins but act as guides for the public.

Of course, this involved some less attractive jobs like thawing the frozen fish for the dolphins to eat, and scrubbing out the plastic tubs in which the fish were carried but that, they felt, was a small price to pay.

There was just an hour between the arrival of the Cairns train at Brisbane Station and the departure of the Tangalooma Ferry at the Holt Street Wharf, down the river at Pinkenba.

The Wharf was fifteen kays away so they caught a taxi, courtesy of the remains of the fifty dollars Bamberger had given them in Townsville. They made it just in time for the ten o'clock departure and presented their pre-paid tickets to the ferry attendant.

On the ferry, they had another nice surprise: Leda and Steve. The way Gina and David greeted them made Steve feel a little uneasy. He had often been confused when talking with Leda as to whether he was talking to the woman or the Osmium. With Gina and David, it was impossible to differentiate. They carried on like a couple of excited kids, talking about what they were going to do on the Island. They invited Steve and Leda to join their group at dolphin feeding time that evening. Insisted they all got together for coffee when they'd settled in.

All this seemed like two normal students greeting old friends. Yet they hardly knew Steve, and Leda looked about fifty years younger than when they last met. And she was no longer a blonde; she was a redhead. They didn't seem to be aware of any of this. And they didn't ask where Luc was or what Steve was doing so far from Winton? It was definitely odd.

When they'd run out of chatter, Gina and David went off to buy breakfast; soft drinks and chocolate bars from a cupboard in the main cabin that served as the ship's snack bar.

Steve asked Leda if they knew they had Osmia inside them.

"No," said Leda. "They have complete freedom of will, but we have tampered with their memories and implanted a few new ones. And, when necessary, we can govern their actions."

Steve watched the carefree students.

"What will happen to them afterwards?" he asked.

"Nothing," said Leda. "They will go to sleep, and when they wake up, they will remember nothing. They will be fine."

Steve wasn't convinced.

"You're sure?"

"Of course," said Leda smiling, "I've already done it to one of you puny humans."

Steve was suspicious. Had he been under the influence of a marble?

"No, not you," continued Leda, who seemed able to read his thoughts. "I need you in full control of your faculties.

The first half of the journey to Tangalooma Island involved a slow crawl down the Brisbane River so that the ferry's wake wouldn't disrupt the trawlers working the river. The Captain, who, strangely, was French, kept up a running commentary on the sites they passed on the river; from the time of first settlement to the reclamation of land that was still going on and which would increase the size of the Port even further.

Leda and Steve joined Gina and David on deck to watch the passing scene, but neither the view nor the commentary seemed to please Leda. She became quiet; almost morose.

"Is something wrong?" Steve asked.

"Why do you do all this?" she asked. "Why don't you learn?"

"Do what?"

"All this," said Leda, spreading her arms to indicate the two sides of the river.

On either side the shore was heavily industrialised: Concrete works, Chemical plants, Paper works, Coal Loaders, the Caltex Oil Refinery.

"This is what is killing your planet," Leda said. "Can't you see?"

She seemed genuinely puzzled by such short-sightedness.

Even when the ferry hit open water, Leda's mood didn't improve. Perhaps that had something to do with the fact that somewhere on the mainland, near Sugarloaf Mountain, there was either a bush fire or they were burning off the cane fields ready to harvest the sugar. Whatever the reason, it sent a huge pall of smoke across the sky that reached almost all the way to Moreton Island. Steve gathered from the expression on Leda's face that she didn't approve of that, either. It wasn't until the Tangalooma Island Resort itself came into view that Leda brightened up.

Moreton Island on which Tangalooma is situated is ninety-eight per cent national park, and the resort clings to the edge of the island on its north-western shore. Its construction is mainly of concrete, but careful planting of trees and shrubs means that it almost disappears when viewed from the sea. It looks to the approaching tourists more like a small Polynesian village than a concrete and steel resort.

As the Catamaran slowed in preparation for docking at the wharf, alongside which the dolphins were fed each night, Gina came and stood next to Leda.

Without preamble, Leda said,

"Phone."

Gina handed it over without question or hesitation. Leda dialled and spoke to the receptionist at Rydges on Southbank.

"You have a woman sitting in your foyer named Kelly MacDonald," she said. "You can't miss her. She's tall, red hair, green eyes, attractive thirty-something."

Leda looked at Steve and smiled as if to say: *I don't find her attractive, but I know you do.*

She continued speaking on the phone.

"Could you please give her a message? Tell her the meeting is off. She shouldn't have brought the cops. We'll call her tomorrow."

There was a pause then Leda repeated,

"You heard -*You shouldn't have brought the cops.*"

The Receptionist had obviously thought she had heard wrong. Leda didn't wait to explain further. She switched off the phone and handed it back to Gina. Gina stowed the phone back in her pack, and went to re-join David, who was waiting, silent and still. Within seconds they were again pointing excitedly at the resort, the dolphin feeding area; laughing.

It was as if Gina had never left David's side; had never given Leda her phone. Steve was watching the Osmium control in action.

Leda turned to Steve, aware of his thoughts.

"It's a prepaid phone," she said. "Untraceable, and we can't just let Kelly sit there forever."

"Why would you care?" Steve asked.

"I don't," said Leda, "but saying we know there are cops there, suggests that we are there to see them, which means we are not here. And now Kelly will blame the cops and the CIA for messing up. Divide et Impera."

Steve frowned.

"What's that?

Leda translated,

"Divide and Conquer, isn't that what you say?"

Steve shook his head in disbelief. He was being taught Latin by an Alien.

"Sometimes I wish the old lady wasn't a university professor," he said with feeling.

Leda held his hand and squeezed it gently.

"We just need a few hours," she said.

But knowing the other Osmia inside Leda had orders to kill him if anything went wrong, Steve found little comfort in her assurances.

25 - The Redheaded Blonde.

When a wide-eyed Receptionist handed Kelly the message from Leda, she swore; apparently at nobody but actually at Ramirez, who was listening on the wire taped to the inside of her blouse.

"You've blown it," she said, getting up and walking towards the exit, past the bewildered Receptionist who didn't even think to ask if she'd paid for her coffee.

"What's wrong?" asked Ramirez.

"They're not coming; they spotted the police."

"They can't have."

Kelly read the message aloud:

"Meeting off. You shouldn't have brought the cops."

Ramirez was sure nobody had spotted the police. They were posted at too great a distance or blended imperceptibly into the normal crowd.

"Maybe they never intended to meet you," he said, "maybe you were right, and this was a decoy while they went to the Bank. We should move the marbles to somewhere safer."

"There's no way I'm handing the marbles over to you," said Kelly angrily, into the wire.

"Once you get your hands on them, you'll deal me out. I'll be back on the plane to Canberra so fast I won't know what hit me. Send a car for me!"

Onlookers, staring at Kelly yelling at nobody they could see, probably thought she was quite mad. She swept on past them, not noticing, but she stopped when her phone rang.

It was the Assistant Director of ASIO. Again there was no preamble.

"Go to the Bank," the Assistant Director said. "Robinson will meet you there. Give him the marbles. Don't give them to our American cousins."

"Robinson?" Kelly was yelling again. "We gave him the Ahearn marble, and he lost it."

"You lost it," the Assistant Director corrected her. "If you hadn't been freelancing, we wouldn't be in this mess. Now unless you want to end up on a charge, do as you're told."

The Assistant Director of ASIO hung up.

Kelly stood at the curb, fuming, as a police car containing three Tactical Response Officers screeched to a halt in front of her. If Steve and Leda hadn't seen the police before, Kelly thought, they've seen them now.

A female officer got out of the front passenger seat, opened the rear door. Kelly got in. The officer slammed the door and jumped back into the front seat as the car raced off, even before she had fastened her seatbelt.

"I don't know what the hurry is now," Kelly grumbled. "We've missed them."

Ramirez had heard everything, partly because Kelly was wired and partly because they were bugging Kelly's phone.

Knowing Kelly was mad at ASIO, Ramirez saw a

chance to get her on their side. *Divide et Impera*, he thought.

"Don't worry," he whispered in her earpiece, "we'll keep you on the case. We need you."

"Oh great," muttered Kelly. "Now my only friends are the CIA."

And she only realized that she had actually said this out loud when she heard Ramirez chuckling on the other end of the wire.

When Kelly's police car pulled up outside the bank, Robinson, his bodyguard, Ramirez, and Bamberger were already waiting for her.

Robinson smiled his usual, supercilious smile.

"You've been having an exciting time, dear lady," he said.

"No wonder Steve Moss hates you," Kelly snapped back and walked straight into the Bank.

Robinson wasn't offended. He rather liked being hated.

He followed Kelly, Ramirez, and Bamberger into the Bank.

Kelly walked up to the Business Customer Counter ignoring the people waiting.

"Jeffrey Friedman," she said to the teller at the counter.

She needn't have bothered. What with armed police in the premises and Kelly being flanked by a group of heavies, everybody was watching her every move. Friedman was already on his way to greet her at the counter.

"Miss MacDonald," he said, "would you like to come through?"

Kelly headed off to the office where she'd deposited the marbles.

Robinson, his bodyguard, Ramirez, and Bamberger followed in her wake. Friedman joined them there coming through a door that led to the office from the behind the counter area.

"Now, what can I do for you?" he asked, feeling quite important.

"I want my safety deposit envelope," Kelly told him.

"Of course," he walked back to the door through which he'd entered. Bamberger followed him. Friedman stopped at the door.

"I'm sorry, sir," he said to Bamberger, "you can't come in here; Bank Security."

Bamberger held the door open.

"I'll watch you from here," he said.

Friedman looked around the room at the four stony-faced men. He was sure he could detect the bulge of a gun under at least one of the jackets. He decided, under the circumstances, that he could allow this slight stretching of the bank rules. He walked through to the area behind the counter.

Bamberger watched him from the door as he approached the teller who held the second key to the cupboard inside the strong room, where the safety deposit envelopes were kept. Together they disappeared into the strong room for a few minutes then Friedman emerged, carrying the envelope and a large old-fashioned ledger.

Friedman walked back into the customer office, and Bamberger shut the door behind him.

"Here we are," he said grandly. "Your safety deposit envelope. If you could just sign the ledger to say you've received it back..."

He put the ledger on the table.

"If you could just sign there," said Friedman, pointing to a page in the ledger. "As you can see the seal on the envelope is still intact; your signature, written across the flap."

It was a routine Friedman always followed to ensure there were no misunderstandings.

Kelly wasn't even listening to him.

She put on her usual pair of pristine white gloves. She took the envelope and broke the seal, ripped it open and poured the contents into the palm of her hand. Two marbles rolled out and because they were completely round, and shiny, they rolled a little quicker than Kelly expected. She had to scramble to hold on to them before they fell off the table.

She stared at them.

"What the hell is this?"

She was yelling again.

She held the marbles out in the palm of her hand for everybody to see.

"I don't know," said Friedman, his sense of self-importance evaporating. "I didn't see what you put in the envelope."

"I didn't put these in." Kelly shoved the marbles under Friedman's nose. "They're stainless steel. They're round. What have you done with the other marbles?"

"I can assure you, madam," said Friedman, indignant that he should be accused of anything untoward, "that envelope hasn't been touched since you sealed it."

Kelly stared at him. He licked his lips nervously.

Kelly moved even closer to him. In her heels she was half a head taller than him.

"Stick out your tongue," she hissed.

"Wh-What?" he swallowed.

"I said, stick out your tongue."

Friedman stuck out his tongue.

It was streaked with black.

Kelly stared into his eyes

"What's that on your tongue?"

"I don't know," said Friedman. "It was there when I woke up this morning. I couldn't brush it off."

Kelly turned to Robinson.

"Can we talk outside?"

She turned to Robinson's bodyguard.

"Watch him," she said, indicating Friedman. "Don't let him move."

"You stay here, too," Ramirez told Bamberger. "If he tries anything shoot him in the heart. Shooting him in the head would be a waste of time."

Friedman was sure he was peeing himself with fear.

"Mike the headless chicken," said Kelly, for no apparent reason; but Ramirez recognized the reference. He grinned at Kelly. Maybe she wasn't so bad after all.

Kelly, Robinson and Ramirez gathered outside the office door.

"He's swallowed at least one of the marbles," Kelly said, for Robinson's benefit, because Ramirez had already seen the signs of the marble in Dog's mouth.

"What does that mean?" asked Robinson.

"He's under the control of the Osmium," Kelly explained. "The marbles could be still inside him."

"So what do we do?" Ramirez was keen to put control of events back into Kelly's hands. She knew more than he did; certainly more than this idiot, Robinson.

"Handcuff him. Get him to the nearest MRI Scanner and find out how many marbles he's got inside him. I can probably cut them out later without doing any permanent harm. We should also find out where he lives and search the place. He could be hiding Leda and Moss."

"And we should check the Bank Security Cameras," said Ramirez. "See who got this guy to remove the marbles from the safe."

"No prizes for guessing that," said Kelly. "It had to be Leda."

"Sure," said Ramirez. "But how did she know which guy to pick? Somebody must have seen you dealing with him."

"It was Moss," said Kelly, remembering. "I was talking to him at the hotel just before I came here to deposit the marbles. He must have followed me."

"Maybe," agreed Ramirez, "but let's check anyway."

Kelly led the way back in to confront Friedman. She might almost have felt sorry for him, if she hadn't been so annoyed. If Steve was right, and the Osmia took over the brain, he would have no idea what was going on right now.

"Mr. Friedman," she said, "I'm afraid we're going to have to handcuff you and take you to have an MRI Scan."

"Why?" wailed Friedman.

"We think you might have been drugged,"

That seemed the easiest way to explain it without revealing too many details.

"Possibly by a beautiful young blonde woman? German?"

The blood drained from Friedman's face.

"I had dinner with her last night," he said. "She came in enquiring about getting money from Germany and I bumped into her later on the street."

"Did you take her home?" asked Kelly.

"Yes, to my place."

"You'd better give us your address, Mr. Friedman," Kelly said.

The high rise apartment building where Jeff Friedman lived was both the perfect place to hide and a terrible place to be trapped. The building had only two ground floor entrances, which the Tactical Response Group had covered before Kelly, Ramirez and Robinson had even got there.

On the other hand the building was huge, with a mixture of owner-occupiers and hotel guests, so nobody ever noticed who was coming or who was going. Nobody, that is, except the Doorman.

He knew everybody and everything, and he confirmed that Jeff Friedman did have a house guest. They'd arrived home together two nights before and left together in the morning. But last night she'd returned before him and she had her own key. Mr. Friedman had got home at the usual time and left for work as usual. As far as the Doorman knew, the woman was still in the apartment.

The Tactical Response Group didn't want to take any chances that might let Leda slip through their fingers. First they switched off the lifts. Then they went up both sets of fire stairs at the same time. On the way up, they checked the corridors on each floor. They assumed that Leda wouldn't have a key to any of the other apartments so if she had seen them coming and hidden on a lower floor, hoping to let them pass, she would have to be in the corridor.

In this painstaking manner, they slowly made their way to the fifteenth floor before switching the lifts back on to let Kelly, Robinson and Bamberger joined them. The trio stood back while the Tactical Response Group gathered around Friedman's door, opened it with his key, and burst in with the maximum of noise and threat.

"Tactical Response Group, come out with your hands up."

No response.

They moved through each room in the apartment, searched it, yelled

"Clear!."

And moved on.

They even moved out onto the balcony.

"Clear!"

There was nobody on the balcony, nobody in the flat.

The Commander of the Tactical Response Group came back to the corridor to report, rather superfluously, that the flat was empty. The flat was so small that Kelly and the others had heard everything. Kelly walked into the flat, pulling on her white gloves.

"Nobody touch anything," she commanded.

She did a quick but thorough search of the flat. She started in the kitchen and particularly checked the refrigerator and the freezer to check the marbles weren't being kept in cold storage. She checked drawers, cupboards and wardrobes.

In the bathroom, she eventually found something interesting. The sink was stained red, and there was a set of hair curlers in the bathroom cupboard.

She picked a couple of boxes out of the bathroom bin and brought them back into the living area. One was the box for the curlers; the other had contained hair dye.

"For some reason she's disguised herself as me," Kelly announced. "Probably to get into the Bank and get the marbles. We've been looking for a tall blonde with straight hair. We should be looking for a tall redhead with curls."

26 - The Sanctuary.

By this time the tall redhead and Steve had settled into their Deep Blue Apartment at the Tangalooma Island Resort with its view directly over the wharf and the Dolphin Feeding Area. They were eating a late lunch, or early dinner, in the Beach House Café, which was the only place on the island where you could eat, outside of the usual lunch and dinner times. They were eating at this unusual time because they didn't want to miss the dolphin feeding.

Their table was outside, right on the beach, with a stunning view across the bay to the mainland. The Dolphin Feeding Area was just a little further back up the beach but it was empty at this hour. The dolphins were fed just after sundown, and the feeding was strictly regulated. No dolphin got more than twenty per cent of its daily intake, to ensure that it needed to continue hunting and would not become dependent on being hand-fed. For the same reason, juvenile dolphins that accompanied their mothers each evening at feeding time weren't fed at all. They had to learn how to hunt for themselves first.

Leda had bought two loose-fitting Hawaiian shirts. Steve wore his over his khaki bush shorts. Leda wore hers over a very revealing bikini that she certainly wouldn't have dared to wear a few days earlier.

After lunch, they returned to their apartment where Gina and David were waiting for them. Both of them had the standard Tangalooma Resort Uniform issued to the Eco-Rangers who supervised the feeding of the dolphins; a blue shirt with an insignia and a white flash down the sides, worn over wetsuit pants, and sandshoes for their feet.

Gina was also wearing a bum bag around her waist of the type many people wear to carry phones, wallets and money when they are in clothes without pockets. The Eco-Rangers wore these bags to carry the fish they fed to the dolphins.

The bag was empty, but for some reason she could not have explained, Gina couldn't resist putting it on as soon as she was selected to be one of the supervisors at the dolphin feeding that evening.

There had only been one position vacant, and Gina and David had decided whose it was in their usual way - rock, paper, scissors. As usual too, Gina had won but, unusually, David was quite upset about missing out. Gina was comforting him, telling him he'd have a chance the following evening. Steve wondered if David would get that chance if Leda was going to carry out her plan in the next few hours.

In fact, Leda was about to put her plan into action immediately.

Leda let them all into the apartment, told Gina to help herself to a coke in the fridge and told David to follow her.

Gina went to the fridge, took out a coke and went to the balcony to drink it and watch the sun, as it slowly began to drop towards the mountains on the mainland.

She seemed totally unconcerned when Leda and David went to the bathroom and stayed there for a hell of a long time; and when Steve heard a thump, like somebody falling.

Leda opened the bathroom door and asked Steve to help.

David was lying unconscious on the bathroom floor.

"What happened to him?" Steve asked.

"He's just asleep," Leda explained, although Steve thought that unlikely.

He tested David's pulse, listened to his breathing. Both seemed normal.

"Satisfied?" Leda asked.

"Why is he asleep?" Steve asked.

"He has given up his marble. He is programmed to sleep for twelve hours. After that, he will wake up and remember nothing. He'll be fine. Help me carry him to the bed."

Steve and Leda carried David into the bedroom and laid him gently on the bed, where he slept, completely relaxed.

They went back into the living room. Gina was still on the balcony staring out at the slowly setting sun.

Leda called to her.

"Gina, haven't you got to do something? Thaw the fish for the feeding tonight?"

"Oh yes," Gina sounded as if she had completely forgotten.

She came back into the apartment, put her empty coke bottle on the table and headed for the door, apparently oblivious to the fact that David had disappeared.

"Don't forget the dolphin feeding tonight," she said. "Make sure you get me as your guide.

Leda walked up to Gina.

"We won't be feeding the dolphins tonight," she said. "We were too late trying to get a spot. But don't worry. We'll be watching you."

Leda gave Gina a gentle peck on the cheek and as she did so she dropped a handful of marbles into her bum bag.

They made a clatter, but Gina didn't seem to notice.

"Okay," she said. "Gotta get back and make sure the fish are thawed. Can't feed dolphins frozen fish. Bye."

And she was gone.

"Maybe it's time you told me exactly what the plan is," said Steve although he was beginning to have a pretty good idea.

Leda agreed.

"It's time I told you everything," she said. "There are six Osmia in the bag Gina has around her waist."

That wasn't true. There were actually five Osmia because contrary to what she was telling Steve, there was one part of the plan Leda was never going to reveal to him, and that was the location of the eighth marble.

She continued.

"Gina will take them to the cold room and put one into each of the fish she will take with her for the dolphin feeding. As the public feed the fish, they will transfer the Osmia into the dolphins. Afterwards, Gina will return here and she and I will give up our Osmia. That's where you come in. We will both fall into a twelve hour trance, like David. You must take the Osmia to the water. Wade in anywhere where it is dark. The Osmium dolphins will find you and take the remaining Osmia."

Steve had suspected Leda was going to hide the Osmia in the dolphins. As soon as Gina and David had started their chatter on the ferry, he knew. He just hadn't expected that all the Osmia would go. That they would just withdraw from the human race.

"What choice do we have?" asked Leda. "Your species aren't ready to be helped by aliens. Sooner or later we'd be captured by Kelly or the CIA or ASIO. They'd probe us and experiment on us. Steal our secrets and keep us captive in the interest of Public Security."

"But what about the planet?" asked Steve. "What about global warming?"

"It will only get worse," Leda agreed. "One day, maybe soon, it will get so bad the world will be ready to listen to us, and we can come back."

"How will you do that?"

"There are lots of places that people and dolphins inter-react around the world. We'll work it out."

Steve still wasn't convinced it would be as simple as that. "How will you know when to come back?"

Leda laughed, but it wasn't a laugh that held any mirth.

"Oh, we won't miss it," she said. "We'll see the storms, feel the seas warming, and rising. Don't worry. We'll know. Besides, tomorrow you'll get Leda back. She'll need you."

"Too right, she will," agreed Steve. "A week ago she was a little old lady dying of cancer. Now she's a…"

He searched for the words as he looked Leda up and down in her skimpy bikini.

"A love goddess," he concluded.

Leda didn't smile at the compliment. In fact she looked sad.

"She still has cancer," she told Steve. "Telomeres, the enzyme we introduced into her DNA so that her body would rejuvenate, is also the enzyme that allows cancer cells to grow forever. She looks younger, but her cancer is getting worse. She is too far gone. Whatever happens, she will soon die."

At first Steve was shocked; then he thought it was probably just as well. The trauma of waking would probably kill her anyway.

"Oh no," said Leda. "We have left her with certain memories. She will know certain things. I think she will be happy. She will have beaten the Military-Industrial Complex at last."

Leda smiled but Steve just felt an overwhelming sadness. He put his arms around Leda, not knowing if he was hugging an alien, a little old lady who was dying, or just hugging himself because he felt so alone.

Jeff Friedman, on the other hand, was feeling anything but alone. In fact he was wishing fervently to be left alone. All day he had been prodded, examined, stuck under an MRI machine, interrogated and bullied, but in truth he could tell his captors little they didn't already know.

He recounted how Leda had picked him up, how they'd kissed, how he'd choked. Then, how he'd woken up thinking it was the next morning when it was really thirty-six hours later, as he now knew.

In the intervening time, he had attended work and carried out his duties perfectly; except, of course, for the fact that he'd handed over the safety deposit envelope to a woman who bore only a passing resemblance to Kelly. Had he been in control of his mind and body at the time, Friedman would have recognized that it was a different woman.

Further proof that Friedman had no control over

those events was the fact that he had not signed out the safety deposit envelope in his usual way when he handed it to Leda. Nor had he registered the new envelope which he had given her to seal and sign before he put it back into the strong room.

All this gave Kelly, and the others, a strong picture of how people behaved under the influence of the Osmia, but little else.

Examining the Bank's security cameras was more productive. They saw Leda with her red hair and were able to produce an image of her that could be distributed to the police and, if things became desperate, to the public.

Even more productive, they looked at the security vision from two days earlier.

They saw Kelly arrive to deposit the marbles in the strong room and they saw who was following her. It wasn't Steve. It was Leda.

As they stared at her, Ramirez told the operator to freeze the image. The time code showed 15.45, a quarter to four.

Ramirez didn't bother to check the flight schedule for flights from Brisbane to Townsville and back. He knew it wasn't possible for Leda to be in the bank at 3.45, meet Gina and David on the ferry from Magnetic Island to Townsville, and then be back in time to seduce Friedman.

"So who did Gina and David meet on the ferry?" Robinson asked.

"Nobody," said Ramirez, "They didn't meet anybody. They made it up. They were like Friedman. They had the marbles inside them. It's the only explanation. I actually talked to two Aliens and I didn't even realize it."

He was disgusted with himself.

Kelly agreed with his conclusion. But how did it help?

They didn't know where Gina and David were, any more than they knew where Leda and Steve were.

"Somebody must know where they were going," said Ramirez. "Phone her parents, phone the hostel where they stayed last night. See if they discussed their plans with anybody."

The call to Townsville was pointless. Gina and David had been programmed not to discuss their plans. Calls to her parents should have been more immediately productive. They knew about Gina and David's plan to work at the Dolphin Reserve; Gina had talked about nothing else in the weeks leading up to their trip. The problem was that Gina's father was a leading Vascular Surgeon at Sydney's Royal North Shore Hospital. He was in Theatre when the call was made and obviously his phone was switched off.

Gina's mother was playing duplicate bridge with the ladies at the Mosman Bridge Club, and the Club had very strict rules about mobile phones. They must all be switched off until play was completed and the scores were being compiled.

That wouldn't happen until nine o'clock Sydney time. Although Brisbane didn't have Summer Time and was an hour behind Sydney, Kelly and the others still had a long wait before Gina's mother would switch her phone back on.

There was nothing to do but to phone around all the backpacker hostels and cheap hotels and motels in the Brisbane and Gold Coast area, in the hope of finding where Gina and David were staying.

Steve also had time on his hands.

The dolphins weren't fed until after dark. Leda was sleeping, David was in a coma, and Gina was excitedly getting instructions on how to supervise the public feeding of the dolphins.

Nobody with a cold or flu was allowed near the dolphins, which could catch all types of human illnesses. No Flash Cameras were allowed on the beach. Both the staff and public must be free of all insect repellents, deodorants or sunscreens because dolphin skins were very sensitive. People must wash their hands in the disinfectant bucket before handling the fish that were to be fed to the dolphins. And, finally, dolphins prefer to eat their fish head first.

Gina practiced this mantra and technique, completely unaware that she had previously placed an osmium marble into the mouth of the fish she was holding, and that it had now worked its way down into the fish's stomach, where it was waiting to be swallowed.

While all this was going on, Steve had nothing to do but sit and think as he gazed out over the blue water. He hadn't expected that all the Osmia were going to ground, or more accurately going to sea. He had expected that he would be needed to protect them in some way while they got together and formulated their plan to deliver nuclear fusion to the world.

He agreed with Leda's assessment that the CIA and ASIO would want to keep the Osmia and their secrets to themselves but he felt there had to be a way to circumvent that.

It sounded crazy, but he wanted the Osmia to save the world.

Instead they seemed only intent on saving themselves; or waiting until the human race was in such dire straits that they could step in and take control. This might be better than annihilation, but it felt awfully like subjugation and slavery.

And what about Steve himself?

When all the Osmia were safely swimming the oceans of the world, what happened to him? How was he to avoid spending the rest of his days banged up in some Military prison for being - god knows what they'd throw at him - a traitor? a renegade? He felt like he was back in the Middle East, fighting a battle he knew he couldn't win, for a cause he no longer believed in, but with his sense of duty forcing him to see it through to the bitter end.

Eventually, he came up with a plan.

He was pretty sure Kelly thought Leda had implanted a marble in him. If that were true, of course, he would have no control over his actions. He couldn't be held to account any more than Gina or David would be; any more than the rejuvenated but still dying body of Leda would be. All he had to do was convince everybody that he truly had been under the influence of a marble.

He went back to the Deep Blue Apartment where David was still in a coma, and Leda was still sleeping. He opened David's mouth and wiped some of the osmium tetroxide off David's tongue with a tissue. He then rubbed the tissue over his own tongue.

He looked at his tongue in the mirror. He could barely see any osmium tetroxide but it didn't matter. There would be traces there. Kelly with her swab and pathology would find it. They'd believe he'd swallowed a marble.

His next problem was to decide when he'd swallowed it. It had to be before he knocked out the CIA Agent in the Park. He decided it was just after he had "forgotten" his driver's licence at the Royal on the Park and returned to his room.

He would tell them that on the way he'd seen a little

old lady fall in the hotel corridor. She had been wearing a scarf, an oversized dress, and running shoes. Steve thought it would be a nice touch to remember that he'd thought it was strange; that an old lady was wearing running shoes. He'd placed her on a seat in the corridor, and she'd kissed him to say thank you. After that he'd turned to walk away and then he remembered nothing before waking up next to David, Leda and Gina in the Deep Blue Apartment.

Satisfied that he now had as good a plan as he could devise, Steve took a stroll along the beach. As he walked, he deleted all the messages on Luc's phone. Claiming he'd swallowed a marble in Brisbane wouldn't explain those.

With the phone empty, he removed the SIM card and then threw both the phone and the SIM card as far out to sea as he could manage. He looked around to make sure that he hadn't been seen, then he returned to the apartment to wait.

At the Mosman, Bridge Club, Gina's mother was a little irritated. The bidding had shown that she and her partner had just about all the points. They were bidding towards a slam. They were strong in hearts and spades. Her strong suit was hearts, which she'd bid first. She had wanted to play the slam. Instead, her partner overbid her seven hearts and bid seven spades. In the best hand of the night, she was reduced to being the silent partner.

Gina's mother sat there with gritted teeth, watching her partner win trick after trick. Obviously she was going to make slam.

Gina's mother would have made slam. She was so angry she felt she just had to go and pee.

So while the hand was being played out with her partner winning all thirteen tricks, Gina's mother went to the bathroom. While she was there, she took the opportunity to check her phone to see if that irresponsible daughter of hers had called her.

Instead she found the call from the police.

It was Robinson who had called Gina's parents, and it was Robinson who announced to the assembled group that Gina Bennett and David Symonds were on Tangalooma Island, feeding dolphins.

Ramirez immediately saw the implications of this. Dolphins are warm-blooded mammals, like humans and Danny's dog. The Osmia were going to hide in the dolphins. Robinson found that unlikely.

"What could they do in dolphins, stuck out at sea? It would be like sending themselves to prison."

Kelly, however, agreed with Ramirez. In any case, she said, they had to find Gina and David, regardless of what they were up to. They should get a police helicopter. They could be on Tangalooma Island in about half an hour.

Robinson ordered the policeman with them to have two helicopters standing by. They'd need that many to get all of them to the island.

As everybody grabbed their equipment, Ramirez gave the policeman his last orders.

"Call Moreton Island Police Station; have the local cops pick up Symonds and Bennett. Tell him to hold them. We're on our way."

Robinson wasn't sure this was a good idea, but Ramirez was insistent.

"They'll hear the helicopters coming for miles," he said. "They'll run. We may never find them again."

"On an island?" queried Robinson.

"On an island with dolphins," Ramirez said.

27 - *The Race to the Bottom.*

Lying on one side of the bed in the Deep Blue apartment, Leda woke suddenly, as if she had been shaken. Steve was sitting in a chair, watching her. David still slept motionless on the bed, barely breathing. Leda sprang to her feet.

"There's no hurry," said Steve. "Dolphin feeding doesn't start for a good ten minutes."

Leda was searching through Steve's bag. She pulled out his gun and holster.

"The police are coming to arrest David and Gina," she said, offering Steve the gun.

"You can give them David. Don't let them take Gina until she has finished feeding the dolphins."

"I'm not shooting cops," Steve said flatly.

"Take the gun anyway," Leda put it into his hand.

He stuffed the gun down the back of his pants and covered it with his Hawaiian shirt, and then he took his wallet out of his bag.

"Hurry," said Leda.

"Hurry where?" asked Steve. "Where are the cops?"

"There is a police station right next to this building,

haven't you seen it? Right before you come to the restaurants and Reception."

Steve wondered why he hadn't noticed the police station. Perhaps because it was behind the hotel buildings and he had always walked along the beach? Luckily, Leda had been more diligent.

She pulled on a wide-brimmed hat to hide her hair and headed for the door. Steve followed her out.

They exited the apartments by the rear entrance and turned left, towards Reception.

The Police Station was almost directly in front of them, although Steve could be forgiven for not recognising it. It looked like a modest, wooden, holiday shack, except for a small sign and a notice telling people that, in the event that the station was unattended, they should call Redcliff Police Station on the Mainland.

While Leda turned left again and headed for the beach, Steve stepped onto the veranda of Police Station. He waited for Leda to disappear out of sight into the gathering darkness, before he knocked on the door and walked in.

Just a few seconds earlier, the police station had received an urgent call from the Mainland. The young Constable had taken the call and handed it over to the Sergeant, who was listening carefully and taking down notes as Steve approached the desk.

Steve heard the Sergeant repeat Gina's and David's names.

The Constable came to the desk to speak to Steve, who pulled his wallet out of his pocket, not his gun.

He waved his SAS ID under the Constable's nose and indicated the Sergeant on the phone.

"That'll be the Mainland, telling you to arrest and hold Gina Bennet and David Symonds," he said.

The Sergeant hung up the phone.

"What do you know about it?" he asked, and closely inspected Steve's ID.

"I've been tailing them for several days. Symonds is in one of the Deep Blue apartments. Number seven."

He pointed towards the apartments.

"He's passed out. Under the influence of drugs, I'd guess. Whatever it is, he won't give us any trouble. You can handcuff him before he comes to. The girl is down at the beach feeding the dolphins."

The Sergeant decided that since David wasn't going to be any problem the young Constable could go and arrest him. The Sergeant would accompany Steve to the Dolphin Feeding Area.

As they walked between the buildings, down to the beach, he asked Steve if he knew what it was all about? Brisbane had told them nothing; just to arrest Symonds and Bennett.

"I can't tell you, either," said Steve. "Sorry, mate, National Security."

They had now reached the paved area that ran the length of the waterfront and was separated from the beach by a roped-off lawn.

On the grassy part, visitors were standing in queues that stretched down to the sand, waiting to feed the dolphins.

At the head of each queue was a plastic bucket in which the visitors were washing their hands. In front of that was a metal bucket containing small herring.

As each pair finished washing their hands, they moved forward and picked a fish from the buckets.

They then waited until an Eco-Ranger came to lead them into the water to feed the dolphins.

The visitors tentatively fed their fish to the dolphins, and the Eco-Rangers handed them more fish from their bum bags.

Presumably one of these Eco-Rangers was Gina, and the fish she was handing to the visitors contained the osmium marbles. The only light on the beach came from the jetty and shone straight into Steve's eyes. Eco-Rangers and visitors alike were all just silhouettes on the beach. He couldn't make out which one was Gina.

Nor could he see Leda, anywhere.

Steve led the Sergeant onto the jetty immediately alongside the Dolphin Feeding Area where there were three rows of seats. Spectators could sit there and get a close-up view of the dolphins being fed in the shallow waters below and take as many photos as they liked, without getting in anyone's way.

As each couple finished feeding the dolphins, they turned and walked back out of the water and across the lawn. Their friends, watching from the jetty, would also get up and leave to meet up with them outside the roped-off area, where they chatted happily and wandered off into the darkness along the beach.

The dolphin feeding was well under way by this time and Steve and the Police Sergeant found a place in the front row, not twenty metres from the spectacle.

With the lights behind him now, Steve could easily see and identify Gina. He could also see Leda, standing in the enclosed area. But she wasn't in the queue with the other visitors. She was standing some way back, waiting, while Gina stood waist deep in water, flanked by an excited couple of Chinese honeymooners feeding the dolphins.

"See the girl standing in the middle?

Tall, Tangalooma uniform, long black hair?" Steve pointed at Gina.

The Sergeant nodded.

"That's Gina Bennett. Not her real name of course."

Steve liked this touch. Gina did look vaguely Middle Eastern; although in reality she was probably part Italian.

"Wait until she's finished, and the crowds move away," Steve advised. "Then we'll grab her. Don't want to cause any panic, do we?"

The Sergeant nodded again. He watched Gina like a wolf watching a baby lamb.

As he stood there, leaning on the railing, he got a call from the Constable. He'd found Symonds. He was handcuffed and in custody, but the Constable couldn't bring him round.

There was nothing to do now but wait.

Just when the dolphin feeding was almost over, and Steve was beginning to think it would all go to plan, two police helicopters appeared out of the blackness, flashing low over the water.

It was like something out of *Apocalypse Now*. All it needed was the *Ride of the Valkyries* soundtrack to complete the effect.

Kelly, Ramirez, and Bamberger were in one helicopter. Robinson was in the other with his bodyguard and a couple of Tactical Response Officers.

They could see the lights in the distance that lit up the feeding area and the beach. The rest of the island was just a dark silhouette against a star-bright sky.

Ramirez phoned the Police Sergeant to find out what was happening. The Sergeant was pleased to tell him that they had Symonds in custody. He was handcuffed but unconscious.

Ramirez cursed softly. That probably meant Symonds had given up his marble.

"Where's the girl?" he asked.

"She's feeding the dolphins," said the Sergeant. "I'll grab her as soon as she finishes."

"No," yelled Ramirez, "grab her now."

Too late. Gina had already finished feeding the dolphins.

She turned and started ushering the two young kids who had been her last charges out of the water. She was chattering happily, asking the kids if they'd enjoyed the experience.

"Yeah, totally! It was awesome."

Gina laughed. She thought it was awesome too, she told them

"She's finished feeding the dolphins," the Sergeant reported quietly into his phone. "She's getting out of the water onto the grass. The place'll be deserted soon. I'll grab her then. I'd rather take her quietly. There are still a few kids around."

"Yeah, ok, fine," said Ramirez and hung up.

It's too late anyway, he thought.

But he was wrong. Gina still hadn't given up her own marble.

The Sergeant walked briskly along the jetty, intending to grab Gina as she attempted to leave the roped-off area but as she emerged from the water onto the beach, she suddenly crumpled and collapsed on the sand.

People rushed to help.

Leda got there first.

"Stand back," she said, "I'm a Doctor."

The crowd, including the Sergeant, hung back as Leda knelt next to Gina, turned her gently on her back, listened to her heart and gave her mouth to mouth resuscitation. She blew just once into Gina's mouth, then sucked.

Gina immediately started to breathe again.

"She's okay," Leda announced, as she clambered to her feet.

The Sergeant was standing right next to her. She looked directly into his eyes.

"She's just fainted. She needs air," she said.

The Sergeant nodded, started moving the crowd back.

"Okay everyone, she's okay. Move back. Move back. Just give her some air."

With the Sergeant's attention elsewhere, Leda, now in possession of Gina's Osmium, quietly backed away and merged into the crowd. Then she started walking out of the roped-off area and slowly away, down the beach, away from the lights, into the darkness.

Ramirez was on the phone again. He could see the crowd gathered around Gina on the ground.

"What's going on?"

"She's fainted. It's okay."

Ramirez knew it wasn't okay. He yelled to the Sergeant to keep everybody away from the body, not to let anybody leave the area; then he looked around for a place to land.

"Put us down," he told the pilot, "Not the helipad. Further up the beach, away from the crowd."

As the helicopter flew low over the beach, it passed over Leda in her wide-brimmed hat, heading away from the crowd. The downdraft from the helicopter blades blew her hat off.

A mass of wavy red hair cascaded down onto her shoulders.

In the helicopter, Kelly leaned forward, electrified by the sight.

Leda looked up at the helicopter as it set a search-light on her, then she ran for the water.

"It's her," yelled Bamberger.

Ramirez yelled into the phone:

"The woman with red hair, running into the water, stop her!"

The Sergeant could see the woman in the helicopter's search lights. He ran, but he wasn't going to catch her.

The helicopter swooped around to try and shepherd Leda away from the water. She ducked and then ran on. She was now splashing through the shallows and heading out to sea.

Bamberger leaned out of the open cockpit of the helicopter and fired, once, twice.

Before he could fire a third time, Kelly suddenly had a subliminal memory flash:

An animal slaughtered; a tree felled; a man shot; a city bombed; an open cut mine blasted; toxic clouds...

She pulled the derringer from between her thighs and stuck it hard against Bamberger's neck.

"Shoot again and I'll kill you," she said.

"Are you crazy?" Bamberger asked, Kelly's gun gouging into his neck.

"She's right," said Ramirez. We want her alive."

Bamberger relaxed. He put up his gun.

But they were too late. Leda had been hit. She took a few more steps into the deeper water then pitched forward and floated face down, motionless.

The helicopter was now so low that Ramirez was able to jump out and land in the shallows.

He straightened up and waded towards Leda whose body was floating in the water, buffeted by the waves. He had almost reached her when a dolphin came out of nowhere...

It rammed Ramirez in the groin so hard he doubled up and collapsed.

The dolphin was gone as quickly as it had appeared, but two more dolphins arrived in its place. One went under Leda's motionless body and lifted it out of the water just enough for her to take a gulp of air. Then she closed her mouth tight, shut down her nasal passages and hung onto to the dolphin's dorsal fin with one hand; she grabbed the dorsal fin of the second dolphin with her other hand.

They carried her out to sea like a high-speed motor boat, causing a huge bow wave as they moved into deeper water away from the lights.

For a short while, the wake left by Leda and the dolphins could still be seen, white against the darkness; then the dolphins dived.

The wake disappeared.

Leda disappeared.

Steve watched all this from his vantage point on the jetty overlooking the sea.

He looked around for a way out. Obviously he couldn't go back to the apartment and feign sleep now; the constable was there with David. Instead, he decided, he would be found wandering aimlessly around in the bush, suffering from amnesia. He slipped through the crowds, around to the back of the Deep Blue Apartments and headed up the steep incline into the bush.

When the first bullet hit Leda, it missed her heart, and she could have kept running. However, she knew if she did, she would probably get shot again.

Even if they missed her heart and the two Osmia inside her, she would soon lose so much blood that her body would become useless. So she closed her larynx to stop water flooding her lungs, dropped her heartbeat to about ten, and fell forward into the water.

When the dolphins lifted her out of the water, she had just enough time to take in sufficient air to enable her to hang on to their dorsal fins long enough to get out into deep water.

As the dolphins plunged below the waves, she opened her mouth wide.

She let go of the Osmium Marbles within her and they fell into the sea.

She re-opened her larynx and the water flooded into her lungs.

Then Leda was allowed to do, finally, what she had already done five days earlier.

She died.

More Osmium Dolphins appeared. They scooped the marbles up from the seabed, then went looking for mates to court and bite and embed with the Osmia.

Kelly stood on the beach, staring out to sea.

Ramirez was still sitting on the beach holding his groin, groaning and trying to get his breath back as the Australian Cops stood around trying to stop themselves from laughing.

Robinson, who had no sense of humour at all, told Kelly to go check Symonds and Bennett. Nobody, it seemed, could get them to wake up.

As Kelly was about to turn away, she noticed a flash of white out to sea. Two dolphins were swimming into shore pushing Leda's body ahead of them.

They didn't stop until Leda was resting on the beach in the shallows. Then, as Kelly approached the body, the dolphins scuffed back into deeper water and disappeared.

Kelly reached Leda, but she was dead. She was also smiling. The Osmia had given her a last memory before she died; she had beaten the Military-Industrial Complex. She had died happy.

Gina's inert body had been taken to the Deep Blue Apartment and laid next to David's.

Kelly examined them both. She assured Robinson that they were in perfect physical shape. They just couldn't be roused right now, but she had no doubt they would awake just as Jeff Friedman had done, given time. And, like Friedman, they would remember nothing.

Kelly walked out onto the balcony overlooking the narrow stretch of water between the island and the mainland.

She could hear the dolphins frolicking in the water and talking to her.

She looked down at the beach.

A figure was shambling along beneath her. He stopped and stared up at her. It was Steve. He had seen enough trauma victims during his time in Iraq and Afghanistan to give a perfect imitation of a man who had lost a piece of his life.

He croaked out to Kelly:

"Kelly, is that you? Where are we?"

Kelly smiled.

It was quite a good impression, and it would probably fool Robinson and the shrinks.

Besides, Kelly would be there to guide and protect him through the interrogation that was sure to follow his reappearance. After all, she owed Steve a great deal.

When Leda had knocked Kelly out, at the gate of the Australian Aerospace Facility, she hadn't stolen the Ahearn marble. She had inserted it into one of Kelly's body cavities in a way that wouldn't leave the tell-tale osmium tetroxide traces on her tongue.

Now that the other seven marbles were safely stowed away in their dolphin bodies, Kelly was the only Osmium Human left.

The mantle of Dominant Female had passed to her. And one day soon, when the time was right, she would call her small band of Osmia back to shore.

Postscript or Prologue?

With none of the witnesses able to remember anything, the top secret investigation into the Osmia was eventually completed and the records then filed, along with all the other unexplained sightings and weirdo experiences, at Area 51.

Steve was discharged from the SAS and moved to Brisbane, where he took a job as a crewman on a fishing boat in the hope that he might one day bump into a dolphin he knew.

Kelly switched from the Australian Federal Police in Canberra to the New South Wales Police in Sydney. She bought a house on Scotland Island, on Pittwater, where she could swim privately with her own pod.

The huge team of agents the CIA had sent to Australia to search for the Osmia were eventually all sent home. All, that is, except Ramirez. He sought and got permission to stay in Australia indefinitely.

Ramirez had realized something nobody else had.

There were eight places in the band that had come to Earth in the wreckage of the Ariane Rocket, and eight Osmium Marbles, presumably, that Leda had eventually gathered together. That meant the DNA that Kelly found on the dead Astronaut, before this whole adventure even began, couldn't possibly have come from any of the Osmia in Leda's band.

There had to be a second band. And there was every reason to believe they were still here, somewhere, in this vast country.

Ramirez had experienced the ultimate thrill once. He had talked to Aliens.

He wanted that experience again.

A Note from the Author

The Osmium Marbles was inspired by two of the great issues of our time: Climate Change and Illegal Immigration. It is not a post-apocalyptic saga. It is set in the normal, humdrum, everyday world of contemporary Australia. The climate change catastrophe took place on another planet, millions of years ago. The illegal immigrants come from across the Galaxy, rather than across the water. But there are obvious parallels with the Australia of today where much of our land is already uninhabitable because of climate change, and where we pride ourselves on turning 'illegal' aliens away from our borders or locking them up.

The story itself came to me as an idea attached to a set of spectacular visual images on an extensive tour of Queensland:

A night sky in the outback, a thousand times brighter than anything one sees in the city.

A shooting star, reminding me of the more than half a million pieces of space junk orbiting the globe, up to 150 tonnes of which fall to earth each year. Most of this debris burns up in the atmosphere or drops harmlessly into the sea. What doesn't, usually lands in Australia.

Parched earth, where once there were huge swamps and where the tracks and fossilized bones of dinosaurs are still visible on the surface of the land.

Natural tunnels, hundreds of kilometres long, formed by the eruptions of a single volcano.

Outback towns, with wide, dusty streets and corrugated iron buildings baking in sun.

The Great Barrier Reef, and green, idyllic, tropical islands.

Dolphins so trusting that they arrive at the same time each night to be hand-fed by humans.

And finally, Brisbane CBD at lunch time: tourists, shoppers, workers, students, joggers - the great and comfortable mass of humanity - going about their lives, apparently unaware of what is happening around them.

Put this all together with a group of Aliens intent on an endosymbiotic relationship with humankind, an obsessive forensic pathologist, a battle-scarred soldier, a bunch of tourists possibly under alien control, and the political tensions between the CIA and ASIO, and you have *The Osmium Marbles*.

I hope you enjoyed reading it.

IB

Sydney, April 2016

Contact Ian on blprod@bigpond.com

Big Fish to Rubber Ducky

Most people plan to make a sea change but never do.
The Bradley and Brook families made a sea change, but
without a plan.

They bought the land sight unseen. It turned out to be an
overgrown cow paddock with a summons for
propagating noxious weeds jammed in the mailbox. They
decided to plant macadamias, just to keep the weeds
down. Which meant they had to stay in the city and work
harder than ever to pay for it all.

Meanwhile, back on the farm, there was nowhere to stay.
So they rented two houseboats on a nearby river. Again,
sight unseen.

The houseboats proved challenging. From the
wheelhouse you couldn't see out the back of the boat or
on either side. The radios only worked when the boats
were within shouting distance, and the charts were
useless. The river itself was tidal. Mooring at high tide
found them marooned on rocks next morning.

And there was one more thing: *Big Fish* was slightly faster
than *Rubber Ducky*. With two competitive men at the helm
what could possibly go wrong...?

For Kate, who was there but too young to remember.

A personal memoir, available now as ebook or paperback
from Amazon and all other major online booksellers.

The Parthian Shot

Primary School teacher Liz Wright has it all -

A successful career, a rich husband, beautiful children; a fabulous house, with an infinity-edged swimming pool, a boat moored at their own private waterfront, and a good friend living next door -

That is, until she is caught travelling through customs with two kilos of heroin in her suitcase.

It soon becomes apparent that her husband is responsible for the heroin. Also, that the police know she is innocent, and are using her as leverage against him. To no avail, because it seems he has abandoned her and moved in with her best friend. With no one to post bail, Liz is sent to Bridgewater, a privately run, Open Prison.

Like all western countries, Australia has experienced an explosion of prisoner numbers in the last twenty years. The response has been to re-open and extend old, dilapidated prisons, and hand their administration over to private enterprise. The result has often been disastrous.

At Bridgewater, with profits taking priority, Private Management has reduced staff numbers, left antiquated security systems in place, and allowed day-release prisoners out, unsupervised. The more enterprising inmates, like sweet, baby-faced Natalie Palmer have worked out how to have free run of the prison, particularly after dark when only two officers are nominally in charge of the entire complex.

When Liz is put into the same low-security cottage as Natalie, the two don't hit it off. Natalie is suspicious of the well-educated Liz. In turn, Liz treats Natalie like one of the cruel, overactive children she has sometimes had to deal with at school.

But they soon realise that by working together, they can both get what they want: a fortune for Natalie, and revenge for Liz.

They begin planning their perfect crime. Made easier, so they think, because they already have the perfect alibi: they are prisoners. What possible mischief can they get up to, locked away as they are?

However, as events unfold, they start to recognise that there are bigger obstacles in their way. It may have been the men in their lives who got them locked up, but it is the women, both inside and outside Bridgewater, from whom they have most to fear.

From the award-winning screenwriter and original Producer of *Prisoner Cell Block H*

Available online at all major bookstores, in ebook and paperback.

www.ingramcontent.com/pod-product-compliance
Lightning Source LLC
Chambersburg PA
CBHW072131250626
47159CB00007B/2656